A Life on Paper

A Life on Paper

stories

GEORGES-OLIVIER CHÂTEAUREYNAUD

Translated by Edward Gauvin

Small Beer Press
Easthampton, MA

Cet ouvrage, publié dans le cadre d'un programme d'aide à la publication, béné-
ficie du soutien du Ministère des Affaires éstrangères et du Service Culturel de
l'Ambassade de France aux Etats-Unis. This work, published as part of a program
of aid for publication, received support from the French Ministry of Foreign Affairs
and the Cultural Services of the French Embassy in the United States.

This work, published as part of a program providing publication assistance, received
financial support from the French Ministry of Foreign Affairs, the Cultural Services
of the French Embassy in the United States and FACE (French American Cultural
Exchange). www.frenchbooknews.com

Small Beer Press
150 Pleasant Street, #306
Easthampton, MA 01027
www.smallbeerpress.com
info@smallbeerpress.com

Distributed to the trade by Consortium.

Library of Congress Cataloging-in-Publication Data

Châteaureynaud, Georges Olivier.
  [Short stories. English. Selections]
  A life on paper : stories / Georges-Olivier Chateaureynaud ; translated by Edward
Gauvin. -- 1st ed.
    p. cm.
  ISBN 978-1-931520-62-1 (alk. paper)
  1. Châteaureynaud, Georges Olivier--Translations into English. 2. Short stories,
French--Translations into English. I. Gauvin, Edward. II. Title.
  PQ2663.H352A2 2010
  843'.914--dc22
                                        2009054291
First edition 1 2 3 4 5 6 7 8 9

Printed on recycled paper by Thomson-Shore of Dexter, MI.
Text set in Centaur 12 pt.

Contents

For my mother

Foreword

Born in 1947, Georges-Olivier Châteaureynaud is the author of nearly two dozen books, and winner of the Prix Renaudot and the Prix Goncourt. He has been translated into a dozen languages but never, until now, into English. He has been publishing for more than thirty years: his fourth book, *Mathieu Chain*, appeared in 1978. In that novel, the author Mathieu Chain hears someone speaking of one of his books, a book that he is certain he never wrote despite it appearing in his bibliography. This small mystery and Chain's attempt to unravel it end up leading the character out of the known world and in entirely unexpected and compelling directions—not dissimilar to the way the simple act of shaving turns the life of the main character upside down in Emmanuel Carrère's novel *The Mustache*.

One of the great achievements of such a novel is that it feels at once oddly real and shot through with the fantastic: the twisty little passages of the everyday crosscut the billows and swirls of the imaginary. The real seems always to be threatening to unravel. Such complex interaction doubly characterizes Châteaureynaud's stories, which offer not only a subtle tension between the real and the imaginary, but also a tension between the calm and the severely odd. As Michèle Gazier has suggested, "These stories are haunted by the twin graces of simplicity and mystery... beneath their almost too seemly exteriors, they burst with madness, strangeness, a sensuality that their prose veneer conceals only the better to reveal."

A compilation chosen from several collections of Chateaureynaud's fiction published over a period of thirty years, *A Life on Paper* provides an excellent and representative sampling of Châteaureynaud's work. Some stories shade far into the fantastic; others seem realistic except for one brief moment or lingering doubt. But in all of the stories gathered here, we have the impression of a focused writer pursuing a personal and highly individual oneiric project. Like Kafka, Châteaureynaud has little interest in explaining away the fantastic or in dulling its claws: the dreamy strangenesses to be found in his stories simply exist and must be taken at face value. At one moment a frustrated poet might suddenly stumble into an impossible museum dedicated to him and documenting his life in painful detail. In another, a taxi driver might reach a street that connects the real world to a void. In other stories, unexplained blight mars both buildings and men, a man suddenly develops ridiculously small wings, an obsessive father has more than 93,000 photographs taken of his daughter, and a dead man has the bad manners to continue interacting with the living. A man might strip naked and then set fire to his house, his clothing, and his birds, and then wander off to nowhere. But, on the other hand, Châteaureynaud might catch you off-guard by offering a seemingly non-fantastical sketch of the life of a schoolboy. This is a world with severed heads still living in sacks, automated firing squads, time travel, tattoos that seem to have lives of their own, and a stuffed woman who occupies a musical instrument case. There are mythical creatures, like undines and sirens. There are dark, perhaps demonic pacts that seem to have been struck over (believe it or not) antique furniture. Through it all we find writers, discussions of writing and art, that allow us to read these stories metafictionally, and glimpse the phantom of the writer as he composes them. In addition, many of the elements of the gothic surface, but Châteaureynaud's tone that is anything but gothic. At times there are moments that strike us as familiar—the tale of a cursed knight, a city that might be out of Calvino, flickers of Vonnegut or even Barthelme, an island that seems half-built from *The*

Tempest and half from Alfredo Bioy-Casares's *The Invention of Morel*—but Châteaureynaud always inflects these moments just slightly, keeping the reader both interested and off-balance.

Châteaureynaud's most sinuous and elegant stories are reminiscent of Isak Dinesen's and their pleasure comes at least as much from the care with which the stories are told and their tone as from the content of the stories themselves. "Each of these texts," suggests Isabelle Roche, "is an embodiment of the short story in its purest form." The longer stories in particular are told with an authority and composure that do not resort to cheap tricks but offer instead moments of genuine subtlety and surprise.

Edward Gauvin's precise and fluid translation does Châteaureynaud great justice. Both in the original French and in Gauvin's English rendering, the prose is scrupulous and deliberately out of step with the post-Beckettian trends of much of contemporary French fiction. But while these stories feel out of time, they never feel old or unoriginal. Quite the opposite: as each story develops one quickly finds oneself engrossed in a fantastical narrative that only Châteaureynaud could write. These are sharp, carefully chiseled stories that initially seem deceptively simple but soon reveal hidden facets and satisfying complexities.

Taking all that into account it is surprising that it took thirty years to bring Châteaureynaud into English. He is an original, and though his vision is highly personal, it is also highly contagious. Before you're done reading, you'll begin to feel highly attuned to the way the real seeps into the surreal, the way the everyday, given just the right push, can collapse into the extraordinary.

Brian Evenson
Providence, March 2010

A Citizen Speaks

A s for the blight, we call it rust for its color. In reality, whether mold or oxide, its true nature eludes us. Does it not assail stone and slag alike? Both zinc and bronze? Even woodwork corrodes here. The leprosy spares only living things: a tree will spend ten years unscathed, slowly rising over a path, but let a branch be cut, treated, painted, and varnished—that branch will be disease-ridden in a few months. So unerring is it that old men's complexions often imitate its taint. That was how my father died: reddish, as though life had singed him. In his final days, I sometimes pressed on, in my walks, all the way to the park's far end, where we'd never before ventured. An ancient statue with a finger to its lips—a faun or *genius loci*—imposed silence on the crabgrass sprouting there. And this corner of nature seemed to obey. By some singular disposition of the place, the wind that blew all over the hill didn't blow there, and I never saw a bird land in that spot. Only my steps, crushing the grass beneath them, disturbed the silence. I drew closer to the faun. Perhaps his nudity explained why we'd been forbidden to play there. On his cheeks, chest, and thighs blossomed brown spatters of blight; hardly the least curious feature of this kind of decay is that it begins from within, making its way from the heart of a thing to its surface. One day, standing before the faun—my father was then at death's door, and I'd come one last time seeking the seclusion I was sure to find there—I had the idiotic but irrepressible urge to stab him with a long stick lying at his feet. My makeshift lance struck him right in the middle of one of the biggest russet spatters, roughly covering his heart had he been a creature of flesh. The rotten marble opened to the pointed stick as would a human breast, and I let go in fright. The lance quivered for a moment at the heart of the statue before falling to the ground. From the wound, with a stirring as of dust, red shavings drained away, a coarse powder of mingled rust and marble that I momentarily mistook for blood. I could not have been more terrified had the faun brought his hands to his chest. Yet still he stared at me with those same mocking eyes, a finger on his lips, as though asking me not to tell anyone about the marvel. My heart beating, I examined his wound more closely and saw that there was nothing left to him but a marble husk, the inside of the statue no longer solid but filled with that strange aggregate so like sand in an arena where blood from carnage had long since dried in the sun. Another shudder passed through me at the thought that my father was the same way, and I imagined his insides, his fragile flesh and organs scraping beneath his skin's reddish translucency. I went home. I was informed of his sudden death. But I was speaking of the city; if only rarely is it so severe, the damage caused by the rust nonetheless leaves unusual and vaguely catastrophic traces on everything within our walls. We who live here can on first glance pick out from among a hundred pictures of unnamed streets the only one from our town. This is because the secret germinations of our façades and rooftops always show through in some sign only we detect. Well before the spatters I've mentioned blossom in broad daylight, wood and stone tarnish, darken imperceptibly. It's as though the sun suddenly loathed bathing this sickly matter in its light. Although many buildings seem new thanks to coats of paint, no doubt remains that the entire city is wasted by this disease, as though by an acid it secretes itself, which will one distant day restore this spot to its initial desolation.

Paris, April 1974

A Life on Paper

The Siegling-Brunet collection no doubt constitutes the most extensive gathering of photographs devoted to a single person. Kathrin Laetitia Siegling was born in London on January 12, 1939. On April 14, 1960, she died in Amiens, where she had moved with her husband François Brunet. She lived, then, some 7,750 days, during which, at the rate of some dozen shots every twenty-four hours, her picture was taken 93,284 times. To the best of my knowledge, the negatives were never preserved, but the 93,284 prints were. Meticulously numbered and filed, they fill five large metal trunks I acquired in 1974, at the public auction of the Brunet estate. Need I add that, at the time, I made off with the lot for a song? Neither principal ballerina nor movie star nor Olympic champion of any kind, nor even muse, to a famous man, Kathrin Siegling never in her life enjoyed any celebrity likely to confer upon her image any market value. Victims of a lack of imagination too common to waste time maligning, Brunet's heirs all but gave away the chests that contained, in its entirety, an iconography unique in all the world: the life of a woman captured and made fast hour after hour, from birth to death.

It seems an opportune time to provide a summary biography and sketch a portrait of the strange, tormented man that Anthony Mortimer Siegling, Kathrin's father, was in the last part of his life.

The fifth child of a Cheshire baronet, he was born in 1890 and fought on the front at Artois during the First World War. The eve of the Second found him successfully practicing business law in London. After a brief engagement, he married Louise Mary Atkinson. He was forty-eight years old. Louise Mary, thirty years his junior, died of puerperal fever shortly after giving birth to Kathrin. The cruel brevity of his happiness late in life explains for me what must be dubbed Anthony Siegling's "madness." Fiancé, husband, father, and widower in the space of little over a year, he never recovered from his wife's death. He could well have conceived a morbid rancor toward the child, as has been known to happen. He did nothing of the sort. *Au contraire*, he devoted toward her an affection legitimate in principle, but excessive in its manifestations—in one of them, at least.

The disappearance of someone dear to us leaves an emptiness to be filled in one way or another. Psychologists call this slow healing "grief work," and we know what risks we run when it is not carried out: asthenia, heightened vulnerability, wasting away...Lost in suffering, Anthony Siegling got it in his head to recover Louise Mary, to resurrect her in Kathrin's barely formed person. Better yet, he would by means of the young girl take possession of all that had escaped him in her mother's life. He would spy upon her, keeping successive images of her childhood and adolescence, opposing their erosion by time's acid tides as no one before him had ever done.

His affluence facilitated the realization of what would have been, for a poorer man, a dream with no tomorrow. As his professional obligations prevented him from pursuing his project with the required diligence, he took on a photographer-in-residence to whom he gave the task of taking snapshots of Kathrin at regular intervals from morning till night. He himself had long practiced photography as a hobby.

Every night, upon returning from the city, he proceeded to develop and print the day's harvest of pictures.

We must imagine what these twenty years of unyielding routine were for him and her. For twenty years, Anthony Siegling never went to bed without first passing through that doorway, bathed in red light, to his darkroom; without having selected, enlarged, developed and fixed, dried and glazed a dozen portraits of his daughter. What could his thoughts, his state of mind have been—his exaltation and, almost certainly, his occasional exhaustion? With his infinite patience, night after night, image after image, was he able, in discerning an almost imperceptible change in Kathrin's features, to surprise time at work? For truly, the mystery of time itself is caught in the continuity of the Siegling-Brunet collection. Kathrin's appearance remains unchanged from photo to photo, and yet the first show us a newborn, and the last a woman dead at twenty . . . But the father's passion, in every sense of the word, cannot make us forget the daughter's. According to my investigation, seven photographers succeeded one another at her side. I located and interviewed several of them. The most intelligent and sensitive of them, John Cory, told me in no uncertain terms that he considered Anthony Siegling criminally insane, that the man had made of Kathrin's life a road to Calvary. She was thirteen when he took up his post at the Siegling household. He lasted only a few months, so great was his dislike for the job. I can still remember the very words he used to describe him. "Monsieur," he told me, "that was not photography. It was espionage, persecution, mental cruelty! The poor child seemed to me a hunted animal . . . There was something about her of a doe who forever hears the twig snapping beneath the wolf's paw. A sweet child, yes, but pale, pale, with a drawn look, a flicker of anguish in her eye . . . And so many nervous tics! She blinked all the time. See here, it wasn't humane to put a little girl through all that. I chose to walk out on the whole mess. I told her father why. He wouldn't listen. He threw my last check in my face. We almost came to blows. Bah! He was insane, that's all there was to it!"

Kathrin died after falling down a flight of stairs at her in-laws' house in Amiens, in the spring of 1960. She had just married François Brunet. She had met him during a ceremony commemorating Haig's Army and the combat her father had seen. François Brunet was a press photographer. The day they met, he was covering the event for a major regional paper.

As for me, despite all the rejections I've come up against so far, I have not despaired of someday convincing a patron to finance the museum of my dreams, where the collection chance has entrusted to me will finally be exhibited in its entirety. For I cannot help but believe the destiny of Kathrin Siegling-Brunet and the 93,284 photos that recreate her now belong to the artistic heritage of humanity.

Lozère, March 1989

Come Out, Come Out

With the help of his cane, the old man went to see if the gardener had indeed opened the valve to drain the pool. On his way back, he passed under the arbor. On the rattan table were cards someone had forgotten to put away after the last hand of liar's poker. He gathered them, replaced them in their case, and crossed the grounds, grumbling.

The sky was still blue, but he felt the autumn coming in his bones. A sudden disgust of winter and cold had overtaken him early, toward his fortieth year and, bit by bit, extended to autumn and its rains. He abhorred the dulled thud of chestnuts falling on the wet lawn, and of his own steps on the matted leaves.

Now he loved only the year's lambent half, spring and summer, which seemed to him shorter every time. Had he been fabulously well-to-do, he would have followed them, in a plane, around the world. Alas, he was but well-off. He lived in a large house, much too far north, that it would have cost him to leave in pursuit of the sun.

Half the year, he left the house as little as possible. Morose, he stewed away by the fire. Books tumbled from his hands. If he rose from his chair, it was to pace in circles and chide his housekeeper who, from the vagaries of his mood, surmised the news he had received that morning. If he was humming to himself, or petting his dog more tenderly than usual, it was a safe bet Francis and Lydia had passed up two weeks at the shore to humor him. If he turned his nose up at filets of sole for lunch and shut himself away for three days straight in his study, it meant that Zöe had chosen riding lessons instead.

Very early on in the winter, often as early as Christmas, he readied for summer. He wished his favorite season, and his house—too large now that his daughters lived far away—to be full of children. He checked names off his lists as he received replies to his imploring letters. He would stoop to anything to persuade his grandchildren to spend the summer with him. He had bought a pony, had a pool dug, and filled the basement with scooters and tricycles, balls of all sorts, BB guns, Indian costumes, croquet, bocce and ninepin sets . . . Anxious to have his heart's fill of the brats, he also invited his nephews, the children's friends, their friends' cousins. He hired a pretty student to watch over the swarm, with whom he didn't really mingle.

His own happiness lay in spying on the children's. In truth, he left the house barely more often in summer than winter. From his study—his favorite observation post—he followed the frolics of his guests with the help of binoculars. Or slipped down secret paths to the hedge from which he witnessed games of hide-and-seek or tag. When he had been sated by bursts of laughter, sharp cries, and breathless whispers, he returned to his lair, opened a great register, the record of his summers as a tender voyeur, and wrote down, on that day's page: *Little Roland had so much fun this afternoon. He was so excited he scratched his arm on the reed grille of the kitchen garden by accident.*

Or perhaps: *They've lain waste to my cherry tree like a cloud of blackbirds!*

Or even: *A big game of hide-and-seek today. Benoît—I was just as awkward at his age—let himself be tricked at every turn, while Lydia displayed her diabolical imagination. Wasn't it her idea to turn over the gardener's wheelbarrow and hide under it like a turtle in its shell? At the cry of "Come out, come out, wherever you are," she reappeared, her hair and back covered with twigs and dirt, a bit stiff, but triumphant.*

He set down his pen and daydreamed at length of other summers, other games of hide-and-seek. Of one in particular.

That day his brothers and his cousins, all girls, had hidden themselves so well he hadn't been able to flush out a single one. And when, weary of searching, he'd cried, "Come out, come out, wherever you are!" none had revealed themselves. They must have planned it in advance. He was the youngest, and easily brought to tears. It seemed he'd wandered the vast grounds for hours, though probably it hadn't lasted that long, shouting, "Come out, come out, wherever you are!" in a voice first confident, then angry, then trembling with fear. The others had chosen their day well: with the maids off and the parents otherwise occupied, only the children remained at the house. The world about the frightened boy was but a silent desert. *Come out, come out, wherever you are! Come out, oh come out of the fold in time or space where you've huddled one against the other, giggling at the little weakling choking on his tears!*

When at last his eldest cousin took pity on him, the unlucky child was shaking with fright in the plain light of day. The others surrounded him, fussed over him, tried to make it up to him. He'd had nightmares for weeks afterward.

The deck of cards in his free hand, the old man stopped in the middle of the lawn, his gaze circling the grounds. Francis and Lydia had been the last to leave, that very morning. The summer had been glorious. For two months, house and gardens had resounded to clamor and commotion. The sun had obediently shone on the pool's blue water, the wooden croquet balls, the freshly painted swing set. And yet this was a fleeting happiness, he knew; this perfect summer would be the last. The children had grown up a great deal since the one before. Next year, if they still agreed to visit, it would be to explore surrounding lands, beyond the Edenic bower. Already they spoke insistently of bicycle rides and swimming in the nearby river...

Then, beneath the foliage of his grounds—still green, but to his clouded eyes faded from within—he murmured in a tremulous voice: "Come out, come out, wherever you are!" And one by one, from behind the groves in their last reprieve and the flowerbeds soon to brown, appeared the creatures he had till now kept at bay. Uncoiling their scaly lengths, spotted with warts and sores, pressing their shriveled snouts between the saplings, they began their advance.

Lozère, May 1986

Icarus Saved from the Skies

The ironies of fate are infinite. Around the time I turned twenty, despite having decided to steer clear of both doctors and women, I met Maude, then a surgical intern, and at her pressing request became her lover.

Don't go thinking I've ever borne the slightest ill will toward the medical body, much less a woman's body. My prejudice extends only to the physician or female likely to see me naked, discover my misfortune, and make it even crueler to bear.

It all comes down to character, they say. In my place, someone else might've rejoiced at what seemed to me a catastrophe. After all, if I'd wanted at any price to rise above the human herd or leave my mark on the world, I certainly could've. But I didn't give a flying fig about being thought original or unique; my only ambition was to blend in with the crowd, flank to flank with my brethren and fellow creatures in the cozy stable of the species. Alas! I was a brother to no man, and no creature was my fellow. In the course of a few days I sprouted wings or, rather, wingbuds. At first naked, pinkish, coarse, and altogether repugnant, these excrescences were soon covered in a chick's yellow down. Thank God for small favors. When I craned my neck to see my back in the bathroom mirror, the down honestly made those extra extremities easier on the eye.

On my first date with Maude, my appurtenances weren't too

cumbersome yet. Unfurled, they spanned about a foot and a half. Folded and pressed flat by a tight undershirt, they could be hidden beneath roomy coats or large, loose-fitting sweaters. My profile suffered a little, but I didn't care. Given the choice, I'd probably have preferred a hunchback's honest hump to these wings which seemed no less suspect for having fallen from the sky, so to speak. What did the heavens want with me? I admit to being terrified. I hid myself away from the world. A rare breed of beginner bird, I feared in every doctor the fowler, if not the taxidermist. Wouldn't they commit me to be studied at their leisure, exhibit me at conferences and, why not, even wind up dissecting me to find out more? As for women... I'd just turned twenty. At an age when people still hesitated sometimes to show themselves as nature made them, where would I have found the courage to show myself as it should never have made me?

It turned out I didn't need courage; Maude took care of everything. Not long after we'd gotten to know each other—that, too, was her doing—she said she'd seen in my eyes when our gazes first met that I wasn't like the others, that "I had something." As it happened, she wasn't far off. I had wings. Her reaction on seeing them played a great part in the continued happiness of our relationship, which lasted for quite some time.

She called me her beautiful bird and, chirping sweet nothings after making love, smoothed my budding feathers. We didn't go out much, nor did we miss it. I felt uncomfortable in public, and she hated the half-pitying, half-repulsed looks I got for my apparent hunchback.

"Idiots! They think you're handicapped," she raged. "If they only knew!"

"Please don't get all worked up, sweetie—people will stare." I tried hard to drag her toward a deserted square or a quieter side street.

"Promise me you'll show them who you really are one day!"

I sank my head into my hunched shoulders. Who I really was? Did

I even know? A cripple? A monster? A future carnival freak? An angel in the making? All I wanted to be was the plain old harmless and ordinary me from before my fateful election.

"One day you'll soar into the light," said Maude, pressing herself against me.

"Yeah, sure ... Let's go home, okay?"

My wings got bigger. Maude was constantly measuring them and sometimes lost patience with how slowly they grew. They were twenty-three inches across on our wedding day, and thirty the day our son was born. Soon they were pushing thirty-five, which, while respectable for a buzzard or a seagull, was pathetic for a man. Worse yet was when Maude noticed they'd mysteriously shrunk a few inches. Two, to be precise. Not only surprised by the decrease, she was truly disappointed by what I, to the contrary, saw as a remission, or even the beginning of a recovery. This was the reason for our first real fight. Tired of hearing her repeatedly call my spontaneous shrinkage abnormal, I pointed out with some bitterness that the initial growth had been no more normal. One word led to another, and soon we were quarrelling in earnest. It wasn't long before I accused her of being more fascinated by my deformity than in love with me. To this she snapped back that I had the wingspan of a waterfowl and was birdbrained to boot.

She'd scored a point there and, beating a hasty retreat, I went to sulk in my office. For reasons fairly easy to grasp, I'd given up teaching to turn toward translation. I spent the better part of my day alone at home. In the days after the fight, I often stopped working right in the middle of something to measure my wings with a folding ruler and some painful contortions.

At first the trend Maude had noticed continued. My aberrant protuberances lost almost an inch a day: half an inch per wing. The next day I calculated that at this rate, taking into account the four inches already resorbed, in nineteen days everything would be back to normal.

I started getting my hopes up. In three weeks I'd be able to go out in short sleeves. Next summer I'd go to the shore again, and swim and sunbathe just like any other vacationer. And if, one of these days, someone else besides Maude were to show interest... A poor way to thank the woman who'd taken me as I was at the worst moment of my life, but my own underlying ingratitude reassured me at heart: I saw it as proof I wasn't on my way to being an angel.

Two more days went by, and my wings lost two and a half inches. The fifth, sixth, and seventh days my condition stabilized, just as it had for long periods before. Then the eighth day landed like a cleaver on the forehead of a lamb: I'd grown back almost an inch. The next day I grew back another, and the third an inch and a half. At night, when Maude came back from the hospital, I didn't even come out of my office to greet her. She respected my dejection, I must admit, without sharing it. Certain that I'd wind up giving in to her, she didn't insist on examining me. Yet the conflicting hopes we nourished no doubt did their part in digging the chasm that would later divide us.

This relapse—the first in a long series—left me exhausted and bitter. I'd thought I was "healed." Far from it. I had to face facts: my "disease" was progressing. Or whatever it was—my idea of it remained quite vague. At worst, I was beginning to dread that my misfortune, though still secret was doomed over time to be obvious to everyone. If my wings kept on growing, the day would inevitably come when I'd no longer be able to hide them beneath tight bandages and a big overcoat. Just how big would they get, anyway? Were they destined to uproot me from the earth one day in the near or distant future? Even I saw myself as repugnant and laughable, my giant wings keeping me from walking.

One night, with tears in my eyes, I asked Maude to cut them off. She let out an exclamation.

"How hideous! And how misguided! An amputation would be a crime against science. You're unique, you—"

Beside myself, I put a stop to the noble words I knew were coming.

"As a doctor," I shouted, "all you did was measure my disfigurement from shoulder to phalange! Please, Maude: I'm not asking you to understand, I'm asking you to save me."

She stared at me incredulously. "Save you? By operating on you? Your wings are a gift, an incredible gift—"

"Oh, really? For years I've lived completely shut away, I wait for night to go out for some air, I've wasted the best years of my life translating trash—are those gifts? Can you tell me how any of that is a gift? What good are these accessories that weigh me down, itch constantly, and keep me from sleeping on my back?"

An unfamiliar smile spread over Maude's face. We were husband and wife, and I'd seen her happy before, but at that moment she was transfigured. Her eyes shone, and I seemed to hear in her voice what I could only call ardor.

"Patience, my love. You have to wait, take the burden on yourself and bear it all, and one day you'll use those wings to fly!"

"But I don't want to!"

"You don't?"

"Not for all the world! I get dizzy just standing on a step stool! Don't leave me like this, Maude, I'm begging you: cut them off!"

Her reply came, determined and irrevocable. "Never."

"Then I'll go see someone else. There are plenty of surgeons in the world."

She shrugged. "You wouldn't dare."

>⊱⊰<

Georges-Olivier Châteaureynaud

She was right. I didn't dare. Many years passed without me ever seeking out another surgeon. I grew old with my wings. At their largest, around my fortieth year, they measured four feet seven inches. four feet seven inches! It was pathetic—clearly not enough to save a 170-pound man from earthly forces. It was, however, enough to slow his fall a bit, if need be. My wings saved my life. Maude and I were on vacation in the Alps. For several months after I'd begged her in vain to cut off my wings, I feared she'd leave me, but she didn't, though we started sleeping in different rooms. I knew I'd let her down. She quite simply no longer believed in me. We carried on an odd relationship, no longer in love but unable accept it.

For hours we'd been making our way along a steep and sunny mountain path. The August sun had just passed its height, and I was bathed in sweat. Few people know just how hot a pair of wings can make you, especially under a polo shirt. The path led along the deserted crest of a ridge. I wound up taking my shirt off. I was walking in front. Without turning to Maude, I fluttered my wings for a moment, congratulating myself aloud for having taken off my shirt. It was delicious: the air ran through my feathers, cooling my back. At the very moment when, overcoming my lifelong fear of the void, I leaned over to see the edelweiss Maude had said she'd spotted, she shouted in my ear, "Fly, damn you!" And sent me hurtling forward with a forceful shove.

My body shattered, I survived a fall that only I could've. Maude understood as much. Since that day, not in order to be forgiven, but out of love (a love grown stronger for having been cast into doubt and confirmed), she has dedicated herself to me, and administers all the care my condition requires with a boundless devotion.

Lozère, February 1991

The Only Mortal

Someone must have made a mistake with his enlistment papers, for François, without having asked for it in any way, got posted overseas, the only draftee in a company of enlisted men. Right after training, they were deployed to one of those countries where the natives were dropping like flies. The situation weighed heavy on the international conscience; it had to stop. The other soldiers were thrilled. Adventure, distant lands, hazard pay . . . François figured on spiders, scorpions, and sunburn for everyone. He was right about the sun and the critters, but in his inexperience hadn't counted on the smells. Once there, he'd caught on quickly: these countries were all about the smell. Stench was more like it. In Europe, organic matter was changeless, numbed by the bracing freshness of the climate. Here it raced toward oblivion beneath the sun's lash. Milk turned quicker than the minute hand on a watch, and flesh to rot the second life left it.

As for fighting: they took a few shots at a shack half-screened by a scrawny stand of trees. It was a farm; they wounded a goat. After the skirmish, they continued their advance and marched into the capital. Crowds and jubilation, wild kisses, cameras, officers interviewed by short-sleeved reporters, parades, twenty-one-gun salutes.

><

Then life at the garrison began. Once more, François had no one to talk to. As a student who'd deferred his compulsory service, he had under his belt long years of literary studies that seemed useless, almost ludicrous, to many. A sense of danger had drawn him closer to his fellow soldiers. In action, he'd felt for them a kind of friendship tinged with contempt. Safety and routine duty distanced him again, returning him to his quietly ironic intellectual solitude. Bastini and Onfret bored him to tears with their soccer talk. Besides, they knew what he thought of it, and so kept him out of their feverish forecasts: would Marseille make the quarterfinals? The only one François could stand was Claveton, hands down the dumbest of them all. That was just it, though: François led Claveton around by the nose, a private second class with a personal bodyguard.

He soon tired of the red-light district's latex amusements and dance-hall intrigues: all that jealousy and drama was pointless since, when it came down to it, the only difference among the women available was price. Well—there was always sightseeing. Soldiers were forbidden to go out alone. That didn't stop François, who had Claveton. Who else would be stupid enough to go with him beyond the safe zone? Guerillas still lurked off the main roads patrolled by the machine guns of the expeditionary forces.

They gave some vague excuse, took a jeep from the depot, and drove down the coastal route, François at the wheel, Claveton on the light machine gun. François had lectured his companion at length, but with Claveton you never knew if what you said to his face really got through his skull. François would only have been half-surprised had Claveton suddenly started gunning down civilians, children, or even iffy-looking camels. Luckily, no one crossed their path.

They covered about twenty miles. Here and there, amidst the ruins of civil war, emerged other ruins: the ruins of yesteryear, bleached clean as old bone, while to recent ruins still clung yesterday's rotting flesh. The sea, intensely blue, lapped at shores of red and ochre pebbles. François had no destination in mind. Claveton hadn't needed one to follow.

Around a bend in the road, an undamaged house swung into view: the first. It stood, below road level, beside a narrow sandy beach flanked by a tree. A real tree, not a dust-choked twig broom stuck in the ground. With its lush green foliage and dark shade, the tree made a striking impression. A steep track led down to the house. François turned the jeep.

"Let's see what's down here. Keep an eye out, OK?"

"Uh-huh!" he replied with grim determination.

François felt obligated to repeat his earlier warning. "You won't shoot without my say-so, right, Claveton?"

"Nuh-uh!"

"OK, then."

François almost parked the jeep beneath the tree, but at the last moment decided against it. The shade was too pretty for him to sully it with his smelly, backfiring machine that leaked grease and dirty engine oil from every crevice ... The shade cast by the house itself seemed to him less rare and delicate, so he parked there. He got out and walked under the tree. Claveton followed grudgingly. His plan, in case things got rough, had been *I'll gun, you run* ... but for that he had to stay close to the jeep. A woman came out of the house to greet them. She was young, beautiful, and unafraid. She spoke French as well as François, and much better than Claveton. She welcomed them, and offered them tea. Claveton shifted his weight from one foot to the other, glancing unhappily at the jeep. He didn't trust her, which worked out well for François: Claveton would've been a nuisance. François suggested Claveton stand guard, an offer he gratefully accepted.

➤❧

The young woman's name was Lalena. Her skin was dark, but not as dark as the girls at the café, or the ones dying in shelters with their children in their arms. She wasn't gaunt or starved-looking. Since she didn't look like a whore, François figured she was rich. That had to be it. How would he know who was rich down here? Anyone more than just skin and bones already was, in a way. Still, he couldn't help but wonder how she'd kept those downy cheeks so plump, those breasts, shifting gently beneath the fabric of her dress, so full.

She spoke to him of Paris, of the Bastille Opera and the Louvre. She was wearing a kind of royal blue bubu and sandals, but he had no trouble picturing her in an evening dress and shiny heels at a gala or premiere. They sipped tea and chatted. An old servant brought a cup to Claveton, who smelled some native ruse and refused it.

Nothing else happened that day. François took his leave when it seemed polite to do so. Lalena invited him back when he felt like it. He promised to seize the first opportunity. In the mess, there were rumors about heading south, where trouble still brewed. He walked back to the jeep. The sun was setting, and the shade beneath the tree less dense.

"So, 'dja jump her?" Claveton inquired.

"Not yet. She's a respectable woman. I'll have to come back a few times."

Claveton's normally dull face lit up in a huge grin. A respectable woman . . . *a few times* . . . He understood at once: target and maneuver.

"You'll come with me?"

"Uh-huh!"

"OK, then."

They made it back to the safe zone without incident.

The possibility Claveton had alluded to didn't happen on their second or even third visit to Lalena. That is, François never did *jump* her, as

Claveton had so delicately put it. On his fourth visit, Lalena led François upstairs. He followed her into a room that opened on a broad view of the sea. It was cool and combined the charms and comforts of a bedroom, a balcony, and a grotto: he felt good there. A vast bed occupied the far end. It was flanked by several shelves, one of which bore a tea set, another a game of *petits chevaux*, and the last paraphernalia for smoking.

"They'll sell anything around your bases," she told him. "I've got something much nicer here...something like a special reserve wine, if you're interested..."

Some men in his company would've sold their souls for a taste of such local specialties. François wasn't as fond of them, but accepted so as not to put his hostess out. He let her ready the pipes, which she did quite matter-of-factly, no island mumbo-jumbo. Then, while smoking and drinking tea, they played *petits chevaux*, which he hadn't done since childhood. He found it infinitely more pleasurable than he'd expected. Was it the hashish? The die struck the wooden board with a thunderous sound, and he seemed to hear the hurrahs of an invisible crowd mingling with horses' galloping hooves. It lasted awhile, then the cavalcade and the ovations faded into some unknown distance. He became aware that he and Lalena had tumbled onto the bed, that they were naked. Her lips at his ear, Lalena twittered sweet, unintelligible words.

Claveton's voice tore François from the happy haze where he'd retreated after disentangling himself from Lalena.

"François! François! It's late! Where the hell are you?" Claveton had gotten over his initial vision of François lying with his throat slit in a ditch, but he was still afraid of missing roll call.

"Your friend's barking," Lalena said.

François nodded. True enough, but Claveton wasn't the only one. Everyone in the company did their share of barking. François rose and began getting dressed.

"François! You there? What the hell are you up to?"

"Coming!"

"Christ, get your ass in gear! It's getting dark!"

"Coming!" François smiled apologetically at Lalena, who smiled back.

"He's right. The road's not safe at night. You'll come back?"

"First chance I get. If not tomorrow, the day after."

She blew him a kiss with her fingertips. "Go on..."

He grabbed his shirt and hurried downstairs. Night was falling in earnest now. Even if they got back safe and sound, they'd still have to get past the guard on duty. François didn't know what Claveton feared more, guerillas or Sergeant Colombani, but the big fellow was hopping up and down impatiently.

"C'mon, c'mon now! Let's beat it!"

"You going to let me put my shirt on?"

"If you're lucky. Hey, what's that? You get a tattoo?"

"Tattoo?"

Claveton's finger, lightly gleaming with gun lube, pointed at François' chest. François dropped his gaze. Under his left pec, almost right over his heart, was something written in blue. He was puzzled for a moment, annoyed, then figured Lalena was playing a prank.

"What does it say? I can't read it."

"That bitch is a regular comedian! It says 'Mortal.'"

"Huh? 'Mortal'? What the fuck? What's that mean?"

"No idea. Get in, we're outta here!"

"Wait a minute, dammit!" François pressed his fingers together like a brush or a palette knife, spat on them, and rubbed the letters vigorously. "Is it coming off?"

"No. Get in and start'er up already, or they're gonna take us hostage on this piece-of-shit road!"

They weren't taken hostage, but they did miss roll call. Sergeant Colombani noticed they'd had no real reason for taking the jeep, and promised to stick it to them when they got back from the action. For now, though, everyone was needed: they were headed south on a peacemaking mission.

This time, a shepherd who didn't respond to their shouted warnings in time had his peace made for him once and for all. They found a penknife on him. A rumor went around that Onfret and Bastini were getting decorated for their little exploit. From that day on, François had to keep a closer watch on Claveton, who was clearly ready to make just about anyone's peace to get himself a medal too. After a bloody beginning (at least for half-deaf shepherds), the campaign dwindled to road checkpoints and supply distribution. Neither Onfret nor Bastini ever wound up with a medal; unofficially, they remained mere criminals of war.

Soldiers cannot afford to be modest. They dress, undress, and wash beneath the eyes of fellow soldiers. The entire company filed past François to check out his so-called tattoo. It was generally considered pretentious and pathetic at the same time. *Mortal, huh? Big whup! What, you didn't know, ya dumb fuck?* François let them ride him without protest. What good was telling them, or trying at least, that first of all, it wasn't a tattoo, and second of all, whatever it was, it hadn't been his idea? The word had appeared on his skin as simply as a butterfly alighting, sudden as a tumor. Words didn't flit about in the air looking for a fleshly page, or sprout from the body like mushrooms from a damp, dark spot; it just didn't happen! And yet it had. Try getting them to buy that: the men of his company, who fled poetry and abstraction like the plague, or even an honest army doctor faced (at worst) with one bullet wound for every sixty cases of the clap...Opening his mouth would've been risky. François was careful to keep it shut. In the end, his "tattoo" was a sorry sight beside Bastini's, and the rest soon lost interest.

François knew—his skin knew—that it wasn't a tattoo. First of all, a tattoo didn't change. You had it, you kept it. Your skin could get old, wrinkled, creased, spotted, and the tattoo ruined, but it wouldn't disappear till you did, into the eternal night of the grave. His own was constantly changing. Clearly no one else had noticed, but he'd quickly seen that its size and color depended on...François was reluctant to say his "mood," but that was how it was. The six letters that made up the word "Mortal" got bigger or smaller, clearer or blurrier, went from dark to light blue, and sometimes almost green, according to his feel-ings at a given moment. Sometimes the letters even grew so clear as to be imperceptible. At first, François was tempted to show Claveton. He stopped himself just in time. Claveton would've been a troublesome witness. He'd have yelled out loud and gotten everyone else stirred up. Or he might not even have understood that the sudden absence of the word on François' chest was as unnatural, as "miraculous," as its presence five hours before or after. For the word always returned. The same night, or the next morning, when François took a moment alone to check, he found it back in its place, seemingly indelible, definitive, fateful, like a stamp on an official file.

They wound up north again. Sergeant Colombani hadn't forgotten his promise. François and Claveton were confined to camp for fifteen days. While everyone else caught up with the easy beauties of the bar district, Colombani made it his job to find them more morally as well as physically wholesome activities.

When the fifteen days were up, the first place they headed was a brothel. Claveton was fine with stealing a jeep, dropping François off at Lalena's, getting busted by Colombani on the way back, and catching a month of extra chores and confinement all over again—but not before getting himself laid.

Several days went by before an opportunity presented itself. This time they didn't have to misappropriate army equipment. Two reporters off to explore the coast gave them a ride in their Range Rover and arranged to pick them up again that night on the way back.

The house was all locked up. François found a letter tacked to the door. Sun and sea wind had already weathered and discolored the paper. In violet ink on the envelope was written François' first and last name, misspelled. Letter in hand, he went to sit down on a concrete bench facing the strip of beach. He read the letter several times. It was polite and bland, nothing like the letter of a witch who wrote disturbing things in magic ink on her lovers' bodies. Lalena had left for Switzerland. She wanted to see him again. She'd left a phone number in Geneva, but the campaign in the south had lasted several months and the number was probably no good now. If it belonged to a hotel, or friends of hers, thought François, surely he could pick up her trail again? He shrugged. Even if he found her, what would he say? *What is this goddamned thing you stuck me with? Don't play innocent with me! This thing on my skin? I caught it from you, and now it won't go away!*

He spent an unsettled afternoon smoking and watching the waves, reading Lalena's letter and draining the bottle of whisky he'd brought her as a gift, thinking about life in general and that damned word in particular, about his bad luck in having to bear, inscribed and spelled out, the final word on the human condition... He'd taken off his shirt. There it was, quite legible, the same blue as the sea. He found it especially despicable that day: insolent, triumphant in the vacuity of waiting. When he was good and drunk, he scratched at the word until it bled, and asked Claveton to burn it with his lighter. All he'd have to do was get it patched up by the medic when they got back, and then they'd never have to speak of it, there'd be a pretty scar in its place; he didn't care about the pain, it was a price he was ready to pay.

Ever cautious when beyond the base's perimeter, Claveton hadn't had so much as a drop to drink. He refused to burn François. Did he, Claveton, have to do the thinking for both of them? What about Colombani? If the sarge found out, he wouldn't let it rest. Self-inflicted wounds or mutilation in a zone of operations, with enemy right next door? You could get yourself court-martialed for that. François flew into a rage. He ordered Claveton to do it. Claveton replied that as a private second class, he didn't have to take orders from another private second class. François called him a dumbass and tried himself to burn the few square inches of his own skin that were poisoning his life. He moved the flame toward his chest, screamed, and dropped it. All he'd managed was a blister. He finished off the whisky to dull the pain. When the reporters honked from the road, Claveton called them over to help. They had a hell of a time hauling François into the Range Rover.

François didn't try to find Lalena after his discharge. The letter with the phone number in Geneva had remained on the beach by the house, along with the empty bottle. Besides, when he gave it more thought, he came to the conclusion that Lalena'd had nothing, or almost nothing, to do with it. Perhaps her skin had only been a catalyst? He had but to close his eyes to remember how soft she'd felt, how sweet she'd smelled . . . That was it: his skin had reacted to contact with hers, and this was the result. Why not? What did anyone know? What did anyone have time to understand about this dark, embroiled world, by the wavering light of their mind and senses, in the span so meanly allotted to them? He figured he'd have to riddle it out on his own. His idea of burning it off hadn't altogether been bad, just a bit crude and brutal. After all, plastic surgery hadn't been created for dogs. When he got back to France, he made an appointment with a dermatologist. If it resembled a tattoo, it could be removed like a tattoo. The night before his visit, he was full of hope. The nightmare was about to end. He would forget this ridiculous affair, all that pathos in such poor taste, and once more be a normal, decent man who thought about death only once in a while. He took a sleeping pill, drained his nightly glass of water down to the last drop, and slept like a child.

The next day, about to step into the shower, he found that with the exception of his face and neck, his entire body—even his prick, even the soles of his feet—was covered with writing. Scrawled in thick awkward capitals, penned in dainty cursive, even calligraphically scripted, the word "Mortal" a thousand times over bound him in a blue web, like the tangled weave of a net flung on him from above. He knew then he would never be free, and burst into tears.

Later, when he'd calmed down, he called the dermatologist and cancelled his appointment. Slowly, in the months that followed, the flare-up receded; things went back to normal. All that remained on his skin was the one original word, where it had first appeared. As before, it flickered with the passing days—regularly and peacefully, on the whole—the pilot light of a terror now so deep-set as to be inseparable from life's own daily rounds.

Lozère, December 1992

The Peacocks

I still recall: we had such confidence, we'd set out to devour the world, to conquer it all, even the planets and the starry void beyond the skies, it was all our America, a land promised and delivered, and then the quiet, stubborn things wore us down as words wear away an eraser.

We were living in a house in the country, Marie and I and two peacocks. Mornings I liked to let her sleep in, pale in the shadows—an eye, a cheek, a rounded shoulder, a leg sometimes surfacing from the sheets as though from quicksand. I'd step outside. In the yard, a peacock was turning toward the rising sun. I'd whistle, calling out to that handsome idiot: come, come to your master, my colored one, my brightly bedecked swaggerer, come! He'd freeze and fix an empty round eye on me. He'd been dreaming; he woke to my whistle, alarmed at being in the world. His mate soon joined him. They stared at me, waiting for God knows what, or perhaps it was simple—watching and waiting for the golden shower of grain that poured each morning from my hands. I was God. I fulfilled their expectations, reaching deep into a sack for wheat that disappeared into the cracks between the porch floorboards—eat, you dumb animals. There, just like that, then groom your feathers, and peck, or cluck, whatever it is you peacocks do, what good are words now anyway, they'll all be forgotten soon.

I'd close up the sack and lean it against a wall in the foyer. Cross the yard and open the gate. We never forgot to close it at night. In a world now safe as a tomb, I held on to this pathetic, childish ritual. I'd take a few steps out into the road, the king stepping from the Louvre to his death. The road was empty.

The village wasn't far away. If I'd wanted, I could've pushed on to the next bend. I would've passed, lost in the fog, a bell tower; a few chimneys without smoke; an isolated shack, once a military outpost, long loud with grunts. A neighbor had kept pigs there. We'd often stop there on the way to the market, when there'd still been a market. Marie loved little piglets, little kids, little gifts. Whenever we were walking she always found something to pet—a puppy, a kitten, a calf; a lamb to coo over, a child to coddle. I stayed a few steps behind, hands in my pockets, urging her to keep walking. The only small things she hated were her breasts, and complained about them till the very end.

I'd go back inside.

We'd inherited all humanity had to offer. Books, music, paintings—they were all ours. At first, Marie put on a different dress each time she put another record on the player. To listen better, she said, to feel more. Maybe we wouldn't have made it through the early days without acting silly, going a bit crazy. Whenever we came back from a spree I'd open the crates and we'd try out canned food, alcohol, candy, test out fabrics; I was saving the books for later. Marie was bewitched by a music box. She had thirty other ones already, the prettiest...That's not all, I said, wait'll we unload the piano and the wing chair and the desk. We set to it clumsily—her in a nightgown and me in an alpaca suit—and were soon out of breath. The peacocks watched us struggle under the weight of the marquetry—excited, sweating, egging ourselves on with swigs of wine. That night, though the truck was still half full and we hadn't finished setting up—to tell the truth, we never really finished—we set the table among the furniture and crates. And ate, drank, were merry. All that crystal, porcelain, silver, and silk, for us alone. Sometimes Marie draped herself in the biggest, heaviest jewels she could find, and sometimes she wore only one, tiny and chosen with great care from among the thousands in her chest. Sometimes—often—she dined in a wedding dress that she'd throw out the next day, tossing it, sauce- or champagne-stained, into the well behind the house. We had drawers and drawers of baroque lingerie with charming, ridiculous names—Rita, Gypsy, Barcarolle, Lady Luck, Nina, Snowy Lace. I dressed up as a commodore, an admiral, anything flashy and official—gold trim, epaulettes, medals galore—and we'd dance.

At first light we'd go out on the front steps and take a deep breath or throw up. Pale, emaciated, a stray lock falling over her eye, Marie would sit on a step in a black lace teddy cut away around her nipples and belly, her stockings mauve or apple green. She'd just sit there and weep, shaking and shivering in the bitter little wind of dawn. Curious, the peacocks would watch us from the other side of the yard, where I'd built a little hut, and the dazed male would spread his feathers. I'd sit down next to Marie. We'd cradle each other in tears and whispers. Slowly, the sun would chase away the cruelties of dawn. Bit by bit, we'd relax, spreading our legs in the growing warmth, and sleep would come for us wherever we were. One night we drank more than usual and it was death who came instead.

I woke and saw the peacocks in the middle of the yard, pecking away between strands of Marie's strewn hair. From the porch, where it seemed she'd collapsed, to that spot—the barest, most exposed spot, where she now lay—a purple trickle ran across the brown earth, buzzing with flies. The sun beat down, hard and bright. I bent down and veiled her grey lips, her shit-smeared cheek, with a scrap of stocking before lifting her body. All the way to the steps I had to fend off the distressed birds, kicking out as they screeched and pranced around my legs.

I laid her on the unmade bed. Moistening a corner of the bedsheet with a bottle of gin forgotten on the nightstand, I cleaned every trace of dust and vomit from her face, her hair, even her shoulders. But her lingerie was stained. How could I leave her like this? Piece by piece, I stripped away her faded finery and bathed her body with liquor. Then, from the jumbled crates I picked an outfit she'd never worn before, weightless and maiden-white. Did we have white shoes, too? I finally found a pair buried in a closet. I sat her up to wait, like a doll, in an armchair while I remade the bed with fresh sheets. And mad with activity, I cleared the room of everything cluttering it up—crates, trinkets, bottles, clothes—tossing jewels out the window by the handful except for a blue ring I slipped onto her finger with great difficulty. I even grabbed a broom to make it go faster, pushing objects and dust bunnies out the door all at once. When the room was clean, I went looking for her makeup kit and clumsily applied a little lipstick, a little eyeliner, some powder foundation, and everything I could find in the way of flowers for a corsage: two withered satin roses from a hatband. Then, and only then, with one final look around the room to make sure I'd forgotten nothing, and really done the best I could—emptied the ashtrays, dusted the furniture, laid Marie out nice and straight in her Sunday best on the bedspread, dolled up, perfumed, hair neat, arms stretched out beside her body, eyes closed—I left.

In a shed I found two jerricans of fuel I'd been careful enough to store up and more bourbon than it took to get me drunk as I wanted. The sun was going down. The peacocks continued their idiotic circling. Seated on a jerrican in the middle of the yard, across from the front steps, I threw them feed from time to time, taking small sips and waiting for nightfall. The hour came. I'd given it a lot of thought, and it was better to start with the peacocks, take them by surprise instead of chasing them around in the dark with a full jerrican. Luring them over with one last handful of grain, I had no trouble dousing them with fuel. Next I set methodically about the house. First the roof. I climbed up. Hauling up the unopened jerrican with a rope was a bit harder. Still, I managed. Once the shingles were soaked, I got down again and started splashing the front and sides.

Everything was ready. I took my clothes off and drenched them in fuel. One after the other, I threw the jerricans, almost empty, through the window of the room where Marie lay. Naked as a jaybird and shivering, I set fire to my pile of clothes. The terrified peacocks ran around me faster and faster. I grabbed my burning shirt by the sleeve and hurled it at the house, which burst into flames in under a second. I didn't even need a torch to light the peacocks. Dazzled, they stumbled right into the flames in panic and then ran around a few more minutes, zigzags of light, before collapsing.

I opened the gate and started walking. Right from my first tottering steps, the gravel on the roadbed and the cracks in the asphalt cut into my bare feet. Then came the rocks, the twigs, the razor grass along the embankment and, farther off, the high and spoiled wheat among the brambles.

Paris, Jan. 1973-Apr. 1974

Unlivable

Accommodations obsess me. I have what you might call a housing neurosis. Most of my childhood was spent in cramped quarters (my mother sublet the cellar to me and my father), leaving me with a tendency toward claustrophobia no less crippling than the legacy of agoraphobia bequeathed me on visits to my grandparents (father's side), a pair of fanatical balloonists. I'd rather not discuss my other grandparents' house; my asthma specialist says it's best not to think about it.

Without making too big a deal of things, suffice it to say I've gone through a few rough patches. If I tallied them up, the lows of my life as a renter would vastly outnumber the highs. For a while I lived in flames. Well, I exaggerate. They were flamelets, but annoying all the same. At all hours of the night and day, fires would break out spontaneously in my apartment, here or there, behind a painting, inside a closet, under a chair, in the laundry hamper . . . None of my belongings were safe. How often did I find myself penniless, needing a new driver's license, all because my wallet had gone up in smoke along with my jacket while I was asleep? I'd be getting dressed when I'd find my pants scorched to knee shorts, my shirts burned to a crisp, my shoes charred and blistered, my gloves in ashes at the back of the drawer where I kept them. My life was a miniature living hell; I always smelled slightly singed; In fact I was slightly singed.

But you can get used to anything; after a while the continual catas-
trophes became routine. I kept buckets full of sand and water around,
wet rags and even a blanket; when a blaze began, I no longer called the
firemen, but set to it myself with the jaded efficiency of a seasoned
veteran. I could just as well have sat back and done nothing; the fires
always wound up burning themselves out. I'd walk in or wake up only
to find evidence of fires that started while I was out or asleep: rugs full
of holes, blackened walls or doors, furniture it seemed some quickly
sated creature had gnawed. I settled for airing the place out.

I could've complained to the landlord, but didn't dare. I hate com-
plaining. An absurd point of pride! But as I've been told often enough,
everything about me is absurd. Besides, had I brought up the subject
with him, wouldn't he have had good reason to turn against me? After
all, could these sporadic flare-ups really be chalked up to the apartment, or just to me, to some incendiary element I didn't know I had
inside? I don't think of myself as having an especially fiendish or flam-
mable temperament, but these things aren't always easy to prove. We
could've fought it out in court, but justice costs a lot. I opted to keep
quiet and moved without asking for my deposit—three months of rent
that might've been enough to get the place back in shape after I left.

Thus it was that one morning I put on my least-damaged suit.
I decided against slipping my toothbrush into my pocket: although
practically new, its handle had melted the night before. Using the first
excuse that came to mind, I left the key with the super and, walking
out on bits of burnt wood and sooty rags, strode determinedly toward
a new life. An opportunity soon presented itself: a burrstone house on
the outskirts, nestled behind a wall of lilac and wisteria. What a dream!

I signed without even looking. A rash and reckless thing to do, you
might say, and you wouldn't be wrong. But I was afraid that by hemming
and hawing I'd let it get away from me. By all appearances it was a fabu-
lous deal. A real house—two floors over a cellar, surrounded by a yard

and within walking distance of shops and the train—and all for the price of a studio! It had to be jumped on, and I jumped. I admit my heart was pounding. Until then, I'd only lived in efficiencies and one-bedrooms. I'd had countless disappointments—the aforementioned episode being the most flagrant, if not the most atrocious. I remember spending one winter in a garret haunted by an entire family of ghosts. Every night the whole damnable clan would show up and argue in Croatian around my bed. The super filled me in on the story. A few years ago, a family of Yugoslavian immigrants had been living in my room. One winter's night, the father forgot to check the stove before going to bed. He, his wife, his in-laws, and his three children died of suffocation in their slumber. If you've never heard six people hurling insults at a seventh in Croatian at midnight in a room the size of a pocket-hanky pocket, you've never known true noise, the gift of sleep, or impotent homicidal fury.

But a house—even a haunted one—had to be something else altogether. You'd be able to sequester yourself, get some distance from the tiresome quarrels of shades. These were my thoughts as I hurried toward my new home—carefree, for it came furnished.

I was there in a jiffy: less than ten minutes from the station! I'd passed by several stylish boutiques on the way. A well-known wine shop, an attractive deli, a promising bakery. It's easy to tell a quality cake: they're smaller and pricier. I rubbed my hands together. It was all just like the lady at the agency had said!

I went up the Dawn Lane—from now on, my street—and stopped in front of number 40. It was high summer. The lavish wisteria (I go gaga for wisteria!) adorned the garden gate. Behind its festoons of soft mauve stood the house. Okay, so it wasn't Versailles—but it still looked neat and tidy, cute and cozy, dependable and down-to-earth. At first glance, it had a well-cared-for, even pampered air about it. The woodwork and metal had that dense gleam of new paint. I opened the garden gate, stepped inside, and closed it behind me with a feeling of . . . serene triumph, I suppose. Never having prevailed over anything, or even really had a taste of serenity, I had nothing to compare it to. I advanced toward my home. A white gravel path skirted potential puddle spots. A few more yards . . . a dozen or so meticulously tiled concrete steps lifted me above life's mire. A glass canopy sheltered me from whatever cruelty the skies might rain down, which seemed distant indeed on this fine summer day. With a trembling hand I opened the glass door, embellished with the most delightfully *petit-bourgeois* cast-iron grille. The door swung quietly on its hinges. My heart swelled with joy. From now on, my life would be the very picture of what I'd already seen of this house and what I had yet to discover. Well-oiled. Well-insulated. Muffled and padded. Fleece-lined. Downy . . . without a single squeaky or protesting part. From now on, I would come home with the firm and easy step of a man who has a safe haven. I, too, would have a castle, a homestead, a sanctuary.

I went inside. I felt around for a light switch, then paused. Of course the electricity would be off. I had to switch on the current first. The lady at the agency had warned me. The meter was in the cellar, but matches and a candlestick had been left for me in an obvious spot, on the table in the living room, to the left of the foyer. I pushed open the first door to my left and walked into a vast room sunken in shadow. A single detail struck me at that moment. Something we quickly forget when we live somewhere is that all houses, no matter how well ventilated, no matter how well kept, have a smell. This one had none. And yet all things steeped in time—rugs, curtains, even an empty chair or an electrolier—soak up the exhalations of those that live and decay . . . I bumped into the edge of what felt like a marble table, and forgot what I was thinking. Holy—a marble table! I'd only ever known formica and oilcloth. I almost fainted at the thought of setting down my latté every morning on a marble table. In the low light, a coppery glint caught my eye: the candlestick. Feeling along the tabletop, I found a box of matches. I struck one and lit the candle in the holder. The shadows shrank back. The living room, which took up most of the ground floor, had windows on two sides. I drew the blind on the closest one, and daylight poured in.

I turned back to the table. Its legs, too, were made of marble. They weren't the only thing: the chairs all around were marble, too, all neatly arranged except for one, slightly pulled out as if someone had sat down for just a moment to jot a note and forgotten to push it back in. I was breathless with delight. Marble chairs ... how chic! But how fragile those dainty legs—slender cylinders of gray marble delicately veined with white—must have been!

I approached the pulled-out chair and caressed its smooth, chill back with my palm. I pulled my hand away and took a step back. Did I dare—clumsy old me—make use of such marvels, sit on them, move them around at the risk of smacking them into things, tipping them over, or breaking them? They had to be heavy. I moved back and, hesitantly, tried to weigh the one I'd already touched. It resisted my efforts. Surprised, I tried again, this time with both hands, but without success. I braced myself and strained my muscles, grunting like someone rooting up a stump, but all in vain. The same thing happened with the next chair, the one after, and the one after that. The eight chairs were one with the marble-slab floor. They wouldn't lift or even budge an inch. Taken aback by this anomaly, I knelt down to take a closer look at where their legs met the floor. As far as I could tell, it went seamlessly from floor to chair without a break.

I was filled with an immense bewilderment. I sat down on the partly pulled-out chair, perching there on a single cheek, since it was too close to the table to sit in comfortably, and let my gaze roam about the room. Only then did I become aware of the radical strangeness of the place where I found myself. In addition to the table and its two rows of chairs, the furniture consisted of a large dresser, a sofa, two recliners, and a coffee table. With the exception of the windowpanes, a mirror, and a few fixtures like doorknobs and window latches, everything in the room was made of gray marble.

I stood up and walked toward the sofa. It was less furniture than sculpture representing a piece of furniture. The artist had done his utmost to mimic the little particularities and imperfections of an actual sofa: a slight droop to the cushions, dull and shiny spots, the almost invisible scratches of a cat startled by a child's sudden entrance...I bent over and saw that the sofa was also one with the floor. In reality, they weren't so much a table, chairs, a sofa, two recliners, etc., but a single "sculpture." The dresser, too, was but an outcrop of the primary deposit, and when I tried to lift a vase on the mantel, it wouldn't move. It clung, if that is the word, to its base like the stub of a sawn-off branch to a tree, or like a finger to a hand. The complete eccentric who had built this house had patiently freed the chimney, the vase, and all the rest from a single enormous block of marble. The room, perhaps even the entire house, formed a whole under a layer of wood, burrstone, and roof tiles.

When I'd switched on the electricity and toured all the rooms, I returned to the living room and stood before the mirror over the mantle. I looked so pitiful I couldn't help sticking out my tongue. Just my luck! I'd rented an inimitable work of art. But all I'd needed was a place to live, and art was unlivable. While exploring the house, I'd come across a kitchen fit for a power-mad prince, with a stove and a sink Michelangelo would've been proud of, a bathroom cut from the same quarry, and a bedroom to go with it. On a bare mattress, a stack of sheets and blankets awaited the prophesied hero able to unfold them and make the bed. In the cellar, beside a misleading boiler, the handle of a coal shovel would stick out at the same angle forever from a pile of fireproof pellets. Beneath the roof, the attic was cluttered with picturesquely decrepit old toys, sewing dummies with their shoulders pocked by fake needle holes, steamer trunks thrown open on a jumble of treasures and inextricable relics. Everything was light gray, veined with white, and cold as the grave.

I lasted three days in my marble house. I'd bought a comforter and slept on the floor. I ate cold meals and didn't shower, since nothing worked besides the lights. Even the bulbs, in their hollow marble globes and housings, only gave off a dull and gloomy glow.

When I got up the third day, it seemed my skin had taken on a grayish, white-veined tint—marbled, so to speak. I've often thought I was too sensitive, but what could I do about it? I ran out to the yard. I didn't look gray in the daylight. I was the same as I'd always been—a bit pale, perhaps, as if I'd just suffered a slight onset of anemia. Suddenly I craved sunshine. Burning sands. Blue water. Tanned bodies. Thatched huts beneath the trees. A thatched hut, I thought, how marvelous! A house of leaves and straw, open to every passing breeze. A house alive with the hum of insects, geckos on the walls and hens getting tangled up in your legs and a dog snoring under the table. Ah, the good life in a grass cabana! No worries, no cleaning, no upkeep...When the thatch rots, you set the whole thing on fire and build another a bit farther off. Friends come and help, and when the work's done you sing, drink, dance...

That same afternoon I left the travel agency and stopped by to give the keys to the house back. As per the contract, I had to forfeit my deposit. No matter what I do, I always end up losing my shirt. Bah! My head was full of thatch-roofed huts, sarongs, and leis. Maybe one day I'll tell you the story of my grass cabana and Hurricane Julia.

Lozère, October 1988

A Room on the Abyss

Fox is life's chosen one; he's six and always losing his balaclava. In such cases, the rules say to go bother Mrs. Bernard, the matron, and get bawled out. Boarding school is tough when you can't even tie your own shoes. Life's chosen one finds himself in tears so often he hasn't time to forget how they taste.

He doesn't know why life has chosen him, and what role it has in store. It'll do what it wants with him. Six isn't the age to be asking such questions. But chosen him it has. He doesn't doubt it for a moment. When he thinks about it, too many signs confirm his intuition. First off, he's almost died three times, and he's only six! Ordinary little boys don't waver so often between river and shore. Next, his papa left. Not to work far away, or wage war, or recover from some illness—all valid reasons for a father's absence—but just up and left, for good, forever. That, if nothing else, is a sign of election: a phantom father, alive and well God knows where, but always referred to in the past tense, as if already dead. And then there's his red hair. Funny, having red hair when your name is Fox, right? Hardly: every recess ends up a foxhunt. But his mother once showed him a book, written by a certain Mr. Fox, whose hero also has red hair and is named Carrot Top. Carrot Top is precisely what the young boarder's bullies call him. So elsewhere, in a world beside our own, he'd be the hero of a story? Perhaps one day, when he's

43

learned to read, opening the book like the door to the house where he was born, he'll go home.

At school, night has fallen. Wind bends the branches of the court-yard's chestnuts to the windows of the study hall. The housemaster is reading the paper. From time to time, he casts a weary gaze over the class. Everything is peaceful. Comics are passed around, games of hangman and tic-tac-toe are carried on in low voices. A few students from the provinces are writing their parents. At the back of the room, not far from Fox, the son of the king of Tanganyika is dreaming of savannahs and gazelles. In truth, no one's sure if that blackamoor is really the king's son, or if he's even from Tanganyika. Rumor has it, is all, and the boy in question neither confirms nor denies a thing. In his indifference, or the daze of the uprooted, one detects a wholly royal reserve. The purported prince in fact numbers among the institution's disinherited, who get to go home only three times a year: Christmas, Easter, and summer. A well-dressed black man always comes to pick him up out front.

"Psst! N'Mambo! Is that the ambassador?"

Unhurried, N'Mambo crosses the courtyard, suitcase in hand.

"N'Mambo! Psst! N'Mambo! If you go hunting, shoot an elephant for me!"

The boy vanishes into the vestibule, that airlock decked with diplomas and potted plants, smelling so sweetly of freedom and furniture polish.

N'Mambo's wandering gaze meets Fox's. Life's chosen one gives him a half grin, which N'Mambo vaguely returns. Fox slides down the bench toward the black boy. "Psst! N'Mambo!"

"What?"

"Your father—"

N'Mambo's gaze returns to the issue of *Coq Hardi* open before him. "Please leave me alone. I am reading."

"It's a lie! Your father's not the king."

N'Mambo shrugs. Fox is dumbfounded. The words just came out of his mouth. "N'Mambo—"

"Shut up. You're bothering me!"

"I was just kidding. Your father is the king."

"Leave me alone!"

"He is the king, he is!"

"Teacher!"

The housemaster looks up.

"Teacher, Carrot Top is bothering me!"

All heads turn toward the culprit.

"On your feet, Fox! Bothering our classmates now, are we?"

"It's a lie, teacher! I didn't say nothing!"

"I've got ways to keep you busy. Write this sentence down a hundred times: *I will not bother my classmates.* Now get started!"

Fox sits down, but stands right back up again. "Teacher..."

"What is it now?"

"I don't know how to write."

The class snickers.

"Then draw tallies. I want two hundred, nice and straight in sets of five. You can count, can't you?"

"No, Teacher," Fox whispers.

The snickering gets louder.

"Do it anyway! I'll tell you when to stop. Everyone else—silence!"

Fox sits down again. He takes the penholder he's never yet used out of his desk. He tears a sheet of paper from his notebook. He dips the pen in the earthenware inkwell and draws his first tremulous tally line. On the third line, he makes a blot. He hasn't got a blotter. He tries to dab at the stain with his handkerchief but only manages to make it bigger. He rips the sheet up and tears another from his notebook. Another row of lines, another blot. Despair overcomes him; tears spring to his eyes, tumble to the paper, blur the lines and the blot. He huddles over the desk, hides his head in his arms. Soon he's asleep, cradled by the class' gentle clamor, nose pressed to his sickly lines.

The Turk is only ten, but he's the strongest kid in the schoolyard. No one, not even the biggest boys, dares attack him. Strong as a Turk, the expression goes. The Turk, who's from Courbevoie, established his reputation once and for all by knocking an older student out the first day of class. The older student had been picking on the Turk. The Turk turned pale—everyone saw. He turned pale, and then he lashed out. Life's chosen one greatly admires the Turk. When kids attack Fox, he turns red. He turns red, and then he runs. That's no way to behave.

Fights are among the students' primary concerns. Generally speaking, boys at the boarding school fall into two types: the weak and the strong, victims and their oppressors. A few individuals stand outside these basic classifications. The Turk, because he never abuses his prodigious strength, and N'Mambo, because in some vague way the others are afraid the king of Tanganyika will send his Zulus to lay waste to the school if his runt gets pestered too much.

This morning, while waiting in line in the courtyard, the students saw a new boy go by, a blackamoor like N'Mambo, led by the caretaker. They noticed that the principal hadn't bothered to walk the boy to class himself, as he had N'Mambo. So the new boy wasn't a king's son: they vowed to have some fun at his expense during recess.

With the exception of N'Mambo and the Turk, everyone got into it, even Fox. The big bullies didn't leave anyone else much of a chance to pick on the new boy. At last, when they were muddying his cap and emptying the contents of his satchel into the toilet, Fox had plenty of time to prance about behind them like the rest of the pack, shouting *Bamboola-Ayaya-Bamboola* at the top of his lungs. Then he saw the Turk standing to one side and watching him with a funny look on his face. Contemptuous, or disappointed, or both at once. And suddenly his joy at having finally changed sides evaporated. He chanted *Ayaya-Bamboola-Ayaya* a moment longer to himself before turning from their quarry and running off to hide in a dark corner of the playground.

Now it's eleven at night. In his bed at one end of the children's dorm, Fox tosses and turns in his sheets without falling asleep. His misgivings have stayed with him since the incident. After what happened, he is no longer quite sure of being life's chosen one. Although he's told himself over and over that it's for keeps, and that the Turk has nothing to do with it, he no longer believes as much as before. He wonders, argues with himself: c'mon, he's got nothing to fear, life would warn him if it was going to stop choosing him! In any case, he'd have to make a lot of mistakes—worse, and bigger ones—for it to stop playing secret favorites. But it's no use: he worries, chews his lips, turns red beneath the sheets. He snivels a little, then falls asleep, shattered.

Maman's whole body is shaking, and she crushes Fox's hand as they cross the street. In the shops where she takes him on Saturdays, her nose stings, her face is bathed in sweat. He often grumbles: he'd rather stay home and play.

"No, you're coming with me." As soon as they're outside, she grabs his hand and squeezes it hard, very hard.

"Maman, you're squeezing too hard!"

She loosens her grip. "I'm sorry, sweetie. Did I hurt you?"

Fox takes his crushed hand back. He wiggles his crumpled fingers, moist with his mother's anxious sweat.

She takes his hand again a few yards later, and starts squeezing. He doesn't say a word.

Maman throws up a lot. She can't keep anything down. The doctors have ordered tests that reveal nothing. One of them wanted to take out her gallbladder anyway, but another one said no, her gallbladder wasn't the problem. It was fear.

When Maman gets too frightened, she sends the boy off to boarding school, or to the countryside with a nanny, or to her parents. As soon as she feels better she fetches him, and it starts all over. The mad dashes, the anxieties, the fatigue, and the memories—and by her side all the while, a living portrait of the one who left, whom she banishes time and again. Beneath a burden too great and too greatly beloved, she soon crumples. One morning she vomits up her coffee again, her hands trembling on the key to the small garret where they live. Nine by nine, it holds a table and two stools, two cupboards, a bed, a hideous corner divan with built-in shelving, and a bucket for necessities. Across from the door, the window opens on a dizzying balcony. Woman and child, betrayed, live up in the sky itself, but the sky reeks. Even without the bucket, odors rise from the building depths in summer and invade the balcony through a duct imperfectly plugged with cork. The woman locks the door and heads down the dark, narrow corridor with her son. She shoves him into the delivery elevator, which serves the rooms and stairs once used by maids. They cross the little courtyard and emerge on the boulevard—so big and noisy!—and suddenly her ears are buzzing, her heart hammering, fear knots her throat, she grabs the boy's hand desperately and squeezes.

It is Friday night. Unless his luck takes a really bad turn, Fox isn't in danger of staying the weekend at school. He'll leave tomorrow at ten-thirty. Maman works Saturday morning. He will go back to the apartment alone. The concierge will hand him the key on his way in. He'll wait for Maman on high, flipping through his *Mickey* comics.

That night, if she isn't too frightened, they'll go see a movie at the Regent. The next day they'll stay in. Maman will do her bills at home. If it's not raining, he'll play on the smelly balcony.

But right now it's Friday night, and he's bored. Almost horizontal on the bench, he catalogues the contents of his cubby: a chewed-up pencil stub, two wads of gum (one pink, one green) stuck up against the top wall, a scrap of blotting paper. Nothing useful! Sitting up, he spots N'Mambo's fuzzy head. He'd like to talk to him about his father, if he weren't sure it'd cost him his permission to leave this weekend. Stop! Don't say a word to N'Mambo!

He shrinks back. A student has just sat down beside him. Changing seats in study hall is not allowed! But of course the Turk isn't afraid of anything. Fox is very scared of getting left at school. "You can't—we'll get punished!"

"The prefect didn't see a thing. And if he pipes up, I'll say it was all me."

"What do you want?"

"Just to talk a little. You look bored."

"I don't have anything to do."

"You could read."

"I can't."

"You're old enough. Didn't you ever learn?"

"Yes."

"Well, then you can."

Fox shakes his head. He's always changing schools. He has come to terms with this nomadism. Quite simply, he always has to start from scratch. B-a ba, b-e be: like a nonsense song everyone sings.

"Let's see." The Turk leans across the aisle, borrows a book, and opens it before them. "Here, try. Follow my finger, and read."

"N-a ... Na ... n-o ... no ... Nano?"

"Nano's the kid in the picture. Keep going."

"Nano ... and ... Na ... net ... te."

"Nanette. She's the girl."

"Nano and Nanette ... are ... in ... the ... ya ... yard!"

By the time study hall is over, Fox has figured out eight lines. The Turk closes the book and gives it back to its owner. Out of instinct, Fox tries to stop him.

"What's your problem? You've got the same one."

"I do? It tells the same story?"

"Open your satchel."

Fox obeys. The Turk pulls out a book the same size as the other, flips through it, and then sets it down open before them. "Well?"

"Nano ... and Nanette ..."

Fox's face lights up. Nano and Nanette are still in the yard, and it's still summer, their dog, Pataud, is still a good dog, the sprinkler still leaking and wetting, leaking and wetting Nano's feet.

As he heads up to the dorm, Fox is happy. He knows how to read. Nano and Nanette are in the yard, forever.

Just behind the cage of the delivery elevator, in a recess in the lobby, two scalped Indians are hiding. They watch Fox, seedy and menacing, nodding their bloody heads in the shadows. Quickly, before they can catch him, he hurls himself into the elevator, slams the door, and pulls the accordion grate shut. Standing on tiptoe, he pushes as hard as he can on the button marked eight. The elevator tears itself away from the floor with a screech. Down in the lobby, the Indians are probably stamping their feet with rage, sticking out their tongues, shaking their fists at their escaping quarry. Fox shuts his eyes. His heart is hammering. But another terror awaits: after the third floor, he starts getting dizzy. People seem to take it for granted that elevators never go higher than the building's highest floor. For adults, at least, this is a rule without exception. Fox isn't convinced. The elevator, he thinks, could easily shoot right by the final landing without even slowing down. Hoisted by unthinkable pulleys, it'd keep going, bursting through the roof, scattering birds, zooming through the clouds, higher and higher, farther and farther into the frozen reaches of the sky. Fox holds his breath. At every landing, he hears a click from the rickety equipment somewhere under his feet. Click . . . six. Click . . . seven. And then . . . then? His knees tremble. He plasters his body against the wall. Click! The cage comes to a stop at last.

A soft reddish glow bathes the room through curtains of printed cretonne. Fox is in no hurry to turn the lights on. The dangers are all outside; nothing can reach him here. An outer shell, an inner sanctum, a pitiful Eden he's routinely banished from, his mother's every relapse reenacting his own Fall.

He puts his satchel on the bed. He crosses the room. He pours himself a glass of milk but spits it out at once: it's sour. He climbs up on a stool to pull back the curtains, a blood-red scrim that hides the sky. In vain, he searches for the sun. He turns his back on the window and sits cross-legged at the table. There are his toys, in a wooden box under the bed, but he doesn't feel like playing. Maman will be home soon. They'll eat together: ham and Floraline, like always. Maman puts his books in the cupboard—the big one, whose doors are blocked by the bed. He knows how to push the bed aside and open it. He's done it before. Once he even took down the ragged little book that holds all the secrets. It's a yellow book, with no pictures. He turned it over in his hands for a long time, before regretfully putting it back. But today he knows how to read it. He repeats the incredible words to himself: *Today I know how to read!* So the day does come when eyes are opened and secrets revealed, when order comes to chaos . . . Fox nods. How many such dawnings does a life hold? Can you die without having your fair share, without fathoming the marvelous truth? Fox is beside himself. What if he's about to die, right here and now, struck down before the very first veil is even rent? He scrambles from the table and races for the cupboard. The sound of steps in the hall, the rattle of keys in the lock; he stands petrified in the middle of the room.

"Maman?"

"Did you make it home all right? You know how worried I get..."

Bures, Dec. 1981-Feb. 1982

The Gulf of the Years

In the train, the passengers spoke in hushed voices about the hard times. A young woman with a yellow star sewn to her breast briefly lifted her gaze from the dressmaker's pattern she was studying. The boy across from her pulled the latest issue of *Signal* from a worn satchel and unfolded it right in front of her face. She lowered her eyes.

Through the window, Manoir watched the few cars, quaint and yet almost new, on the road beside the tracks. He started at the sight of a military convoy. He checked his watch, then settled back. It was still early. The bombing wouldn't start till later that morning. Far away, young men were waking in their barracks ... or were they on their feet already, assembled in flight suits before a blackboard with their wing commander? Early rising schoolboys of fire and death. They were twenty, in fur-lined boots and leather helmets, blue wool and sheepskin. They drank tea and smoked *gauloises blondes*. Manoir's best wishes went with them. And yet, in a few hours, one of them would kill his mother.

Manoir got off at S. He walked up the Avenue de la Gare, turned left at the town hall, and passed the post office, then the elementary school. He hesitated, but not over which way to go. As a child, he'd pretended he was blind in these streets. He'd try and make his way to school from home with his eyes closed. Sometimes he walked right into a lamp-post, or someone's legs. He cheated, of course: from time to time he opened his eyelids just a bit, long enough to see where he was. But one night he'd managed to make it only cheating three times.

He checked his watch again. In five minutes, a little boy would emerge from his house a few streets away. On the front steps, his maman would kiss him as she did every morning. Satchel in hand, he would cross the small yard. With one last wave, he'd head through the gate and be on his unhurried way to school.

It was seven-fifty. School opened its doors at eight. Would it take him ten minutes to get there, or just five? If he missed him—God, what if he missed him? Manoir spotted a boy in a cape, then two more, an older one leading a younger one by the hand, and two more after that ... they were coming out of the woodwork now. Still sleepy, eyes unfocused for the most part, pale and huddled against the cold morning, children were converging on the school. Manoir panicked. They were coming toward him down both sides of the street at once, the bigger ones sometimes hiding the littler ones from view. All he could see of some—hooded, wrapped up in scarves or balaclavas—was their eyes and a bit of nose poking out from the wool. He recalled a yellowish coat, maybe even a beret? Yes, he was sure of the coat. But two out of every three boys were wearing berets.

The crowd of children grew, overflowing the sidewalk for a moment. Manoir almost wept with frustration. None of these children were the one he was looking for! The flood slowed; most of the flock had passed. He'd missed him; he'd let him slip by beneath a brown coat or a black cape. All was lost. His heart broke. The street emptied. He ran into a few breathless latecomers ... and over there, that shape! He dashed forward. An ugly yellow coat. A beret pulled halfway down his forehead. A loose-knit gray scarf. And that odd, almost moony walk, that dawdling step! He should've known. He slowed his pace, trying to still his beating heart. The boy was only fifteen yards away, now. Their paths were about to cross. The boy looked up at the man. Something—a familial air—had awoken his curiosity. Manoir stopped right in front of him.

"Jean-Jacques?"

The boy took a step back. "How come y'know my name? I don't know yours."

"You're Jean-Jacques Manoir, aren't you? Right? You don't know me, but I know all about you. You're eight years old, in third grade, and your teacher's name is Mr. Crépon. He's got a tiny mustache and is very strict. See—I know all about you!"

At once intrigued by the stranger's omniscience yet worried about being late, Jean-Jacques hopped from foot to foot. "OK, but I'm going to be late. Mr. Crépon's going to make me do lines!"

Mr. Crépon didn't make him do lines as often as he might have. His customarily iron rule softened for the three fatherless boys in his class.

"C'mon, Mr. Crépon's not as bad as all that. If he punished you every time you were late or busy daydreaming instead of working—"

So the stranger knew that, too! The boy gulped. "Wh-who are you?"

"I'm your cousin. Your father's cousin. Don't you think I look like him?"

"Yes, you do," the child replied after looking him over. "But I still don't know you. And my dad's dead."

Manoir nodded. "He died in the war. He was a hero. He got medals: a round one, with a green and yellow ribbon, and another with a green and red ribbon and little swords. Isn't that right?"

"Yes!"

"C'mon, I'll show you something that'll prove I'm his cousin. You know the ring your dad always wore?"

"A ring? I dunno..." Jean-Jacques blushed. Through the fabric of his pocket and the handkerchief he'd wrapped it in, the signet ring he'd brought in secret to show his friends seemed to be burning.

The cousin's eyes gleamed with irony. "You must have seen it. A gold ring, with a little *château* on it, like your name—a *manor.*"

Jean-Jacques gave in. "Yeah, I've seen it before."

"I've got the same one! Look!" The man took his hand from his pocket, fingers spread, and held it out to the boy. A signet ring, exactly like the one the boy had stolen from his father's desk but moments ago, gleamed in the gray day. "See, there's my proof."

"Why Jean-Jacques! Jean-Jacques, you're really going to be late to-day!"

A woman stood before them: a neighbor, the same one who would come fetch the boy after school, after the tragedy. She was speaking to the boy, but looking the man up and down. She did her best to help the young widow: here a pot of broth, there some wool from an old, unraveling sweater. She'd believed the mother and child alone in the world. But who was this man who looked so much like poor Mr. Manoir?

"I'm a friend of the boy's mother," she said. "And you are...?"

"Manoir," the stranger mumbled. "Jean-Pierre Manoir. *Enchanté.*"

"He's daddy's cousin," Jean-Jacques announced. "I didn't know him, but he knew all about me."

The woman hesitated. If it weren't for the resemblance...She didn't dare insist, but she vowed to get to the bottom of this. "I'll drop in on your mother, Jean-Jacques. You should hurry, or Mr. Crépon will yell at you again."

The cousin had other plans. "Jean-Jacques isn't going to school this morning. We're going home together."

"You know Yvonne, of course?"

"Jeanne, you mean? My poor cousin's widow is named Jeanne."

"Jeanne, of course. I'm losing my mind."

"No, we've never met. The hazards of fate . . . But I'm eager to meet her at last. So, if you'll excuse us—"

"Please. Later, perhaps? I'd planned to visit Jeanne this morning anyway." The woman walked off, her fears allayed. Now it was curiosity that gnawed at her. Jean-Pierre Manoir, cousin of the deceased. He looked just like his brother. He'd turned up just like that, with his hands in his pockets, but where from? A cousin fallen from the sky . . . What if he were a Gaullist? A parachutist from the FFL? A terrorist? One didn't quite know what to call them. Shouldn't she stay away from Jeanne's this morning? But then she'd never find out a thing!

Manoir took the boy's hand. Jean-Jacques let him, and this act of trust overwhelmed the man. He quickly wiped his tears away with the back of his free hand. The excited child skipped beside him.

"Are you going to stay for a long time?"

"I don't know. Do you want me to?"

"You'll have to play with me."

"Count on it. Do you have many toys?"

"A whole chest full! And comics, and a train—say, how come you know me if you don't know maman?"

Manoir chuckled, stalling. "Well! You think of everything, don't you! Look, the bakery's open. Do you want some cake?"

"There is no cake."

"Of course there isn't. Some sweets, maybe?"

"It's not real sugar. Maman says they make your tummy hurt."

"I see. But you like them anyway, don't you?"

Jean-Jacques smiled secretively. He didn't really mind them so much, those fake-sugar sweets that made your tummy hurt.

Manoir walked inside the store. The baker watched them with curiosity from behind her empty glass jars. She saw the boy go by every day. Sometimes she sold him sweets made with saccharin. The father had been killed in 1940. The man looked so much like him! His brother, no doubt.

"Good morning, madame. We'd like some sweets."

"Of course. Green? Yellow?"

"A few of each. Let's see..." Manoir pulled the few coins he had left from his pocket. "As many as these will buy."

"That'll be a hundred grams."

"Excellent!"

"Do you have ration coupons?"

"Coupons? Oh no, I—I hadn't thought..."

The baker scratched her forehead. "A pity. I could give you the cracked ones? Without tickets..."

"Of course. Whatever you can spare."

On the doorstep, Manoir handed Jean-Jacques the little bag.

"Thanks."

"Call me Uncle Jean-Pierre, if you'd like."

"Thanks, Uncle Jean-Pierre."

They walked. Jean-Jacques crunched into the broken sweets with relish.

"You know what's good? The raspberry ones."

"And the hard mint ones, and the little eggs with liqueur centers. But—"

"Your father sent me your photo. I don't have it anymore. I lost it in the war."

"Oh. Was I a little baby in the photo?"

"No, not a baby really, or I wouldn't have recognized you. You were five or six."

They were getting close. At the next intersection, on the left, they spotted the house.

"Ow! You're hurting me!"

"I'm sorry." Manoir loosened his grip. Seized with feeling, he'd been crushing the child's hand. His heart was pounding. His mouth was dry. They rounded the corner.

"What's wrong? Are you sick?"

"No, no."

From this angle, the greenish grille, spotted here and there with rust, half masked the millstone and stucco facade. He'd remembered the building being taller, larger, perforated with broad windows like so many eyes wide open on Eden. In reality, it was tiny: the smallest house on the street, nestled in its few acres between two bulging villas that drowned it in shadow.

"C'mon, we're here."

Jean-Jacques dashed off and swung briefly from the handle of the bell. It let out a feeble ring. A minute went by before a window opened upstairs.

"Jean-Jacques? Why aren't you at school? Who is that with you? What's going on?"

"It's daddy's cousin. I met him on the street."

Manoir reeled at the sound of his mother's voice. He couldn't, he wasn't strong enough to see or speak to her. He'd faint, right there on the sidewalk. He had to get away. But his legs refused to obey. With one hand he hung on to the gate and closed his eyes. A thin figure appeared. He was trembling all over, his eyes clouded with tears.

⊰⊱

"Monsieur?"

Manoir desperately swallowed his tears and smiled. His mother was as old as she'd ever get: thirty. The bomb would crush a short young woman with even features and skin already dulled by grief and worry. She had but an hour left to live, and stood up straight in her seamstress' blouse over which she'd slipped a man's jacket much too large for her.

"Monsieur?"

She, too, was trembling. This man looked so much like her husband! He'd never mentioned this man, but how could they not be related? He spoke. His very voice, his tone, awoke echoes. He introduced himself. He explained. He was in fact the only relative of the deceased. A few months before his death, he'd written his cousin; he'd even enclosed a photo of his young son with the letter. Manoir caressed Jean-Jacques' hair. The boy let him. Unfortunately, Jean-Pierre Manoir had lost the letter and photo with his belongings near Sedan, in the chaos of the retreat.

Manoir ostentatiously underlined his words with gestures of his ringed hand. Jeanne gave a start.

"Pardon me, but that ring—"

At that moment, Jean-Jacques, who had been watching the two adults silently, chimed in. "Yeah, did you see it, maman? He's got the same ring as Papa. The exact same one!"

Manoir held out his hand. "We ordered them together from a jeweler in P——. Michel drew the chateau on the setting himself on a page of his notebook."

The truthful part of this new lie chased away whatever doubts lingered in the young woman's mind. Her husband had indeed had his ring made in P——, from a sketch by his very own hand. Still, despite everything, it was strange that he'd never brought up this cousin, a dozen years his senior, whom he must have been close to in his youth, it seemed ... But above all, she was inclined to rejoice in this visit that interrupted the monotony of her day and this revelation of a friendly presence in the desert of her life. She became suddenly aware of her unkempt appearance—this blouse, this shapeless jacket, really! She apologized; she'd been about to sit down to work at her machine. She did a little sewing; her war-widow's pension was quite modest.

They went inside. The impostor's throat tightened as he inhaled the old smells he'd never forgotten and staggering traces of which he sometimes came across by chance on the street. Quince cheese, a canary cage, wax polish, and vegetable soup, and from Jean-Jacques' room, the slightly acrid reek of mouse droppings. The smell of sec-ondhand clothes, for in these penurious times, Jeanne gathered, recut, and repaired more old clothes than she made new ones. The smell of the oilcan for the sewing machine. There it was. The big black Singer with its gilt chasing sat enthroned in the living room, amidst a mess of spools and needles, chalk and scissors. But he remembered a room reserved for special occasions, where you went only if you had to, in a pair of felt slippers . . . that was before, of course! Before the war, and his father's death. The living room had been turned into a workspace, and the slippers peeked out from under a sofa.

Jeanne led them into the kitchen. He sat down in the chair she offered as though his feet had been cut out from under him. The walls, hung with plates, spun around him.

"Jean-Pierre? I can call you Jean-Pierre, can't I? After all, we're related. You look quite tired!"

"Yes. The trip—"

"Did you come a long way?"

"A very long way, yes."

He was overcome with dizziness. He closed his eyes, opened them, tried to smile. She'd turned her back on him and was heating water. Then, standing before the pantry shelves, she pushed aside empty jars and gave each white tin box a shake beside her ear.

"Let's see . . . No more tea, of course. No more real coffee, either. Herbal tea, then, or chicory."

Bit by bit, Manoir's dizziness wore off. The walls slowed their spinning, the plates grew still. There were three, covered with a thin film of grease and dust. The first showed an interior scene: a woman, like Jeanne at that very moment, busying herself in her kitchen. In the second a traveler from the last century, cane in hand, broad hat brim hiding his face, made his way through the woods. The last was a rebus. From where he was sitting he couldn't see the elements very clearly. A note on a musical staff, a pond . . .

"There, it's steeping. It's lime-blossom. Oh, wait, I've got a treat after all."

She pulled a plate from another cupboard. Manoir recognized the dark amber, almost brown sections she used to cut from a block of fruit jelly for his afternoon snack.

"I don't make it as often as I used to. It takes too much sugar. But Jean-Jacques loves it. Where has that boy gone now? Jean-Jacques?"

A clatter of steps echoed in the stairwell. Jean-Jacques appeared.

"What were you up to?"

"I was cleaning my room so I could show Uncle Jean-Pierre."

"But Jean-Pierre isn't your uncle. He's your father's cousin."

"Yes, but he said—"

"No, that's fine," Manoir interrupted. "I'm a bit too old to be a cousin."

"And we'll play, right? Like you said. I cleaned my room just so we could."

"Leave Jean-Pierre alone. Here, have some quince cheese. You, too, Jean-Pierre. Help yourself."

Man and boy started in. The pieces were a bit sticky. Jean-Jacques licked his fingers. Manoir hesitated, then, giving him a complicit glance, did the same.

"*Maman?*"

"Yes, dear?"

"Am I going back to school today?"

"Well . . . not this morning, at least."

"Not this afternoon, either!"

"We'll see. I'll see. Oh, the tea's ready." Jeanne had taken out two bowls. Jean-Jacques didn't much like herbal tea, and he'd just had breakfast. It didn't stop him from digging into the quince paste. For his part, Manoir was dying to have seconds but didn't dare.

"Help yourself, Jean-Pierre! Really!"

"With pleasure. It's delicious." He took a broken piece from the plate.

"Hey, are you coming back?"

They were in Jean-Jacques' room. Jeanne was working below. Jean-Jacques was lying on the linoleum near his toy chest. Manoir set down the little tin airplane he'd been studying.

"Of course, if your mother wants me to."

"She does, I know she does!"

"And why is that?"

"Because you're family. When you've got family, you visit, right?"

"I suppose so. I don't really know. I don't have any—except you two."

"Just like us—all we have is you."

Manoir leaned over the chest, and reached for a box of cubes. "But sometimes you live too far away to visit often."

"Do you live far away? In the free zone?"

"That's right. In the free zone."

"So we won't be able to see each other."

Manoir had opened the box of cubes. He'd already found three faces that represented parts of a single picture. A rodeo scene, no doubt.

"I'm moving."

"Really? Neat! So we'll see each other often, then? We could go boating. Maman won't take me. But you will, right?"

"We'll go everywhere! The circus, and the zoo, and the Ferris wheel at the fair."

"The Ferris wheel! It makes me scared to look around even when we haven't left the ground yet!"

"You won't be scared with me, right?"

"No! Definitely not!"

Suddenly the sirens screamed. Man and boy froze.

"Hear that? It's the bomb warning!"

Manoir checked his watch and nodded. Jeanne's urgent voice reached them from below.

"Jean-Jacques! Jean-Pierre! The sirens!"

"Come."

On the threshold, before closing the door, Manoir took one last look at his childhood room. The red eiderdown on the bed, the white mouse nibbling at the bars of its cage, the plaster coin bank in the shape of a dog on the dresser, the Kipling poem in its gilded pitch-pine frame. Good-bye, good-bye forever this time.

They went down. Jeanne was waiting for them at the foot of the stairs. She wasn't alone. The neighbor stood next to her. Curiosity had brought her over, and the sirens surprised her on the front step.

"Hurry up! Didn't you hear the warning!"

"Yes, but it's not for us. I bet they're going to bomb the station."

"We're just next door! Come over, my cellar's deeper underground, and my husband did a good job shoring it up."

"We don't have time," Manoir cut in. "Listen—they've started!"

The engines' roar had grown louder. In a few moments, the

squadron would pass right over the town. Muffled explosions broke out.

"It's the AA guns," Jean-Jacques shouted. "Blam! Blam! Vrrr! Vrrr! Blammm!"

"Hurry, downstairs!"

Jeanne grabbed the boy. She opened the cellar door and headed down the steps. Manoir stepped aside to the let the neighbor by.

Jeanne lit a small lamp. They were seated on old crates. The ground trembled without stopping. With each detonation, shockwaves shook the walls. In a corner of the cellar, empty bottles clinked.

"They're bombing the station. We have nothing to fear."

"If you say so!" The neighbor was missing her reinforced shelter and her sandbags. Jeanne was quiet. After a momentary brush with fear, Jean-Jacques had regained confidence before "Uncle Jean-Pierre's" demeanor. Manoir smiled. He felt great peace within. Events once gone astray were about to resume their rightful course.

Above, a bomber had been hit. It veered, losing altitude. To lighten the load, the pilot ordered all bombs to be dropped. For a moment, the bombs rocked in the air as though uncertain, then the wind on their fins stabilized them. They were falling straight down now, with a whistling that grew ever higher in pitch. The first ripped the street open two hundred yards from the house. The second crushed a gas truck at the corner of the street. In the cellar, the neighbor, the bearer of bad news, opened her mouth to cry out. Jean-Jacques pressed himself against Jeanne, his face buried in her breast. Manoir rose, threw himself upon them, and held them.

Bures, 1980

The Dolceola Player

Blandeuil thought he should take advantage of his trip to Eparvay to ask his fellow natives what it meant to have been born there, rather than somewhere else. He saw now that a feeling of deep, intimate belonging to this place had never left him, even when he'd fled ten years ago.

Without a word to anyone, he'd taken the dawn local with his dolceola, still new then. The first scratches on its case dated from that day. God! So many others had followed...

It was nevertheless curious that *flee* was the word that sprang to mind. For, after all, he'd left neither jailers nor enemies behind. His parents had pampered him, he'd had lots of friends, and when they'd talked about the future, Xenia hadn't seemed to envision her own without him. He might have been within his rights to say he'd gone off to win fame and glory. And won it he had, in a way.

He bit the inside of his cheek, as he always did at the thought of the publicity given over to the event. Years had gone by since then, and he hadn't yet fully recovered; perhaps he never would. He had to harden himself and endure, was all. But he knew he never really could...Endure, yes, with great difficulty. But harden himself enough—no. Turn to stone—no. He'd always suffer from odd things, things that as a rule no one else suffered from, things they prided themselves on instead...

Georges-Olivier Châteaureynaud

After the final bend in the road, he saw the town. It had grown, but all he noticed was that it had no suburbs. Besides, suburbs mark the steady growth of a town beyond its medieval walls, and no walls encircled Eparvay. No historic ramparts, no history...yet it wasn't modern, either. Blandeuil had never in his travels seen anything as quaint, outdated, and almost backward as Eparvay—an affluent backwardness, of course, but incorrigible nonetheless. It seemed no new construction had been started there since at least the '20s. Of course, the way they spoke, dressed, and behaved there wasn't like in the '20s, but it wasn't the '90s, either. Everything was insidiously out of step, or somehow off ... On reflection, the notion of want best expressed the strangeness: something was wanting. Something was missing from the sky, the air, perhaps the light. But Blandeuil had only realized this far from Eparvay, when he'd discovered Paris, Rome, London, New York, and Tokyo. Now that he was headed home, everything seemed normal and legitimate; he found the rest of the world strange in hindsight.

He slowed and parked his car on the Avenue de la Republique. Everything was just as he remembered it. It was all clean, quiet, and peaceful: residences of dressed stone, wrought-iron gates painstakingly painted slick black. Here a concierge might dust a hard-to-reach spot at the meeting of two iron volutes. Here the vestibules smelled of wax polish and fresh flowers. Here was here, the only real *here* Blandeuil could imagine, every other place on earth never having been anywhere but elsewhere.

Blandeuil tugged the bell on a town house. An unfamiliar concierge came to the door. At the sound of the bell, Blandeuil's parents appeared on the landing atop the flight of steps in the inner courtyard. He lifted his gaze toward them (the landing was high; at that moment Blandeuil remembered there were fifteen steps). He told himself he could predict his parents' every act down to the last detail. He'd often amused himself with this little game as a boy. He'd spy on them, then bet in his head: *in a minute, maman will take off her glasses and scratch the tip of her nose, then say, "In the end, if you weigh both sides . . ." And Papa won't let her finish her sentence. He'll say, "My poor dear, your scales are off, I'm afraid!"* And he'd be right: Madame Blandeuil's reckonings were always off. Reckonings material and immaterial alike. Her food was inedible, and she was as tone-deaf to logic as some were to song—that is to say, irremediably.

There, raising his gaze to the landing, Blandeuil made a silent bet he was sure to win. They wouldn't come down to meet him; they'd show their joy some other way, their way. Hugging each other, shoulder to shoulder, as befit parents witnessing the return of their eldest son. Maman would bring a hand to her head (*That's right—whatever was I thinking? I had an older boy, and here he is!*) while papa would lift his left arm up partway and wiggle his limp fingers a bit, as if stroking an invisible horse.

Blandeuil's parents matched his expectations exactly. Far from being annoyed, he was grateful, for once, that they'd stayed so much the same, and he only just managed to hold back his tears.

At dinner that night, they didn't bring up his little adventure, and he was grateful to them for that as well. At least there was one place in the world where he could forget it ever happened, where no one threw it in his face. Oh, strictly speaking, people weren't trying to be mean. They thought they were being nice by reminding him of his amorous exploit. Nor would they have minded had he given them exclusive details. How she'd been in private, the starlet, that most beautiful of all women, and to start with, was she as beautiful up close as they said, was she really perfect? After all, she *had* to be like the others, sculpted from the same clay, the same flesh. Softer—silkier, probably. Still, in the end he'd merely held a woman with a finer finish than the others in his arms . . .

He tried to keep a game face during all this chatter. He'd dodge questions like punches, and at the first opportunity break off the conversation, fleeing with his unsharable memories.

Whether they'd planned it jointly or not, his parents never broached the torturous subject. They only discussed his career, which they'd followed from afar, like the path of a star of the umpteenth magnitude.

"But really," his mother exclaimed yet again, "why ever did you pick that instrument?"

"Maman, can I help it if the dolceola only reaches a limited audience? God himself put it in my hands. He made it, so someone has to play it. There were only two dolceola virtuosos and, ever since the other one died, I'm the best—the greatest! All these years I've given concerts in all the capitals of the world!"

It was true: he'd given a concert in every capital, in front of thirty people.

That night, while dining on his mother's disastrous fare, he suffered not from having once held the most beautiful woman in the world in his arms, but from being henceforth the uncontested virtuoso of a somewhat ridiculous instrument. Bah! When one wound closes, another opens: *c'est la vie!* He'd poured himself a full glass of margaux, and was about to gulp it down in compensation when his parents informed him of Xenia's death.

Around one that morning, Blandeuil woke up again and got dressed in the half-light of his rediscovered childhood room. How could he ever have thought he'd sleep as if it were just another night, no more or less peaceful than any other, when Xenia was dead? He didn't even know how she'd died. His parents hadn't said, and it made him suspect the worst. Suicide, or something like that... He began biting his cheeks again. Suicide was suicide. Had Xenia committed suicide because of him? No. Surely not. To begin with, he didn't even know the date of this supposed suicide. It must've happened before the papers announced his affair with Lola Balbo. Even if it had happened after— even if it'd happened the same day—what would that have proved? Quite simply, he wasn't worth suicide. The observation reassured him so much that he continued with this train of thought. He was just another guy—why hide it?—a loser, even. That gratifying adventure with Balbo had been sheer accident. She'd kidnapped him! She'd been taken with him the same way a very rich woman, weary of mink and ocelot, one day dons a rabbit fur coat on a whim. His naïveté had entertained her for three weeks. Then she'd sent him back to his dolceola. He hadn't really been the worse for it; the whole time he'd been away from Eparvay, he'd had it in the back of his mind to come back to Xenia one day. But Xenia was dead.

In Blandeuil's memories, nights in Eparvay smelled of lilacs, and the air was often soft as a lover's stole. That night, he thought to sense beneath the sweetness and softness the whiff of roadkill. He shrugged it off. He'd always been too sensitive; it was one of his countless tragedies. On his too-tender soul, everything immediately left a mark. He urged himself to be tougher. All women were mortal. He hadn't seen Xenia in ten years, and it hadn't made him shed a single tear. He'd thought about her, vaguely, from time to time, when he felt a little too lonely. In Kuala Lumpur, for instance, before going on stage. Through a gap in the curtain, he'd looked out at the vast, almost empty room, a face with almond eyes surfacing now and again from an ocean of plush crimson. He'd thought about Xenia there.

Blandeuil let his steps carry him along. Ten years had gone by. Most of his friends were probably tucked away in orderly slumber right now, one hand on a wife's breast. Most, but not all. There had to be a few left drifting from bar to bar, like in the good old days.

The Parrot was closed, and the Blue Rabbit now little more than a brothel, but at the Nautilus, Blandeuil found Javier sitting in front of a gin and tonic. Odds were he would've found him there on any of the three thousand six hundred and fifty nights that had slipped by since the last time they'd seen each other.

"Well, look who it is!" Javier murmured. "You son of a bitch..."

Lola Balbo, no doubt. Blandeuil regretted not staying in bed. This drunk was going to congratulate him for seducing Lola Balbo. He'd probably use a different word. But the salacious gleam in Javier's eye winked out as though doused by a breaker of gin and tonic.

"So... how's the dolceola going?"

Relieved, Blandeuil replied that yeah, it was going pretty well, tours and concerts... "How about yourself?"

"Me? Ahhh...The gin-and-tonic makers can rest easy as long as I'm around!" Javier guffawed. Then: "Did they tell you about Xenia?"

Blandeuil nodded. Javier said no more.

There was a party at Bordenave's that night. Javier wouldn't have gone alone—Bordenave annoyed him, with his airs of a man who'd worked and succeeded—but with Blandeuil, why not? Everyone would see that he hadn't come to nibble from Bordenave's hand, but to keep Blandeuil company. Bordenave had moved; the former stockbroker now lived atop Belvedaire—that's right, old pal!

They bought two bottles of gin and left the Nautilus. They were in no hurry, stopping every hundred yards or so to knock back a swig of liquor.

At the foot of the hill, right before attempting the steep hill up Belvedaire, Blandeuil felt on his cheek the cold breath that came, winter and summer alike, from the nearby chasm.

"Remember how scared we were as kids?" he asked Javier, pointing to the old fence overgrown with Virginia creeper that blocked off access to the rift.

Javier nodded. "We'd climb the railing, and whoever went the farthest down . . ."

"Yeah . . . Bordenave was the best."

"You think? Anyway, that's where."

"That's where what?"

"Xenia. She beat out Bordenave! She went all the way down, head-first."

Blandeuil's breath caught for a split second. At last, he knew. So it was here, in this chaos of rocks and moss, at whose bottom roared an underground river they called the Tartarus. He relived their games on the edge of the abyss. It could've been yesterday. It was. Ten years, twenty, the blink of an eye, and an entire lifetime were the same. He saw the gaping rift, its lips half-hidden by a mess of roots, vines, and tiny trees clinging to the walls; heartened, defying the vertiginous jungle, he saw them all again, Xenia in ankle socks and ponytail, Javier already pale and jaded, Bordenave the brave, and all the rest, even himself, awkward as though he'd had his dolceola in his arms all his life.

Bordenave greeted Blandeuil warmly and Javier less warmly; Javier annoyed him, with his airs of a man who drank and went slowly to seed. A small circle soon formed around Blandeuil. His childhood friends asked him about his trips and his concerts, but he could tell quite well they had something else on their minds. He listened to them with half an ear. They inspected him in light of the articles that had been in the papers a few years back. So this was the face—that build, those shoulders? hardly impressive, really—that Balbo had favored? That mouth, those hands had traveled the thrilling, trembling body of a star? Blandeuil grew flustered and wound up stopping in the middle of a sentence. There was a terrible silence. All eyes were on him, his audience hanging on his every word, as though the tale of his triumphant tour in Tierra del Fuego actually interested them. And then someone, God knew who, said Xenia's name. The circle broke; his listeners scattered, leaving him alone in the middle of the living room. He realized that, the whole time, he'd been holding the bottle of gin he'd started. It had seemed to him a casual, fashionable accessory. Suddenly it seemed vulgar. He looked around for Javier, to see what he'd done with his bottle. Javier had vanished. Was he sleeping it off in a corner? Or had he already headed back for the Nautilus, the cozy nest of his dereliction? Who knew? Blandeuil was really alone now, bottle in hand, cheeks burning, in the middle of a no-man's land of waxed parquet flooring. He brought the bottle to his lips, and, not really knowing whether he was doing it to look composed, or to put a finishing touch on the disaster, he took a long swallow of gin.

Later, sprawled in a lounger in the corner of the drawing room, he was finishing off the bottle when Philomena came to talk to him. Philomena, pretty Philomena! More beautiful than Xenia, maybe even more than Lola. Blandeuil wondered which of his friends had had the privilege of marrying her. He didn't have to think hard; it was probably Bordenave, a phoenix among hosts in this neck of the woods.

"W-well, p-pretty Philomena . . ."

She laid a ringed hand on his wrist, encircling it almost tenderly.

"You know, we often talked about it with the others..."

She fell silent, watching him from the depths of her eyes.

"Huh? About what?"

"Xenia. You. And we all came to the same conclusion: that you should join her."

"Join her? But—"

"What are you doing here? Not here, at our house, but here on earth, I mean. What are you doing? What do you think you're doing?"

"Hey! P-playing my music!" Blandeuil objected. "You're looking at the best do-dolceola player of our generation!"

"Poor thing! No one needs your dolceola; you can't even dance to it! But Xenia needs you—down there."

Panicked, dumbfounded, Blandeuil tried to pull his arm back, but Philomena was strong, infinitely stronger than he.

"Down there?"

"There, at the bottom of the chasm, on the dark banks of the Tartarus, where she wanders, weeping..."

Philomena pulled him to his feet and forced him across the room. As they passed the buffet, he left his empty bottle there. Bordenave and several guests—Xenia's closest friends, and perhaps his own, he thought in the drunken haze where he wandered—fell in behind them. They left the villa and started down the slope. Wasted as he was, Blandeuil never knew where he found the strength to break free of Philomena's grip. Still, he got away and started to run. Behind him rose cries of disapproval, but no one came after him. What, and break an ankle? No thanks! The Bordenaves and their guests shrugged and headed back for the villa, exchanging cynical comments. Blandeuil, however, reached the bottom of the hill, out of breath but intact. He let himself fall to his knees before the fence around the chasm. He was so weary, so drunk, that he fell asleep right there, his nose in the creeper, as though an avalanche of sleep, pouring onto him from the heights of the Belvedaire, had buried him.

The cold, redoubled in the wee small hours, woke him. Eparvay was still asleep. No one saw him cross town hunched over, trembling, spitting, and coughing. When he reached his car, he saw he'd left his dolceola out in the open on the backseat all night, and he hadn't even locked the doors. Luckily, Eparvay was such a safe place... and who would go to the trouble of stealing a dolceola? He sat down at the wheel and started the car. He turned halfway round to brush the dolceola's scratched leather case with his fingertips. He hadn't waxed it for a long time. Too long. He had to take care of it, as he did the instrument inside. Did they still make them? He wouldn't have sworn on it. And when the day came for him to retire, would there be another to play it after him? He entertained the idea of opening a school for the dolceola. He'd reached the point of wondering who'd help finance such a project when the absurdity of it hit him. A dolceola conservatory! Why not an Egyptian embalming institute, while he was at it? He couldn't keep back a chilled little laugh that turned into a coughing fit. He needed a nice hot coffee. The cafés would be open in the next town over by the time he got there. He cranked the heat up all the way and drove off slowly. The roads were clear, but it would have been stupid to get into an accident now, at the very moment he was leaving Eparvay forever.

Lozère, October 1992

The Pest

I'd known him forever, but I never knew his name. He was neither brother, cousin, nor friend to me, oh no, least of all a friend, despite the insufferable, nauseating expression of tenderness that lit up those piggish little eyes whenever his gaze settled on me.

Time and again, he'd ruined my life. I'd even made an attempt on his, but his filthy little fingers clung tight and fast to his filthy little life. He got away every time and came back to taunt me with it, with his repellent potbelly, his teary eyes, his incurable acne, his falsetto, his grubby rags, his inevitable shopping bag bulging with old oysters and plastic conches.

It was his fault I'd become a pariah. Every time a chance had come up for me, he'd chased it off, or embarrassed me so much I couldn't seize it, mired as I was in him and his grotesque notions. How many women had withheld their smiles, how many potential investors their trust, how many taxi drivers their services in the pouring rain—and all because of him? Oh, how well I understood them! I would've done the same: a man who knows, or is known by, someone like him is obviously disreputable.

Let's be honest: not everything in my life was that hopeless. Sometimes he was here one day and gone the next. It so happened that he'd leave me a few months or even years of respite. Disbelieving at first, I'd rejoice suspiciously. A day without him was already a blessing.

Two, three—I wouldn't yet dare believe it but bit by bit regained my confidence, I straightened up, I sneaked peeks at women passing by: he wasn't there to elbow me and loudly pronounce the crudest commentary on this or that aspect of their physique. A week went by, the skies cleared, my smile came back, I whistled, I hummed, I snapped my fingers, I laughed out loud alone in the street, I began making plans for the future again!

Now and then I had the chance to get these plans underway and, more rarely, to see them through. That's how I managed to start several businesses and two families ... alas! He always wound up coming back, unbridled, more monstrous and destructive than ever. In a few days he'd reduced it all to nothing. My wife would chase me out. My business would collapse. The mailman would hurl my mail at me from far off, as though at a plague victim, and if I were so imprudent as to protest, my own dog would take the mailman's side and bark at me. I'd find myself homeless, ruined, and riddled with debt, alone ... no, not alone, that would've been too good to be true! There he'd be, obnoxiously loyal and loving.

Once I tried to place myself under the protection of the law. Still reeling from a incident more unpleasant than usual, I walked into a precinct and asked to speak to the desk sergeant. A patrolman greeted me. I launched right into my tale: "Officer, I'm the victim of harassment."

"I see. What form does this harassment take? Insults? Infringement of civil liberties? Death threats? Insistent, unwelcome sexual advances?"

"No, no," I replied. "He doesn't lay into *me* so much as people I meet ... He annoys them, shocks them, frightens or disgusts them, and their contempt and disapproval reflect on me."

"But you're not the one harassing them. It's him, right?"

"Absolutely! But you have to understand, he's not really harassing them. He's happy just acting like a lout, while treating me in such a friendly and informal way that my acquaintances can't doubt our closeness. A closeness I formally refute, officer!"

"Hmm. I see . . ." The policeman scratched his forehead for a moment, silent.

"Actually, I don't," he began again. "To tell the truth, I don't see at all. Could you be a bit clearer, more precise: how is this closeness shown?"

I dropped my gaze. "He . . . he caresses my hands, gazes fondly at me, gives me the most excessive, extravagant compliments!"

". . . and?"

I blushed. "Oh, this is absurd! He says my skin is lily-white and soft as a peach, that I'm aglow with health, that my teeth are gleaming—"

I bit my tongue long enough to clear my throat. "He praises my wit, my manners, my diction, my knowledge, my fashion sense, the—the freshness of my breath!"

"And these compliments irritate you?"

"To say the least, sir!"

"So why don't you just slap him in the face?"

"I have! I've insulted him, slapped him, half strangled him, smacked him silly, left him for dead again and again—"

"That bad, is it?"

"Yes!" I said, nodding frantically, heedless of the fact that in the policeman's eyes I was changing from victim to victimizer. "I've often thrown him to the ground and trampled him, twisted his ears and nose, broken his fingers, even tried to poke his eyes out!"

"But you never managed?"

"No—well, I thought I did once or twice, but sadly, no!"

"In short: you'd like us to intervene?"

"I want it to stop! I want him to go away! I want him to leave me alone!" I'd raised my voice. The patrolman scowled.

"Calm down now, mister. Mister... I'm sorry, I didn't catch your name?"

I stated my name. He noted it.

"And this individual... What's his name?"

It was inevitable. We were bound to reach this point sooner or later. I felt sheepish, helpless. "I don't know, officer."

He frowned. "You don't know?"

"He never said."

"How exactly do you know each other?"

The pointlessness of my approach was suddenly clear to me. How could I have thought my agony might be relieved by an outside party? I was quiet for a moment. But the officer was getting impatient. I had to give him an answer.

"I met him at Buttes-Chaumont. Well... I think it was Buttes-Chaumont."

"You're not sure?"

"It's just that it's been more than thirty years since he first showed up in my life, officer. After all that time, I'm not sure anymore. I could just as well have met him in the little square on the rue de Crimée—I was there a lot too back then—but I'm leaning more toward Buttes-Chaumont, since—"

The patrolman cut me off. "Buttes-Chaumont it is. Well? What happened then?"

"I was playing in the sandbox with a few other kids when he appeared. In the wrong clothes, even back then. Grubby and pimply. His nose was running, and a few big snotty drops had fallen on the half-chewed waffle in his hand. He stepped into the sandbox, walked right up to me, and made a great show of friendship: the first of many! He sang praises of my sandcastles, marveled over the stickers on my little bucket, and grabbed the other kids' rakes and shovels, piling them up at my feet like spoils of war. Then he made me eat his waffle.

I got a cold the next day, lice the day after, and two weeks later came down with chicken pox. My troubles had begun."

My voice broke into a sob. Recounting the first station on my long road to Calvary had moved me to tears. I took a packet of tissues from my pocket and blew my nose loudly. Just above the edge of the tissue, I caught the officer's look. It didn't seem quite as compassionate as I might have expected.

"Of course," I said, folding the tissue back up neatly, "if you've never been through that, you couldn't understand."

The patrolman coughed gently. "I understand."

"You'd have to have been through what I've been through. The sandbox was only the beginning of an endless series of encounters. If only you knew—"

Carried away by the desire to convince the officer it was essential he intervene, I gathered myself to tell him everything in the greatest detail.

He stopped me right away. "Let's skip that for now, OK? Where does this man live?"

I grew flustered, and dropped my gaze again. Bad enough that I didn't know my tormentor's name. But how could an outsider ever accept that I'd put up with him under my own roof? For live together we did, for long periods, against my will, of course. I'd change my locks every week, but he'd get in somehow and impose his awful presence on me. If I moved, he'd find me. Even if I fled to the far ends of the earth, it wouldn't be long before he happened by.

"Usually, you'll find him wherever I am. I mean, at my place, since right now I work at home stuffing envelopes because of him," I said, trying to control my trembling voice.

"At your place? You mean you live together?"

"Not exactly. We don't really live together, strictly speaking. He's just . . . there most of the time, that's all."

The patrolman took a deep breath, then shook his head. "One last question, if I may: do you have a history of psychiatric illness?"

"Excuse me?"

"Have you ever spent time in an asylum?"

"Never, officer! I don't think you understand. I'm not insane! In fact, I am in full command of all my faculties. I'd have to be, to put up with what I do without losing my mind."

"We'll see about that."

When I managed to escape the hospital eight days later, I was worried. The doctors had succeeded in raising my doubts again. Did my tormentor really exist? I hurried back home on foot from the distant suburb where I'd been shipped despite my protestations, mulling the question over seriously. If he didn't exist, I was insane. Moreover, doubting his reality meant doubting my own—I felt my reason waver, unsteady as a child's loose tooth beneath a probing finger. If he did exist, my health but also my misfortune would be confirmed, for everything led me to believe he'd be around as long as I would.

Once more—for the thought had crossed my mind many times before—I was tempted to put an end to myself. Only an abiding uncertainty about the nature of the afterlife—and also, let's face it, a certain natural pusillanimity—had always stayed my hand. I'd suffered enough, and been kept from acting often enough (and therefore from acting wrongly), to go straight to heaven if there was one. But if I got up there only to find him, that groper, that toady, in all his sniveling bonhomie, ready to stick by me for the rest of eternity, well, it wasn't worth it. But that day, my despair almost won out.

Despite myself, my steps led me to the river's edge. Night was falling. The waters seemed to be calling me through the gray mists, promising me a blessed oblivion free of everything, especially that despicable puppet who'd ruined my life.

Drowning isn't usually considered a barrel of laughs, but as I was frail of body and a poor swimmer to boot, I was hoping for an easy death without too much suffering if I went about thirty feet out. Besides, the harsh winter would come to my aid. I stood a good chance of succumbing to sudden pulmonary congestion, or something of the kind, before the water reached my chin.

I'd taken a few steps down a half-submerged stone staircase toward the water when a voice rang out in my ears. I'd have known it anywhere. It'd been the cause of each of my innumerable defeats. It was the voice of bad luck itself.

"Oh, it's you! What a pleasant surprise! I was just taking a stroll, and thinking about you, in fact! What are you doing here?"

In the mist that rose from the river, I was flooded by two contradictory feelings: relief at being able to dispel the doubt the doctors had instilled in me, and rage at finding myself back in a life that horrified me.

My reply rang out in the still air. The sound of his execrable voice had swept aside every last hesitation. "I'm going! I'm leaving you forever, you hellish creature!"

"What? You're not thinking of—you can't be! You don't have the right! A man like you can't let down the hopes he's raised in others!"

I burst out with a cackle and took another step into the icy water.

"You silver-tongued clown! 'A man like me'? 'Hopes I've raised'? Fuckall, I say! Without you, I might've been something … I'm not sure what. But at least I would've lived! Too bad! I'm going to drown myself and escape you in death, you pestilent meddler!"

"Stop! You poor man! Think about those who'll grieve for you! Who've loved you, who love you still!"

"That's right, keep talking!"

Still cackling, I took two more steps. An icy hand squeezed my belly. O river Seine, make quick work of me! I leaned forward and pushed off with my heels. Terror struck my heart, and my entire body rose up prickling against the vise suddenly tightening around me. But I was sincerely determined to die. From here, it looked painful but brief. All I had to do was take a few strokes from shore and let myself go under.

Not far away, something heavy hit the water with a massive splash. I couldn't believe my ears. It was him! The fool had jumped in!

He surfaced, shook himself like an elephant seal, and reached out his hand.

"Get away from me," I screamed. "I don't want you to save me, you filthy piece of trash!"

He shook his big head. "You're wrong, you—"

"Get away!" I hit him again and again with all my strength. He went under, then resurfaced almost immediately, huffing and spitting. "Get away from me, you bastard!"

"I can't! I can't swim!"

"What? But you jumped in—"

"So you'd save me!"

"Me? Save you? That really takes the cake! Save you?" Beside myself, I began hitting him again. A few of my blows landed. His face was covered in cuts and bruises. His blood flowed freely.

"Save me!" he cried, one last time. "It's the only way to free yourself!"

I don't know what came over me then—what reversal of the soul, what sudden clarity—but I gave up on suicide and saved him.

It wasn't easy. He was a fat slob and didn't lift a finger to help. But we hadn't had time to drift very far from shore. I hauled him onto the steps, and we stayed there for a moment, moaning and shivering, miserable. Finally, we made our way back up the bank, hanging on to each other.

"Real smart," I said. "We're going to get sick now."

"Probably. But if you get better, you'll be free. I give you my word."

He spoke the truth. We ran to the nearest bistro. They undressed us by the stove, rubbed us down, covered us in blankets, served us grog, and even called us a taxi. He let me take it on my own. I have never seen him since.

Lozère, December 1988

Delaunay the Broker

All things there are the same, but the same as what, I could not say.

He walked into my antique shop one September afternoon. I knew right away he hadn't come to buy. I have an eye for these things. Even taking a certain fashionable negligence into account, he wasn't well-dressed enough. In truth, he was neither well nor poorly dressed: he simply couldn't have cared less for his appearance. His kind is rare among my clients. I have no complaints about this. I hate mediocrity in all its forms.

So, he hadn't come to buy. I was making ready to turn him away with my customary skill when our gazes met. Make no mistake—I am by no means insensitive to the promise in a gaze . . . In fact, I've an eye for that, too. He wasn't like *that*; I would have staked my life on it. Something else gave me pause. A lived-in gaze is so rare these days.

I made my way toward him unhurriedly. Nonchalantly, even. Perhaps he was one of those people for whom every encounter is a joust—in which case he'd already scored a point.

"You have quite a collection of handsome items," he said.

Neither upper, nor lower middle class. I have an ear for it. But nothing common about him either. Clear speech, firm tones, fine timbre. His voice confirmed his gaze; this was no ordinary man.

"Very . . . personal items," he concluded.

I appreciated his adjective without letting it show. Indeed, such items are precisely what I sell: it is up to the right person to present himself.

The stranger carefully picked up a mechanical toy displayed on a low table. "Günthermann's perambulator...The lithographs look so fresh!"

He tripped the switch, and the baby whose head surfaced from the stroller shook his noisy rattle. "Charming, really!"

He set down the plaything and turned to face me. "Allow me to introduce myself: I am Delaunay."

"Delaunay...wait—"

"The broker."

"Ah! So you're a real person?"

He smiled in amusement. "So it would seem."

My heart had begun foolishly to beat harder. Like everyone in the business, I'd heard of Delaunay. Rarely does a conversation among antique dealers end without some mention of his name. "And...to what do I owe the honor of your visit?"

He shrugged. "You must know that Raymann is dead."

"That's right, Raymann is dead! What a loss!"

Every guild has its notables. Raymann had been one of the richest and most influential of that roster to which I belonged. Rumor had it Delaunay worked exclusively for him.

"Doubtless. But here I am, without employ," said he prosaically. "I thought of you."

I must have blushed with pleasure. Delaunay had thought of me! At the same moment, however, I reproved myself *in petto*. I practice a difficult profession, in which I must sell at the highest possible price and buy at the lowest. By showing too much joy in his offer, I encouraged Delaunay to overestimate his services, and compromised any anticipated profits.

He must have read these thoughts on my face, for he made a soothing gesture.

"Raymann found it rewarding to work with me," he said with a little laugh. "You will, too—you'll see."

In the months that followed, I saw that Delaunay was indeed the king of brokers—the only one, at any rate, to furnish any object on demand in the shortest possible time, no matter how unusual, no matter how uncommon.

I knew—we all knew—that a mystery surrounded Delaunay. He was known in our little world, known to everyone in it. He rarely visited the auction rooms, he placed no want ads, nor did he rummage around flea markets. No one had ever been able to boast of having done business with him. No one had the slightest idea where he acquired his items. The objects he brought me seemed to have welled up from nothingness . . . or rather from the very desires of those who'd requested them. A client would come and speak to me about some trinket or a little piece of furniture that he'd glimpsed and missed his chance at in a sale once, or that he'd always loved in the living room of an old uncle now deceased, or which he'd simply dreamed of. I tried to get as precise and complete a description as possible of the item in question—shape, size, color, material; often I even made a sketch from the information given by the collector. I endeavored to ascertain how much he might be willing to spend. Then, without any absolute guarantees of satisfying his desire—for it would have been tactless to dull its edge—I did not rule out the possibility of hope.

I had only to give Delaunay the sketch and the description then. Eight to ten days later, he would bring me the coveted item. It always met in every way the wishes of the client who, overcome with joy, usually settled up without turning a hair. I grant you, our services cost a pretty penny. But for our regulars we procured what they had themselves described as marvels. It was only fitting that they pay marvelously dear.

Delaunay had his limits. He was not to be asked to track down a Norman wardrobe or an abbey table of solid wood. When I ventured to do so, at the beginning of our arrangement, he was adamant: "I won't carry large objects. Jewelry, paintings, silverware, lamps, small bronzes, old dolls, glass paperweights, books, albums, miniatures—any and as many of these as you want; light furniture at the most, a footrest, a pedestal, but nothing heavy or cumbersome. After all, you're not the one crossing the bar."

"Bar? What bar?"

"My point exactly," he muttered.

He was too valuable for me to run the risk of alienating him. My profits had tripled since he'd walked through my door. Nevertheless, my curiosity was keen. But each time I raised the question of his sources, he interrupted bluntly.

"Have you ever had a broker who let slip a word on the subject? You have the buyer, I have the item, together we sell it, and for a tidy sum! What more do you want?"

As I'd returned yet again to the topic, he grew incensed. "I'll tell you this much: even if I revealed my suppliers, it wouldn't do you any good . . . Now back off or I'm gone!"

His behavior was understandable, but it infuriated me. I am curious; it's in my nature; I've chosen to spend my life in the business of curiosities. I sought neither to poach on Delaunay's territory nor to evict him from it. I only wanted to know. I suspected Raymann had died without knowing anything about his broker's secrets. The idea that the same thing might happen to me was intolerable. I brooded over this entire days at a time in my shop. That's how I am: a brooder, easily obsessed. Capricious, but persistent. Passionate! Now that I think back on it, was I perhaps in love with Delaunay? I'd understood at once that he wasn't part of my brotherhood, and I'd suffered too much in the past from such incompatibilities to expose myself once more to the inconveniences they occasioned. I'd committed myself; yet my entire temperament as an antique dealer urged me to discover what he hid from me. I had to make up for it somehow. It occurred to me that I might do him one better. I'd send the mighty hunter Nimrod on a wild-goose chase!

I took up pad and pencil, and gave my fancy free rein. The result was a snuffbox whose cover was adorned with an engraving that depicted neither a hunting scene nor a libertine tableau—motifs too common to try a sleuth of his talents—but instead a semaphore tower set atop a hill in the heart of a pleasant countryside. Such snuffboxes couldn't have been so common as to be easily located today. In any case, none had ever passed through my hands. To perfect my snare, I specified that my imaginary client wished the body of the object to be made of rowan wood and the lid of ivory or, failing that, horn. I wrote these desiderata beneath my drawing, added this to an actual order for a silver, helmet-shaped sauceboat, preferably on a pedestal base, signed Boulanger if possible, and had it all sent to Delaunay.

Delaunay called at the shop three or four times a month. He never came empty-handed. If he happened not to have located an item yet, he was diligent about bringing me a few charming or original baubles that always sold quickly and turned a nice profit. I'd sent him the messenger on Tuesday. He dropped by Saturday morning.

Delaunay opened his valise and removed a helmet-shaped sauceboat on a pedestal base, hallmarked pre-Empire, and signed Boulanger. I'd sold the piece for nine thousand francs, and counted out three thousand for him on the spot. I would settle with him later for the little knickknacks that rounded out his delivery: a toiletry bag from the time of Louis-Philippe and a gaily decorated billiard cue in its sheepskin sheath.

"Oh! I almost forgot!" he said, stuffing the money in his pocket.

He held out an object wrapped in newspaper. A feeling of unease overtook me. Even before undoing the paper, I knew what I'd find inside. At a certain level of insolence, luck no longer amazes us; it terrifies. I finished opening the package and took hold of the snuff-box with a trembling hand. It was indeed as I'd imagined and drawn. The body was of rowan wood. The rectangular lid of yellowed horn was embellished with an engraving of unsophisticated workmanship, depicting a semaphore atop a knoll in a rural setting.

"The scene is simple and the etching clumsy," said Delaunay. "Mid-nineteenth century, no doubt. But your client wanted a semaphore, and got one! The configuration of the arms on the tower means 'T.' I suppose some Thénard or Tournier, in charge of a signal post, wished to keep some souvenir of his vacation."

"It's perfect! Perfect!" I said expressionlessly. "My client will be satisfied..."

"My commission, then?"

"Right away!"

I added four hundred francs to the three thousand I had already given him.

"No new orders for the moment?"

"No ... not yet. Really, this snuffbox ... It's most uncommon. You have a knack."

"Yes, yes," he agreed absentmindedly.

He pocketed the bills, shut his suitcase, bid me farewell, and set off at an easy pace.

From that day on I knew no sleep. The incident had made the facts plain: all this was unnatural. I should have realized earlier, of course. Even the cleverest, luckiest, most well-connected and zealous broker could not repeat such *tours de force* week after week. For even if the af-fair of the snuffbox with a semaphore had impressed me the most, the truth was that Delaunay brought me the most eclectic and singular curios every week.

I didn't for a moment think him a thief. But then how did he locate the very *personal* merchandise I asked of him with the required promptness and precision? I'd sooner have believed he'd made a deal with the devil! I don't believe in the devil, but none of the theories I'd put together held up, and I was dying of curiosity.

I waited until I'd taken a few more orders and passed them on to Delaunay, and then I put Lambert on his trail. Lambert was a private eye. I'd made his acquaintance during a love affair that was, as they say of certain illnesses, painful and protracted. I'd learned to appreciate his seriousness and his discretion. I charged him with tracking Delaunay's every step and keeping me informed from day to day of all his movements. Shabby behavior, maybe—but I wanted to put my mind to rest on the subject.

One, two, three days went by without a call from Lambert. Furious, I phoned him at his agency. I got his secretary. The girl told me her boss had stuck to Delaunay like gum to the sole of a shoe. So to speak, that is, because Delaunay hardly ever left his place. When he did, he never went far. He frequented a restaurant, a movie theater, and the public library, all a stone's throw from where he lived. He lived alone in two rooms and a kitchen on the highest floor of a modest building. He had no visitors, and barely spoke a word to his neighbors. Lambert hadn't deemed it necessary to inform me of the poverty of his findings. He'd thought it better to wait and learn more before calling.

I was quite concerned by what was in my eyes a crucial point: "All right, so he isn't going anywhere for the moment. But does he make any calls?"

"No. Never. He doesn't have a telephone, and never uses the pay phone in the street."

"What? But there's no such thing as a broker without a phone! He never gave me his number so I'd leave him alone, and he's not in the phone book, but he *must* have a phone!"

"Mr. Lambert checked, Mr. Thyll. Mr. Delaunay is unlisted because he doesn't have a phone, simple as that."

Staggered by this revelation, I hung up after insisting that I be kept abreast of the smallest wrinkle in his routine. I was more intrigued than ever. I'd pictured a frenetic Delaunay, moving heaven and earth, making calls day and night . . . but he loafed around all day, caught flicks, read paperbacks. He was taking it easy, just as if he wouldn't soon have to deliver a World War I English officer's hat in mint condition; a statuette (the subject didn't matter) about eight inches tall and, most importantly, of jade without any saussurite, and more olive than green; and finally a silver sugar bowl with a display stand in the Villard style.

Five days after my call, in the early evening, while I was closing up, Delaunay appeared, suitcase in hand. He seemed weary. It certainly wasn't from exerting himself for my sake! Ever since my call to order, Lambert had phoned me every night to say that Delaunay hadn't changed his quiet habits in the slightest.

"Well?" I said.

"I'm still missing the sugar bowl," he said. "Next time . . . But the rest was no problem."

From his suitcase he pulled a heavy object wrapped in newspaper and a splendid box for a regulation English army cap.

I remained seated long after he'd left, my head in my hands, unmindful of the hour, and of an appointment awaiting me on the other side of Paris. In front of me, atop my desk beside a brown woolen cap encircled by a broad red ribbon, an eight-inch hermit in olive jade, standing firmly on his crooked legs, seemed to taunt me with a good-natured condescension.

➤❮

Eight days later, Delaunay brought me the sugar bowl. And yet I knew perfectly well from Lambert that he'd kept on going to the movies or, locked away in his room, reading the books he'd gotten from his local library.

I admit that what follows is not to my credit. Nevertheless, you must imagine my state of mind. I no longer thought of anything else. Sleep escaped me. I lost interest in life. Usually quite the gourmand, I picked at my profiteroles, and I must have seemed so tormented that those around me began to worry for my health.

One afternoon, while Delaunay was at the movies, I broke into his apartment. I'd arranged everything with Lambert. He'd had the keys copied and kept watch in front of the building.

I was exceedingly uncomfortable. After all, the escapade could cost me quite a bit. My shirt grew damp with sweat just thinking about the headlines: Edmond Thyll, Well-Known Antiques Dealer, Caught Red-Handed in Burglary. But you had to know what you wanted, and I wanted to know.

The door to Delaunay's opened easily. I slipped through the gap. I closed it without a sound, and started to explore the place. The place: a bare and cheerless foyer, two tastelessly furnished rooms, the kitchenette of a bachelor who takes most of his meals out. I'd been expecting a broker's lair—that is, a mess. Crates stuffed with bric-a-brac, piles of empty frames, tables and small pieces of furniture awaiting restoration, jam jars full of odd bits of molding and keys kept just in case ... But nothing of the sort. No artistic touches. Nothing in the least picturesque. It was clean, well-ordered, impersonal to an unusual degree. The best broker in the business put out his cigarettes in complimentary ashtrays of enameled metal, with ads in the bottom, and kept his pens in an empty mustard jar.

I cursed my own foolishness and slumped into a chair. What had I been hoping for? That Delaunay might have been so kind as to scrawl his secret on the wall? I stayed seated for a long moment, contemplating his pitiful furniture with a confounded eye. And little by little the notion of writing made its way into my mind. Delaunay might not've written his secret on the wall, but maybe he'd written it somewhere else. He lived alone. Lonely people write. I myself began a novel after every break-up, only to abandon it joyously each time I found a new companion. The human heart is a vase filled with humors and tears. One good blow, and out splash its contents. Neglect it, and it rots; parasites proliferate, spin out their filaments, mount an assault on the walls, scale them, and spread...

I leapt up and ran to the bed. In the drawer of the bedside table, I found a large spiral notebook. I opened it to a page at random and read, in a low voice, the first lines my eyes fell across:

> *All things there are the same, but the same as what, I could not say ... The streets I pace, the squares I cross there resemble ours as the reflection of a bridge in a river resembles the bridge itself. The slightest thing destroys its order, as a shift in the wind will wrinkle the bridge's image, or the brush of a bird's wing strike it from the water's surface. All things there are the same, but the scenery dissolves and resolves itself ceaselessly beneath the gaze of an observer himself caught up in the current. The instant the reflection unwrinkles, the second the breach opened by the bird's wing is filled, the cockleshell of my consciousness has already slipped downstream.*

These lines might have seemed obscure, but I was certain right away of holding, in this notebook, the key to the mystery. I tucked it in my coat and left the apartment.

That day I photocopied the notebook, and read it that night. I meant to have Lambert replace the original the next day, and I'd already called and told him to come pick it up in the morning, but this turned out to be unnecessary. I'd just opened up shop when Delaunay walked in.

He headed straight for me. "My manuscript! Give it back!"

"What are you talking about, my friend?"

He shook his head menacingly. "You broke into my apartment yesterday afternoon—you, or someone you hired! A manuscript was stolen . . . the manuscript for a novel. Give it back, if you know what's good for you."

"What makes you think—"

He cut me off in a voice trembling with anger. "Who else could it have been?"

I'm no warrior. I gave up trying to outsmart him. "All right, all right, I'll give it back."

Despite himself, his face expressed an unspeakable relief.

I took the notebook from the desk drawer where I'd placed it while waiting for Lambert. Delaunay tore it from my hands.

"Why did you do it?" His voice was almost as tense as before.

"I wanted to know. Now I know."

"It's only a novel!"

"A fantastical novel, then."

"That's right. A fantastical novel."

In that moment he hated me—I am sure of it—but his desire to deceive me as to the nature of the notebook forced him to keep his hatred in check.

"It was inspired by my work," he went on. "You've read it? What did you think?"

"It's a . . . disturbing tale. I'd like to know how it ends."

"You'll find out if it's published someday."

". . . or by reading the newspapers. But in that case I'd be the only one to know what story had just come to an end."

Georges-Olivier Châteaureynaud

Our gazes met head-on. He was the first to lower his eyes.

"You'll have to hire another broker," said he, lifting his gaze once more.

"No one could ever match you. If you agreed to stay, I'd increase your percentage. I know—"

I shut my mouth. I'd almost added that from now on I knew how much each piece cost him. I couldn't think about the pages in the notebook devoted to what he called "the bar" without trembling. I had never read anything more terrifying.

"The money's secondary," he said. "I want to work in a climate in of trust. And I no longer trust you."

I have never seen him again since that morning. A few weeks later, I learned that he'd teamed up with Nedelkovich, one of my most gifted competitors.

All I have left of this little adventure is the photocopy of Delaunay's diary. I made another copy, and had them both bound. The first I keep by my bedside. I often reread it, and reflect upon it. The second is tucked safely away in a deposit box, where these pages will join it when they come back, in turn, from the binder's. Let posterity make of them what it will. As for me, I believe I have done my duty in thus preserving a part of the only diary of the fantastic in the history of literature. For God knows what may happen to Delaunay and his notebook, and to the pages that he will, without a doubt, keep writing every day, every night, upon returning from his expeditions.

Lozère, April 1988

The Excursion

We didn't know who he was. We never do know much of what goes on. We're too far away from it all. Be it fashion, progress, war, or people's reputations, few things make their way out here. Everything is foreign to us, as though we took part only on an honorary basis in the human race. All we know is wind and rain and the sound of waves on the rocks. Our few visitors find it sad out here. They never stay. After the excursion, they hurry back quick as they can to civilization, to the sunny shallows, as though out here were the depths: the depths of what, God alone knows.

But they're wrong. It's not sad out here—well, maybe just a bit, in an infinitely gentle way. You have to be born here, and not have known anything else. Then you'd understand, you'd see how it cradles and calms you, lulls you to sleep for life. Your eyes stay open, but you're actually asleep, and all is well; nothing, almost nothing really reaches you, rain falls in a curtain of pearls between you and the world, the wind half drowns out the voices and cries.

I don't know how we found out he was famous. He wasn't the kind to brag. Maybe all he said was that he was in music, and that was enough to ring a bell; then we rummaged around in a closet and came up with an old magazine. A closet at the inn, no doubt, since it's always visitors who bring the books and magazines alike. There's no delivery service here. There isn't even a post office. We entrust our letters to the pharmacist. He stocks up on remedies at the branch depot every two or three weeks. But we rarely write. Who would we write, and what would we say? As for letters *to* us . . . well, no one writes us, either. You can't make reservations in advance, not even for the excursion. You come and work something out on the spot with one of the fishermen . . . So most magazines are at the inn, where they've been forgotten or left behind. The innkeeper saves them. Sometimes, when we stop by to see her for this or that, she pulls them out of the closet and we flip through them together. How terrifying, how bewildering the tumultuous world they depict! Each time I've taken a peek I've thought back for days on the drugged athletes, corrupt congressmen, and two-timing princesses that haunt it, on the dictators, serial killers, and terrorists . . . and I think how lucky we are to live here, if only just, in the murmur of the wind and the light tap of rain on our roofs.

As for him, his music had made him famous: it existed like the wind or the rain, since he, too, was in the papers. We got a kick when we found out, since he was the first. Not our first visitor ever, of course, but the first to come bathed in the same aura of fame he enjoyed back beyond the curtain of pearls. The first to matter. You couldn't tell from his face. Without the innkeeper's magazine, how would we have guessed there was music in that head? Music of his very own, like a matchless scent? For we, too, sometimes sing songs or hymns. But it's not the same. I've often thought I'd liked to have heard his music. Maybe I wouldn't have liked it. In the big cities, crowds might flock to his concerts in the big cities, they might call him *maestro*, but can we tell beauty from its opposite? Do we know what we like? At any rate, I'm sorry never to have heard his work. If I really wanted . . . there are recordings, after all. All I'd have to do is get them through the pharmacist. I'd find someone to lend me a record player, or order one at the co-op . . . everything's always very complicated, though never really out of reach. That's the worst part. Nothing's really out of reach, but nothing ever gets done. A pity . . . I'll probably never hear his music.

He arrived one night on horseback. He dismounted, or fell off, more like; happens to all of them, after ten long hours in the saddle through dune, marsh, and peat bog. The innkeeper's used to it. She serves them soup and puts them to bed. They sleep in the next day, and when they make a showing at last, it's to go down to the port, one hand on their aching backs. There they wait, nursing a mug of mulled wine, for the fishermen to return. It might not be their favorite, but the barman hasn't much else to offer, so mulled wine it is. Between sips they watch us in the low, dark room. Their gazes dart about, lingering here on one face, alighting there on another, their nostrils flaring. Back home, in their well-lighted cafés and eateries, where everything is new, clean, smooth, and gleaming, it doesn't smell of rain, tides, mulled wine, and mildew like it does here. The odors disorient them, doubtless even sicken them a bit. Then they study us with a curiosity tinged with worry. It's true that we live in the nearness of myth, that since childhood the air we breathe has been as though suffused by it, so much so that visitors start imagining things. They tell themselves that what they've come in the middle of the journey of their lives (or for some, even later) to find, we've always known, which confers on us a certain . . . if not superiority, then uniqueness at least. But it's not true. They have no reason to envy us. We and they are equally as helpless, as naked before it. What advantage will the fisherman who takes them out tomorrow have over them, once they settle on a price for the excursion? Well, he knows where he's going. He'll take them to the edge of that mystery they alone will brush. On the way back to port they'll no longer be the same; there'll be something feverish in their eyes that wasn't there before. The skipper's gaze won't have changed.

The maestro did what all the tourists do. He sat himself down in a corner of the bar and, after ordering, asked the barman, who said, "Of course, a number of fishermen take people out for a price. Just wait till the boats get back, and I'll point out a dependable soul." The maestro seemed reassured: it was just like he'd been told it would be. So he nursed his mulled wine, setting his mug down and rubbing his hands together between sips. He waited a long time. He had many more mugs without losing patience. I've often said that in the bar at port you don't feel the hours pass. The sands of time there are so flowing and fine-grained they never stick in the neck of the glass.

Only three or four sailors make the trip, due to low demand and the very real danger, even if you take all the necessary precautions. But it's not just that. Those who used to go but don't anymore will tell you it's too hard. Before the spectacle of utmost pleasure and utmost pain, you must carry on, never quite knowing what has caused it. "It's cruel," they say, "it's filthy. You can't stomach it for long. It's not about the money." Those who keep making the trip rarely speak a word. As they grow inured to their singular trade, they say less and less about it. When they're too old to go out to sea, their silence betrays them; you can pick them out as they while away afternoons, even entire evenings, at the bar, mute, back hunched, pensively rubbing their hands before a mug of wine gone cold.

At last, the barman indicated someone with a jerk of his head. The maestro rose and timidly approached the skipper. It was Esmeraldo. I was there, at my usual spot, and watched the scene from afar. It went on for too long. I was struck by the sight of a maestro used to having the world at his feet speaking humbly as a beggar, and at length, to an uneducated fisherman whose hands were chapped by the sea. It wasn't a complicated transaction. All the trawlers asked about the same price. They came to an agreement at last. The maestro hadn't gotten a raw deal. Esmeraldo wasn't the most taciturn of the ones who went. He still spoke willingly when spoken to, and sometimes even laughed! In pointing him out as someone dependable, the barman was merely cleaving to popular opinion. But in light of what happened next, it's clear Esmeraldo wasn't adequately hardened to the task, hadn't cut himself off enough from the world, sealed himself in silence and in-difference. To ply this trade, it's best to let yourself go beast-dumb. That's why they no longer speak, why words must be torn from them. For them, silence is essential. They know it protects them, out there and back here. It's clear now that the lengthy conversation between Esmeraldo and the maestro the night before they left was too much. Anyway, they shook on it, and arranged to meet early the next morn-ing at the port. The maestro walked out, tottering slightly from the mulled wine.

Esmeraldo never confessed exactly what happened out there the next day. We pieced it together from his trailing sentences, his sighs and shrugs and muddled denials, and also that conversation of theirs.

Georges-Olivier Châteaureynaud

Not its content, which we would never know, but the simple fact that it had lasted much longer than needed. The only sure thing was that Esmeraldo was at fault. Nothing like this had ever happened before. The boat might have capsized, and no one survived, but *this* couldn't have transpired had the skipper been aware of his responsibilities— had he kept watch over his client, protected the man from himself. No need to be a psychic to see that the maestro wouldn't settle for the same excursion as everyone else: a few seconds of rapture and torment, writhing like a worm against the ropes lashing you to the mast before the skipper plugged your ears again with wax like in his own and you returned to port, broken, radiant, initiated. The maestro wanted more. Much more. That was why they'd stayed and talked so long that night at the bar. The maestro had negotiated, insisted, even begged maybe, and Esmeraldo had given in. The next day they'd hugged the shore too closely, and lingered too long in those perilous waters.

So the maestro, too, was to blame in the matter. Why had he come here, anyway? What had he wanted to confirm? We would've had to know where he was at in life to tell. It's said artists are like temperamental machines that work fine for a while and then suddenly stop, for obscure reasons. Too much fame, not enough, too much love, not enough...What keeps them going? What fuel? What fire? No one knows. That flame can gutter out, go astray, get lost. In some people it seems to last their whole lives, and still be burning strong, when one day something else goes missing, or breaks down: a single organ, or a whole body pushed too hard. With others it burns and blazes and suddenly stops, the tank empty, the boiler snuffed out, and there they remain, alive but from then on inert and sterile. Had the maestro broken down? What led us to believe he'd been driven more by worry than curiosity was that he clearly hadn't told anyone where he was going. Otherwise someone would have come looking for him by now.

Someone still might soon, for when a man like that disappears, it doesn't go unnoticed. They must have been looking for him. Someday they'd pick up his trail and follow it here. Then a helicopter streaming rain will drop from the sky to land on the field where our children play. Its arrival will sound the death knell for our way of life, and for what we are, in our way, the last to preserve. At a rare town council meeting, or what passed for one, no one cherished any illusions on the matter. If we just let things continue, we'd soon see a helicopter full of detectives, worried friends and family, and journalists brandishing cameras: our way of life would be blown to smithereens. All of it. For the world beyond the curtain of rain, which had until now been more or less unaware of our existence, neither respects or really tolerates any other world. It is a jealous world. What it names, it kills. Its people claim or hope for the opposite, but the truth is bleak and simple: their cameras despoil all they gaze upon, and destroy all they depict. When the reporters learn where Esmeraldo took the maestro, nothing will stop them from going and filming it from a helicopter. And they'll come back unharmed with their freight of dead images, for the noise of their rotors will drown out the song that turned our illustrious visitor into the village idiot of sorts that he has since become.

In order to keep these things from happening, we decided to wipe out all traces of the maestro's brief trip here, as a child might a chalk line from a blackboard with one swipe of a sponge. His path never brought him to us. Esmeraldo and I have been appointed by the council to see him back to his own kind. We've prepared a sign for him with his name on it, and we will hang it round his neck before abandoning him in the middle of a big city, blowing dumbly into a comb, as he has done unceasingly since his return from the sirens' isle.

Palaiseau, September 1999

La Tête

Permit me to remain anonymous; my name would mean nothing to you. My profession, however, is not unrelated to the story I am about to tell. I am a doctor. I've seen many a woe in my line of work. Some I've eased, and in other cases forestalled what, without my intervention, wouldn't have been long in coming. Well, you'll say, that's all you can ask of a doctor, and I quite agree: we save those patients of ours whom death vies for distractedly. Should its interest in the game be aroused, all our efforts are in vain, and death reaps another victory... It was fifteen years ago—the summer of 1905, to be exact—while in the exercise my profession, that I made the acquaintance of a young man who introduced himself to me as Bennett Riven. He was a stranger to the small seaside town where I had my practice. I knew as much at the first sight of him in my waiting room, crowded that Saturday as any other. After twenty years of being a doctor in a small town, one knows, or can at least place, everyone. By all counts a strapping lad, he wasn't one of my regulars nor, I would have sworn, among those of my two competitors. I say "strapping" because I've known few people with his physique. On seeing him, I remember thinking that if the whole town had his constitution, I could've tucked the key under the mat and retired. Twenty years old, with a marble worker's shoulders and a peasant's cheeks, the neck of a glassblower and hands big enough to throttle a horse. He had health to spare; I would have bought some if I could. Still, something was the matter, since there he was in my packed waiting room. I took the time to study him, and in his blue eyes, with their corneal patina of faience, easily identified a brightness and fixity of stare that, in such an irritatingly vital giant, could have but one cause: terror.

What a fickle thing is a man, no matter how settled in his ways. Simply arouse his curiosity, and he forgets his compunction, his seriousness, and soon thereafter even his duties. In my newcomer's eyes, I'd chanced upon an expression that so intrigued me I examined Mrs. Blanc-Dubourg with appalling absentmindedness; the most unsuitable noises might have come from inside her without my so much as batting an eye. One sole question preoccupied me: in this time of peace at home and abroad, what could possibly have so badly frightened a boy of twenty years built, for all appearances, to live a hundred more? After seeing Mrs. Blanc-Dubourg all the way to the front steps in apology, I strode into the waiting room with the imperious air of someone about to abuse his power and pointed at the young man.

"You're next!" I said in a tone that brooked no rebuttal.

He rose. From all around came astonished sighs and a rebellious rustling of knees. In all fairness, he shouldn't have made it into my office for another two hours. Sweeping the room with an icy gaze, I silenced any inclination to revolt. Was I not the master of my house?

The party concerned, whose already ruddy cheeks had further reddened, gathered a canvas sack from beneath his seat. He held it close to him and preceded me into the office I'd pointed out with a movement of my chin.

I never begin an appointment before my patient and I have taken our respective places on opposite sides of my old leather-topped desk. This desk, as my patients are dimly aware—this desk is the gulf that separates sickness from health. I hold out my hand to them across this desk, and if my patients are obedient enough, and lucky—if I'm lucky—I pull them gently across to my side, to life . . . But what am I blathering on about? The young man was sitting across from me—that's all that matters. He remained silent, eyes lowered, chest canted forward, arms hanging between his knees, hands fiddling with the drawstrings of his sack. I used my most confident, jovial tone of voice. A doctor's voice is fully half of doctoring.

"Well, well, my boy! What can the matter be?"

He lifted his eyes, then dropped them again almost as quickly, coughed slightly, and spoke at last in the voice of a lost child.

"Aw, Doc, everything was going swell . . ." He stopped, not knowing how to continue.

"You felt the need to see me."

"Yeah . . ." He fell silent again. Timidity. Shame. Anxiety. A-ha! Often as not, shame + anxiety = venereal disease! I should have hit on it earlier, I thought; a lad like that surely leaves a trail of hearts in his wake. Hearts and everything else, too. I laid a clean sheet of Bristol on my blotter and uncapped my pen.

"Let's begin at the beginning. What's your name?"

"Bennett Riven, Doctor."

"Bennett Riven? R-I-V—?"

"E-N. Bennett."

"Date of birth?"

"November 22, 1885, Doctor."

"Why, you're only twenty! It's the springtime of your life! You're enjoying it to the hilt, I gather?"

"Excuse me?"

"I said I gather you're enjoying the springtime of your life to the hilt!"

"Uh, yes . . ."

"Good! So, you've enjoyed yourself so thoroughly that . . ."

I left the end of my sentence hanging. Would the young lion wind up taking the line I'd thrown? He did nothing. He was beginning to irk me. After all, I'd surely upset good and faithful patients to hear him out, and now he threatened to be a waste of time...

"You can tell your doctor everything, my boy. I'll even go so far as to say: you must. This kind of affliction—"

He understood what I was getting at, and at the same moment, I understood, as he slowly shook his head, that I was barking up the wrong tree.

"No, Doc, it's not that—" Suddenly, his voice broke and he burst into tears. My heart is hardened, as it must be in my line of work, but his distress touched me all the more because I couldn't fathom its cause.

"Come, come! Are you a doctor? You're not the one who should decide if this is worth crying over. I'm here to help, but I can't do a thing if you won't tell me where and why it hurts."

"It's not me, Doc, it's him—"

"Him? Who?"

Bennett Riven kept right on sobbing as he placed his sack on my desk and undid the drawstrings. He reached in and pulled out the most horrifying thing I have ever seen. I leapt back so fast I knocked over my chair.

"Madman! Killer! Go! Get out of here now! Take that thing away!"

I groped about the desktop for the brass bell that would summon Edgar, my nurse-gardener-errand boy. My patient saw my hand, and his voice became pleading.

"Please, Doc, don't! I'm not a killer or a madman. I just came to get help! For him, Doc! For him! He's alive!"

And in a barely audible whisper, the thing he held aloft with fingers clenched around a lock of black and gleaming hair confirmed his words:

"It's true, Doctor. I'm alive... Have mercy, for the love of Christ, have mercy!"

At the time, I was a robust fifty years of age; should such a scene occur today it would surely kill me. As a student, then intern, I'd seen far worse than a severed head, but this wasn't the same. In such cases, context is everything. During my studies, anatomy was all parts and pieces. My friends and I examined and handled these in a university setting, under the supervision of our professors, and with their support. Besides, the body parts smelled of formalin, and that powerful, distinctive odor dehumanized them—"thingified" them, if I may...What my patient now thrust into my face was no anatomical part, but well and truly *a man's head*. I would have preferred a hundred times over for it to give off the wholesome odor of formaldehyde rather than a blend of rotting flesh and the cheap cologne it had been sprayed with. But above all—above all! The sliced-off head moved, wept, and spoke. Or rather, it shivered, sniveled, and whispered. The free play of its functions—facial mobility, lachrymal effusions, phonation—was considerably impaired. But the simple fact that these manifested themselves at all flew in the face of what the entire medical establishment took for granted. That said, I am a progressive and an optimist; if it's proven tomorrow that babies will henceforth be born from their mothers' ears, that's where I'll await them. The decapitated head spoke? So be it!

"Who is it?"

"His name's Henri Languille, Doctor."

"Yes—I'm Henri Languille!" whispered the head.

"Languille? Never heard of him! Where did you get it?" I asked the young man.

"You called me a killer—well, he's the killer!" he replied. "As for me, I'm apprenticed—well I was, till recently—to Mr. Deibler, the executioner. Mr. Deibler and me chopped Languille's head off on the twelfth in Orleans."

"The twelfth? It's the twenty-fourth! That's almost two weeks—well, go on. What happened?"

"Dr. Beaurieu in Orleans and my boss agreed to try something out. Even Languille was on board with it. Weren't you, Languille?"

"I admit I was, I was," Languille mumbled.

"So it was settled, then. Right after the execution, Mr. Deibler would ask the head, 'Can you hear me, Languille?' And if Languille could hear him, he'd blink."

The scientist in me bridled at this simple-minded protocol. "What were you trying to prove? A blink could quite easily be nothing but a reflex! And besides, guillotines cut off heads, not ears!"

"All right, but anyway he blinked . . . and he's still blinking now!"

I had to face facts: twelve days after his beheading, Languille was still blinking away.

"Fine! The experiment was a success, if you must. Then what?"

"After that, I did something dumb. The whole thing had gotten me all turned around. He could still hear, see, think . . . What was going on in that bodiless head? Do you realize—? Anyway, I was supposed to bury him on my own, Mr. Deibler was already on the train back to Paris, but at the last moment I wanted to try the experiment again, just to see."

Bennett Riven fell silent. At the end of his fist, the head was silent, too. A single mysterious emotion held the two consciousnesses in a single embrace—the hardened killer and the apprentice executioner, so different and yet so close in that instant beyond all guilt and innocence.

"Well?"

"He didn't just blink again, he spoke to me. He said it hurt, that he was scared. Of the dark, especially. The darkness of the grave. I should've put him right back in that coffin of raw wood, with his uncomplaining body, and nailed it all up tight and buried him and not given it another thought, but put yourself in my shoes . . . I couldn't. After all, Mr. Deibler and me aren't paid to kill them but once. I felt sorry for Languille, because of how he talked about the dark. I couldn't, and well . . . here we are."

Where had Languille come up with those tears, those heavy tears that trailed down his creased and greenish cheeks?

"How did you make it all the way here? What did you do for those twelve days?" I asked Bennett Riven.

"I hid him in this bag I usually use for lunch, and I took him home with me—I mean, to the room I was renting in Orleans. That night we talked a lot. I reassured him as best I could. He was thirsty, so I gave him some moonshine."

"You gave it a drink?"

"I had to put him in a bucket, of course. But it did him good, or so he said. Just the taste of it made his head spin, I mean. And I could keep using the same moonshine over and over..."

That first night, Bennett Riven had understood that he'd committed a great wrong in the eyes of Mr. Deibler, the administration, and perhaps authorities even higher still. Imagine that night and those that followed. A young soul of twenty interrogating himself on the consequences of an ill-considered act, the crushing responsibility he had undertaken while from the shadows on the table that terrified and terrifying presence, that nightmare curio, clicked its teeth from time to time in the quiet of the night.

The next day, the boy did not return to Paris, where his master Deibler was waiting. He panicked and ran away with his charge. Together, one carrying the other, they wandered the highways and byways at random, sleeping in small inns but also in fields, beneath bridges, on the beach. And always, the head complained—it ached; it was afraid of the night, of the day, of everything! It was fear incarnate, absolute, confined to the tiny chamber of a human skull. And it was beginning to reek. Bennett washed it in the sink when he dared take a room for the night, or in a brook, or the sea. But the saltwater stung... In the villages he passed through, he bought lotions and vials of perfume for it. Nothing did any good. The head was rotting alive. The decomposition manifested itself not only in sight and smell, but also in memory loss, hallucinatory episodes, delirium, and fits of dementia. Several times, the head tried to bite its benefactor. Bennett was afraid of it now. He wanted to have done with it, smash the head against a wall or a rock, free it once and for all—even it had been begging him to do so for several days now—but he dared not, and that was why they were here before me. They'd thought a doctor might know how to do it. It was forbidden, of course, but what exactly was forbidden? Practicing euthanasia on a lopped-off head? What article of the law forbade that?

Dear reader, friend and brother! I don't know what you would have done in my place. I know I couldn't let this child leave again with the contents of his tarred canvas sack swinging against his leg. I calmed him, and then sent him off alone toward an altered fate—for I doubt he ever took up his apprenticeship with Mr. Deibler again. After he left, I hid the head and its stinking sack in a cupboard and rang for Edgar. Pleading faintness, I bade him announce that I would see no more patients that day. Then, alone in my locked office, I consulted diverse treatises on pharmacology and toxicology while waiting for my angry and disappointed patients to leave. When at last all was quiet once more, I removed Languille from the cupboard. I spoke to him gently. I listened to him at length. And when I was sure of his resolve, I did what must be done.

Lozère, February 1992

The Styx

In hindsight, I should've suspected something. Strictly speaking, I didn't feel sick, but still, those persistent dizzy spells should've clued me in. I was losing my footing, like at the beach. You walk into the water, it's up to your chin, and suddenly the hard, rippled sand shifts beneath your feet, you feel yourself sinking, right away you close your mouth, pinch your nose, water slaps a cold cap over your head. A quick backward kick and you're up again, like a Cartesian diver ... You know what I mean. But I wasn't at the beach, and there was no water, only air and dry land and life. I was losing my footing in life, on the street, in the office, rising to leave a table in a restaurant, or at home, in my own living room—everywhere. It never lasted long: like the diver, I bobbed back up good as new. I was never unduly worried, as these episodes were so brief. No matter what happens, we feel at heart that it'll pass, we tell ourselves it's just a feeling without real cause or meaning. But in the end, with the hindsight I mentioned earlier—the decisive hindsight my new status grants me—I'm uniquely placed to appreciate that everything has cause and meaning. Now when I think back on yesterday's dizzy spells, I realize they were early warning signs, and that if I'd seen my doctor in time I might not have wound up where I am. Bah! If you have to be wary of the least sensation, the slightest tingling, the mildest twinge in any muscle or organ, you might as well give up and stop living. That was, in fact, what had happened: I'd stopped living. I don't know when it started. My doctor couldn't shed any light on that, either. The day I finally went to see him—for something else altogether, actually—he examined me and, with a certain gravity to his voice, said simply: "My friend, I've got some bad news for you. You're dead."

I didn't get really worked up over it right then. My doctor must've thought I hadn't heard him correctly, for he repeated himself: "You're dead, buddy. Deader than a doornail!"

This time when he spoke he looked at me from the corner of his eye, as though fearing an irrational reaction on my part—a "despair response," as they say.

"Do you . . . understand what I'm saying?"

I nodded. "I think so. I'm dead, right?"

He nodded back, and patted me on the shoulder. "You're taking it quite well. Go home. You'll have to tell your loved ones. I can't do anything more for you now. Please accept my sincere apologies."

His remorse seemed genuine. I felt obliged to say a few reassuring words. "Don't worry, Doc, it'll be fine. Thanks for everything!"

I paid for the visit and left. Back on the street, I tried to look at things and people in a new light. I wasn't quite managing to, at least not quite enough, and silently urged myself to feel more. After all, not just anything had happened to me: I was *dead*. And yet, try as I might with all my body and soul, everything in and around me remained the same, just as it'd always been. It seemed like life as usual. And I admit that, after the initial stages of curiosity, almost impatience even—no doubt childish but understandable—I felt deeply, immensely relieved. I'd finished that terrifying chore through which all things on earth come to an end. We make such a fuss about ourselves, I thought, but ultimately it comes to nothing, less than nothing even, a flower, a passing breeze . . . I congratulated myself on having gotten off so lightly, and for a trifle would've danced in the streets, if I'd known how to dance and dared to do so.

On the way home, I stopped at the funeral home to sort out the service. Mr. Charon wasn't in. His wife received me. I'd never paid much attention to that tall, brusque, chilly woman with a pike's eyes and teeth. I'd never pictured her also running the parlor. There was no mystery to it, really: Mrs. Charon sold headstones and rented hearses the way the grocer's wife sliced off the mortadella and provolone in her husband's stead. It is a trait of mom-and-pop businesses to perfect their union by hitching couplehood to a single yoke from the morning after the wedding till death do them part.

Mrs. Charon had been eyeing me more closely than I had her these last few years. She'd noticed me, observed me, and given thought to my situation and my style. At least that was the feeling I got from our meeting. I left having signed off on all her suggestions concerning my casket and its padding, the order and luxury of my cortege, the site and character of my final resting place. As a reward for my obedience, she smiled, showing her teeth. I couldn't help thinking of the man who spent his days and nights with that mouth, and in my head, doffed my hat to Mr. Charon.

We confirmed one last time the date and hour of the burial, and I went home. You'll permit me to depict only in broad strokes the distress of those dear to me when I announced the event. Naturally, it resulted in cries, moans, sobs, and also accusations, despite the apologies I'd offered to soften the news with: I hadn't done it on purpose, I was the victim here, etc. It was a hideous moment but couldn't have gone otherwise. I was soon sick of it and decided—not without a certain cowardice, or so I thought at first—to go to bed. Later I realized this was, in fact, what my family expected of me. They'd loved me as much as a husband and father could hope to be loved; their pain and suffering were real; if I wanted to make this easier for them, allow them to better manage their grief and roll with the blow they'd gotten, I had to make an effort, too: for starters, staying out of the way of my widow and orphans.

I made it to the master bedroom. I took off my shoes, loosened my belt and tie, drew the curtains, and lay down on the bed. Whispers, sniffling, stifled sobs occasionally reached me from the dining room. I let myself be lulled by them and soon fell fast asleep. A brief, but restful sleep: when I woke a few hours later, I felt fresher and more alert than ever. It was really inappropriate, I guess. I was brimming with vigor, champing at the bit while my grief-stricken family's only thought was going to bed. While I'd slept, my wife had made a make-shift bed in the dining room. For herself. There was no way she was going to spend the night by my side. Try as I might to point out that I wasn't tired anymore, that she'd get a better night's rest upstairs, and that if need be I'd take happily to the impromptu bed, she refused to hear a word of it. I stopped insisting when I saw her rolling her eyes the way she does whenever she finds my behavior unbecoming. I can assure you this doesn't happen as much as in the early days of our marriage. In the end, this woman who I've every reason to believe loved me tenderly will always have considered me a half-tamed savage, barely presentable, with a few last-minute manners slapped on. Nor is it inconceivable an impartial observer should agree with her. I can't deny I suggested putting a dead body in the dining room or playing a board game with our children that night. As I said, the poor kids were about to keel over, but they would've given in if their mother hadn't flatly refused, citing the late hour and the fact that they had to get up early for school the next day. I knew her well enough to keep from making the case that some things are worth skipping school for. She saw no reason for children who'd already be missing their father to miss a day of school on top of that. So I let them go to bed. Then, just as she was about to do the same, I wished her a guilty little "Well...Good night, anyway."

"Try not to make any noise when you come in," she said when she saw me slip on a jacket. "You know I can never get back to sleep once I wake up..."

The ceremony took place two days later. Mr. Charon was still nowhere to be seen. One wondered what he was up to. I have to say that Mrs. Charon filled the role perfectly. When it comes to conducting a funeral, courtesy is less important than authority. Mrs. Charon had authority in spades. Something implacable in her kept the cheekiest remarks in check. I can attest to the fact that no one laughed at my burial, and that everything went according to custom, in tasteful gloom.

I'd taken my place beside Mrs. Charon, who was driving the hearse in her absent husband's stead. The cemetery wasn't close by; you had to leave town and cross the river. The journey's length was not without its effects on those who chose unwisely to make it lying down in their caskets, Mrs. Charon explained. When they got there they were often sick to their stomach, about to throw up, and had to wait until they were feeling better to proceed in proper fashion. To avoid all that, Mrs. Charon employed a trick of the trade: the deceased traveled sitting up, like everyone else. In such conditions there was no reason for him not to arrive in good shape and ready to get down to business. So it was I got the best seat, shotgun in a spacious hearse, while my family and friends were squeezed each into their own cars.

Despite the qualities she'd shown that day, Mrs. Charon proved to be no more pleasant than usual. Having seated me beside her, she proceeded not to speak a word to me before the river crossing. To be fair, the coin my wife had put in my mouth would've kept me from keeping up a conversation with the desired elocutionary clarity.

The cortege slowed as it approached the bridge. Mrs. Charon stopped at the toll booth and turned to me. I took the coin from my mouth. I wanted to dry it with my handkerchief before giving it to her, since it was gleaming with spit. She grabbed it from my hand, grumbling something about "morons making a fuss," and tossed it in the basket. The barrier went up. The cortege started over the bridge. It was the middle of the afternoon, but you'd have thought it was dusk. Without my noticing, the sky had darkened while we were driving. Beneath a sky full of somber, heavy clouds hemmed in gold, the river's roiling waters seemed like molten lead. I'd often gone down to the bank as a boy, but I'd never noticed the river's breadth. Was it really a river? It seemed more like an arm of the sea. And this bridge I'd known all my life—only now did I realize what a titanic piece of work it was! Even going at a good clip, it was taking us forever to cross it.

But cross it we did. Once over, the cortege headed down a broad avenue interrupted, at regular intervals, by smaller streets leading to other parts of the cemetery. I'd expected to see a wall, to go through a bronze gate, monumental at that—why not, while we were at it? But no, nothing of the sort. From the looks of it, it seemed the entire bank was reserved for us, the dead, and for a fleeting moment I was worried about the kind of company I'd find here.

The living, it seemed, couldn't wait to get back across the river to their uncertain shore. In any case they dropped me off, I dare say, with a promptness I would've called offhanded if the sight of my loved ones' devastated faces hadn't inclined me to leniency. Back, back to your hopes and fears, poor things—you're not out of it yet! Take up once more the tunic of flames from which another's death delivers us ever so briefly. One by one, they kissed my forehead. I remembered giving my father the same kiss. I'd had the impression of brushing the stone front of a statue with my lips. I felt feverish. After these final kisses, Mrs. Charon signaled to me to get into the grave and lie down in the casket. I obeyed, not at all reassured. Luckily, it all went quite fast; everyone came in turn and cast a handful of earth down upon me. The living have no idea how irritating this is. When they were done—a bit too symbolic a gesture for my taste—I had dirt up my nose and down the collar of my shirt. Indifferent to my sneezing, the assembled were already turning to go, leaving me to my fate or, if you will, my lack of fate. A relative absence, since something was nonetheless happening: it was starting to rain. It wasn't a very deep grave. I pulled myself up the wall without difficulty and ran to catch up with the cortege. I didn't expect to be greeted with open arms, but if I'd cherished even the slightest hopes about it, I'd have been in for a shock. My wife, my children, and my dearest friends all ignored me. Some met me with stony faces. Faced with my impropriety, they pretended not to see me. But, I was sure they could, for in turning from me their gazes wavered a bit before fixing on the horizon, the way a motorcycle will slip when starting on a slick surface . . . Others' eyes widened on seeing me, as though at a mischievous child. Still others waved vaguely, embarrassed; some smiled surreptitiously, some shook their heads and sighed. Annoyance? Contempt? Pity? Did they themselves even know? Yet despite their contradictory attitudes, they drew together to keep me from joining their ranks and hurried toward the vehicles. I saw what they were doing and tried to counter by speeding up my own step. I reached the lot first and got into the hearse with a triumphant laugh. My move surprised the group, who hesitated before getting into their cars. Slightly off to one side, my wife and Mrs. Charon had a brief discussion. Its content escaped me, despite my attempts to read their lips. At last, with conniving grins, they split up. My wife rejoined our children in the most comfortable car. Mrs. Charon got in beside me in the hearse. She quickly threw me the fearsome glance of a pike on the hunt, then started the car. I cleared my throat and tried to cajole her.

"Don't worry," I said, "I'll make sure your fees and costs are covered in full—cash on the barrel."

She didn't answer. My first impression had been right, I thought: she wasn't someone you could bargain with.

She released the emergency brake and pulled out.

"It won't make a difference to you," I continued. "I mean, if I stay or go . . ."

She remained silent. I thought I'd touched on her two soft spots, one after the other: her pecuniary desire and her indifference to others. Boy, was I wrong! The pike has an integrity beyond reproach. Mindful of its mission, it doesn't pretend to hunt small fry through clouded waters and scummy ponds, it lies in wait and snaps them up in its jaws and tears them to pieces once and for all. Mrs. Charon waited until the hearse was rounding the curve leading to the bridge. There she gave a show of determination and sangfroid that left a vivid impression on me. Using the centrifugal force we both felt, with her left hand on the wheel to negotiate the bend, she suddenly flung open with her right the door I was leaning on with all my weight.

I got up just in time to glimpse my wife's face in the window of a passing car. She was biting her fist, eyes brimming with tears. Was she blaming herself for having gone along with Mrs. Charon's plan? I'm not much dumber than the next man, and I understood her reasons. I wouldn't have been any use in the struggles ahead of her: to survive, and raise the children. Quite the opposite, in fact: I would've complicated, perhaps even compromised everything. Already the other cars had passed me in a great squeal of tires. Already the cortege had reached the bridge and the toll barrier they'd never let me past.

I shrugged and, turning from the ramp to the bridge, went down limping lightly to the river. I saw then that I'd never wondered where it began, or where it was going.

Lozère, April 1993

The Beautiful Coalwoman

For an audience of two—himself and the wind—Maxence often hummed the only song he'd ever written.

> *For a knight errant am I, alas*
> *A lady, a squire, and a quest do I lack*
> *Too little knight and too errant, alas,*
> *No one to pray for my soul, alack.*

There were fourteen couplets in all, each as mournful as the last, which he did his best to sing in his most plaintive voice. Long ago—in truth, as long as his youth had held out and he'd passed for a handsome lad—the lament had won him the sympathy of little girls and older women wherever he'd stopped for the night. He sighed. Now women heard his song and poured him a swig of wine before sending him off to sleep alone in an attic or a shed, and little girls no longer listened at all.

Once, Maxence had knelt with six other young men, none yet of age. The war in its impatience harried apprentices, rushing them through training, and the Prince, as he tapped their shoulders with his sword, believed iron would separate the wheat from the chaff. Of these hastily made knights, two would perish in their first battle. They alone, thought Maxence, could have boasted on reaching heaven of never betraying their vows. He tried to remember their faces, but the great wheel of the seasons had rolled thirty times over his memory and the ground where they lay. He suddenly regretted not lying down beside them. He envied those unbearded knights who'd smiled at the augur of death in spring. His own hair had grown, then grayed; he'd known fear and was far from blameless—he'd misused widows and raised a hand to their children.

He must have tensed his thighs against his horse. The animal had strained to speed. *There, there! Easy now! What is it? Do you smell fresh water? Then go ahead, I'm thirsty, too!* Maxence loosened his hold on the reins. A hundred yards away, tall and straight on either side of the path, two oaks mingled branches at the edge of a clearing. As he entered the yellowing vault, he spotted a thatched cottage beside a pigsty at the clearing's far end, and reflected that not the haughtiest lord could have wished a more dizzying arch for his estate than the one these two giants formed in the very center of the sky. Not far from the pigpen, a spring trickled from a pile of mossy rocks, and two small children were frolicking naked in the nearby grass. Children of the poor, their clothes hanging out to dry in the sun. They raised their heads at the sound of hoofs and gave out great shouts of joy when they saw the knight. An older boy that Maxence hadn't seen at first stepped between the children and the stranger.

"Fear not, boy, I only want some water for my horse and myself."

From beneath disheveled hair, two suspicious eyes watched his every move. The backwoods boy's scrawny legs trembled a bit, but he seemed ready to seize his brothers, one under each arm, and dash off into the underbrush. Maxence softened his voice as best he could.

"Don't worry, I won't eat you! My name is Maxence. I am a knight. What's your name?"

The boy didn't say a word. His brothers, excited a moment earlier, and wanting a closer look at the man in metal, were now growing alarmed by their elder's silence. Time passed, fear and discomfort overcoming the little ones in turn, and Maxence steeled himself for the moment when the three would all burst into tears. He was about to set foot on the ground, even if it meant terrifying the little brats, and reestablish his authority, when an old man appeared in the cottage door.

"Well, didn't you hear his lordship, you little ninnies? He's thirsty. You, boy, fetch an ewer, and the rest of you run off and play in the sun."

Maxence dismounted. The old man had reached him but kept a few steps away, beret in hand. Maxence guessed that his servile demeanor hid a burning curiosity and, despite his own weariness, tried to make a good impression. But he saw, from an easing of the man's fawning manner, that he'd been sized up for what he truly was: a knight, yes, but a lowly lord, quite old and poor, from whom there was little to fear and even less to hope. Despite it all, Maxence made sure the long sword hanging at his side struck his greave with a ringing sound.

"Sire, if it pleases you to take your rest here, this house is yours."

"Thank you, old man. Heaven will be grateful for your hospitality toward its humble servant, for I am a Christian knight."

The old man crossed himself at once. In school, Maxence had been taught how to pay his way in the coin of word. The oldest of the children reappeared, ewer in hand.

"My thanks, boy. Tell me, would you know how to look after my steed?"

The boy gazed at his grandfather without answering.

"Of course he does, sire!" said the old man. "Off you go—you know where fodder can be found, and make sure you give the horse a good rubdown!"

The boy walked toward the horse. Maxence told him he could ride it instead of leading it to fodder. The boy smiled at last. Maxence plunged the ewer into the spring's fresh water.

"It's good water, it is, sire," the old man said. "It's kept me in good health for seventy years, it has!"

"Upon my word, seventy years! It must be good indeed—you seem quite sprightly still!"

On hearing these words, the old man couldn't keep from contorting his face in a grin. Maxence saw he would have food and shelter tonight for a trifle.

"My daughter and my son-in-law will soon return from gathering mushrooms," the old man continued. "We've had rain of late, and we'll have wild mushrooms tonight. Water, bread, and a mushroom omelet are all we can offer you, milord."

"I'd gladly make it my daily fare, if it would guarantee I'd stand up just as straight at your age!"

The old man straightened proudly, his face wracked by another smile.

So sore were his loins and limbs from riding that Maxence would have liked to turn in right after supper, but he would have offended his hosts had he begged his leave of them so hurriedly. Thus he spoke graciously of the lands he had seen, his adventures among the Turks, the Germans, and the Calabrese, as well as of a few customs peculiar to these people, and likely to astonish poor folk who'd never been more than a league from their clearing. Then, once the children were in bed and their mother busying herself clearing up, the grandfather removed a flagon of spirits from the dough trough. His son-in-law pointed and said, "If it's the springs of youth you're after, those are the waters that keep him a strapping lad at his age!"

Maxence was drifting off, but the sight of the bottle restored his forces a bit, for he loved to drink, and the omelet they'd shared would have seemed more delicious with a pitcher of wine. The old man filled the goblets and set the flagon down in reach. The liquor was rough but did the job as well as any other. Maxence settled himself against the wall before picking up the trail of his thoughts once more. He was among men now, and knew what his hosts wanted to hear. He answered their desires, telling tales of Moorish serving girls and Italian bordellos, which he readily embellished with far-fetched or flattering episodes. Eyes wide, the forest-dwellers hung on his every word. They pressed on late into the night, he speaking, the others listening, and everyone drinking so much that the old man had long since fallen asleep on his bench when Maxence was at last done with his flowery fables.

"Well, my good men, that's how women are in those lands!"

Across from him, the son-in-law was nodding off, his nose sometimes dipping into his half-empty goblet. "What a life you've had! What women you've seen! We don't have any like that around here . . . Well, there is one, one beautiful woman in these parts, but she's . . ."

Maxence, who wanted only to crawl off to sleep, straightened in his drunken stupor and, as best he could, assumed the air of a great lover hearing tell of a legendary lonely lady. The man hesitated, as though fearing he'd said too much. Maxence pressed him. "Come now, a pretty damsel? You must tell me all about her!"

"A . . . damsel? Oh, I don't know . . . She is a beautiful woman, but . . ."

"But?"

"But . . . how should I put it? We think her a bit of a witch, milord, and she frightens us."

Maxence shrugged. "I've yet to meet a woman who frightens me! Come now, tell me everything! After all, you must, if she's a witch. Do you understand?"

The threat lurking behind his last words overcame the woodsman's scruples.

"Milord, she lives not far from us, on the island in the river. She lives alone. My father-in-law, who has indeed seen seventy winters, claims she's been there all his life. She was already living there, alone on the island, making charcoal, when he was a little boy."

"What are you saying?"

"The truth, milord, as the old man has spoken it a hundred times."

"Then she must be a hundred if a day!"

"A hundred she may well be, but her hair is dark as the crow's wing, and the snow no whiter than her teeth or skin. Milord, it's girls of sixteen who seem crones beside her! I remember, for I saw her once, up close. My father-in-law had told me so much about her that I wanted to see her for myself; I went to the island. And suddenly there she was, standing before me, stepped out from behind a thicket."

"What did you do?"

"I gazed on her a long time. I was a young man, just married, my wife expecting our first child. And yet I swear to you, at her slightest sign I would've left it all behind, wife and child; never would I have come back across the river. But she remained unmoving, unspeaking, in the middle of the path, and I fled. So far as I know, God never wrought a thing so beautiful—the Evil One must have had a hand in it . . . Once home, I pulled my wife to me and held her close. Since that day, I have avoided the banks."

The man fell silent. His eyes, which had shone as he spoke, were once more dull with drink. Maxence wanted to pour him another, but he shook his head.

"Thank you, milord. I've had enough. I should not have spoken of such things. They always make me sad."

"Let's go to bed. It was a beautiful tale, my friend. But do you really believe that woman's a hundred? Your father-in-law is old. Sometimes, toward the end of such a long life, everything runs together in one's head. Was it not the mother, or even the grandmother of the girl you met, that he'd known as a child?"

"I don't know, milord. Were she but sixteen summers, she'd still be too beautiful. So much beauty is a terrible thing: a man's soul cannot conceive of it without being troubled forevermore. Please, I beg of you—forget what I've said. No doubt you're right, no doubt she's but sixteen, or twenty, and shines too brightly for we who share these woods . . . She must be a good Christian . . . I wish her no harm."

"We'll see."

Looking up, Maxence was surprised to find on the face of host an expression of such fear and remorse that he hadn't the heart to worry him any longer.

"Rest easy. I'm a knight, not a prelate. Let us to bed."

The two men rose clumsily. Maxence lay down beside the fire and rolled himself up in a blanket from the couple's bed while, with an uncertain step, the man joined his sleeping wife.

Heads were heavy the next day at dawn. When it was time to say good-bye, Maxence gave the old man a medal he'd claimed to have brought back from the Holy Land, then took the path toward the river.

In the morning mist, man and mount, both half-asleep, trailed the night's dreams. Maxence liked this torpor, the world's melancholy in the early hours of the day. Among his memories of military life, he loved more than the thrills of victory and pillage the uncertain dawns, the hushed sunups when, first to rise, he'd walked at length among his dozing comrades. It was a good hour for lending a hand, when the sentinels themselves were often nodding off. Yet he had felt invulnerable then. He retreated into those slow minutes as though into the heart of an impregnable citadel. Then a bugle would sound at the other end of camp, the sleepers would stir, and Maxence begin once more to fear death.

Before he glimpsed the river, its cold breath bathed his face. He advanced to the edge of the bank with care, so difficult was it to tell, in the gray, mist from water. The island rose up halfway between the banks. Maxence contemplated it at length. His indecisive nature often led to such moments, hours even, of being torn between two paths, neither of which particularly drew him. Why ride beside the river? Why try to reach the isle? Why, in the past, had he followed one man in war and not another? Most of the time, the first banner to go by had been the one he went with, and the same for women. Last night's desire had flown with morning. What was he going to do with a wild-woman he wasn't even sure of winning? And yet he could not bring himself simply to go on his way. He thought he saw a figure on the island, and his horse went into the water.

The young woman raised her head and saw Maxence. His whole body was shaking. Though he'd forded many a river on horseback before, the cold had never affected him so. He wasn't sure the cold alone was to blame for his state; as soon as he'd seen the coalwoman, he'd understood his host's troubled words. He too had been afraid, and ready to turn heel and run from the girl. In the purity of features, that high forehead lightly smudged with soot, Maxence saw the face of all his longings. Everything he'd dreamed of as a youth, and even earlier, in those final days of childhood when desire knows nothing of the flesh and yet calls out to it, were suddenly incarnate before him. The tenderness of those vanished days, toward everyone, no one and the heavens above, awoke in him that morning, his life almost wholly consumed, his graying, wasting life broken by wars and embraces, and tears clouded his eyes. He was about to flee when she spoke.

"The river has chilled you to the bone, knight. You mustn't stay here. Come and dry off in my hut. I'll make a fire. Come, you're shivering, you'll take ill!"

"Y-yes . . . you're right. The river is cold as death."

He shook from head to toe, and his teeth chattered. She took his mount by the reins. He let himself be led. The hut was more wretched than the woodsman's cottage, but he barely noticed. Regiments ran this way and that across his body as though across a battlefield, some mounted on horses of flame and others on horses of ice. He let himself be undressed and put to bed by the young woman like a child by his mother. When she drew away to light the fire and reheat a bit of broth, he remained on his back, staring at the ceiling, a thin coverlet drawn up to his chin. Despite the fever, a feeling of peace flooded through him. He was likely to die, and the thought no longer worried him. His final resting place would be a meager hut of twigs and branches, and the last thing he saw a face like those he'd never dwelled on in the alcoves of churches; so it was, and it was good. When she returned, he drank a bit of broth, then all was dark.

He had no memory of the days and nights that passed. Then the fires the fever had stoked in his body went out one by one, and the black smoke they'd thrown off stopped clouding his mind. The morning came when he could step outside and walk all the way to a nearby pond. He leaned over the water and looked at his reflection between the ribbons of scum on the surface. Though thinner than ever, his hair and beard whiter than expected, it was still him, and he laughed to find himself alive. He heard a gentle voice call out to him, and rose, blushing.

"Sir knight! Sir knight! You're on your feet again!"

Today it was her cheek that was smudged with soot. He remembered their first encounter, and couldn't keep himself from laughing again. Beautiful, yes—but a coalwoman. Still—beautiful! He didn't know what to say to her and cleared his throat.

"You looked after me . . ."

"Yes, sir knight. A long time."

He misread her. "I'm sorry. My purse is empty."

She stopped smiling, and made as if to leave.

"Don't go! What have I said to offend you?"

"Do you think I'm interested in your money? Had you died, I could have taken it freely."

"Forgive me. I am old and poor, and sooner or later, the subject always comes up."

"You tire me."

She moved away. He returned to the hut, upset with himself. When night began to fall, he waited, but she did not come. He fell asleep late that night. That was how she was, the ruler of her little island, and that day he had displeased her. She did not come till the next day, after noon, bringing fish, four gleaming fish spotted green and blue, one of which still jerked among the blackberries she'd gathered along the way and tossed pell-mell into the wicker basket with her catch. They ate without speaking a word. When they'd finished, they went inside. There they shed their clothes and coupled. Then they fell asleep. Night was falling when they woke. They drank some broth and fought over the remaining blackberries before returning to their lover's sport, inventing new games to play.

They were the only two souls on the island. From time to time, said the coalwoman, boatmen stopped to buy some charcoal from her. The yard behind the hut was almost bare: they would not come again for a long while. The days went by. Slowly, Maxence recovered his forces. He no longer wore his coat of mail, but a simple serge tunic the young woman had sewn him. He helped make charcoal, and at night they lay down beside each other like husband and wife. Sometimes he was astonished that so young and beautiful a girl had given herself to him like this, and the woodsman's words came back to him. He had indeed found a strange companion. She spoke little, and some days behaved as if he didn't exist, coming and going or dreaming in the sun before their hut without giving him so much as a word or a glance. Sometimes she suddenly disappeared, and Maxence spent hours, days even, searching for her on the island. It wasn't very big, but the young woman only reappeared when she chose to.

She pretended not to know her age. Maxence teased her, saying that her childhood days could hardly be so long past, that she should remember them, and made as if to look for dolls beneath the bed. She replied in a serious voice that frightened him.

"Oh, but they are, they are! Long, long past! I no longer even remember ever playing with dolls!"

He asked her about her parents, and got no answer; if he insisted, she fled. He would only see her one or two days later, and then thought only of being forgiven for his tiresome questions. Unlike most young women he'd known, she cared not a whit in love for sweet words or vows. She gave and took without flowery phrases, then fell asleep with a smile on her lips. They never once had those lovers' conversations, which are really confessions, and Maxence, whom these had always bored, missed them for the first time, for his curiosity gnawed at him. One time, as he laughingly threatened to leave her, he caught her giving in to the silly nothings said in bed.

"If you leave this place," she said, "no path will lead you anywhere. The world around this isle is empty."

He pretended to play her game. "But then, my beautiful sorceress, what of your buyers, the boatmen? Doesn't the river lead them to the sea after they've stopped at your hut?"

"Yes, because I wish it. You can leave; you are free to do so. Cut down branches and make a raft if you wish. But be warned: the river runs only between dead banks to an ocean of silence."

Maxence tried to lighten the mood. "My dearest, love makes a world without the one we love a wasteland!"

"It is not love, but I," she said gravely, "who will make the world a wasteland for you."

She slipped away, as always when the conversation displeased her. Alone, Maxence went to check on the ovens. He looked up for a moment at the opposite shore and reflected that he'd never seen smoke rising where the woodsman's cottage should have been. No doubt he had misreckoned the length of his ride to the river the morning he'd left, and the next moment, gave it no more thought.

A short while later, winter came. All night, the wind howled round the hut like a hungry dog and in the morning, when the lovers stepped out, snapped at their hands and faces. The river would soon freeze. Already gray lace advanced from either side, just above the water, soon to meet and harden in the middle till the river could reliably be crossed on foot. Then it snowed for three days. The river vanished; frost after frost immobilized the landscape for several long months. Maxence complained of the cold and spoke to the coalwoman of distant climes he'd witnessed in his travels, depicting the golden lives they'd lead if she but agreed to follow him to those lands where the sun shone all year long. She listened to him, but never replied. He himself was uncertain if he wished to bring her along. He often coughed and felt suffocated at night. After his illness and convalescence, he had seemed, briefly, to recover his youth, but since winter's sudden start had felt himself growing older by the day. While his companion braved winter with a smile, his own temperament grew bitter. Eventually he no longer stepped outside, and spent his days by the fire, nursing memories of the Orient. One night at last, he realized he was an old man. He said so to the young woman, who pulled him close. No doubt he had a fever already, for she fell asleep first while he shivered at length in her arms before joining her. When dawn came he rose without waking her. Though he had not used his armor since arriving on the island, he had always taken care—an old campaigner's habit—to keep its pieces in good shape. He donned his armor, harnessed his horse, then mounted her and crossed the river. He went slowly, often getting off to help the creature, who sometimes sank to her chest in the snow. Beneath his helm he wept with cold. His tears froze to his face as soon as they welled from his eyes. He soon realized he wouldn't make it far this way, but the hope of warming himself by the woodsman's fire restored his courage. He squinted at the icy air before him, expecting at any moment to see smoke from their hearth rising through the trees. He saw nothing of the sort, but suddenly, lifting his gaze once more toward the skies, recognized the two giant oaks: no tree in all the woods could have rivaled them in height. He took another look around him: he was standing in the clearing. The frozen spring, which he found easily, was proof. But there was no cottage. He dismounted and got on his knees, sifting through the snow for some trace. Though he dug through the snow with his own hands, nothing remained of the cottage. He stood up again. Considering the clearing, he tried with his mind to efface the snow and recreate the shapes and colors of the autumn forest he still remembered. He was unable to decide, in his confusion, if the attempt was conclusive. His head spun; he tried to get back in the saddle but an even more violent dizziness seized him and he had to give up. The snow had started to fall again, slowly at first, then in large flakes that the wind hurled into his face. He tried to catch his breath long enough to make the shelter of the trees, but his mount didn't give him time: she took fright in the white whirlwind and jerked hard on the bridle. His numb fingers failed to hold her back. She broke free, bucked once and knocked him back in the snow. He tried to get up again, but rose no higher than his knees. He saw his horse one last time, mad with fear, dashing out of reach. Crossing his arms over his dented chest, he let himself fall back. The first flake settled on his right pupil, which didn't flinch, then another fell, and then a hundred more as the snow filled his eyes and his wide-open mouth.

Paris, Apr.-May 1974

A City of Museums

You wouldn't dream of staying here without having booked a hotel room far in advance, for once in town, trying to find lodgings with the locals is hopeless. When the locals aren't innkeepers, they're curators or docents. Housing for the archival students was put up outside town. The lower classes—cleaning women, waiters, municipal clerks—come from neighboring hamlets. At day's end, they all go home in cars or buses. If by chance the last shuttle should leave someone behind, it's quite a sight to see the beeline that last straggler makes for the overnight shelter by the police station. Not that any danger awaits: no city is safer. But fear overtakes the townspeople when night falls. If they only knew what mellowness follows when the putt of the final motor fades away!

How many times have I seen it? It's as if the evening breeze awaits that moment to sweep the streets clean of all the putrid fumes. How many times have I spied that first imperceptible breath, the Spirit stirring in a rustle of wings? I don't know. I'm not twenty yet, but I've prowled these streets forever, it seems. When the wind is on the rise, I step out from the shadows of the carriage entrance where I hide myself away, and take possession of the streets. I head for the old quarter, for the city's sacred heart. The Ancients dwelt there: adventurous bards, pallid monks, mischievous schoolboys or court poets in ruffles, tricorne-sporting hypochondriacs, wild-eyed *petits-bourgeois* . . . I stand before them in my faux leather bomber jacket and worn jeans, and laugh along like a conspirator, I who have yet to write a line. And I walk, heartened, caressed, the breeze gently nudging the back of my shoulders.

There are some fifteen of us, pariahs who hang on within these walls. Dressed in rags, always starving, hounded by the city watchmen, we hole up by day and go out only at night to root through hotel Dumpsters. One fine morning, each of us left hometown, job, or family to come live here like a rat. That's what we're called, too: rats.

I'd long been the youngest of the pack. I was sixteen when I slipped through a barred window into the basement of a museum, a few minutes before everyone headed home. I'd arrived that very morning with a high-school group. From my hole, I watched without regret as the bus drove off and disappeared, carrying my classmates toward their ordinary fates.

Last year, two teenagers joined us one after the other. A high schooler, who like me had let his bus leave without him, and a farmer's son from nearby. Most of us think the high schooler won't last long. He moves slow and makes too much noise. Plus he picks his hiding places poorly. Sooner or later the guards'll collar him. They'll give him a beating and then send him home. Gus, the farmer's boy, is made of sterner stuff. The guards, who learn all our faces from trying and failing to run us out of town, still don't know he exists. Also, Gus already writes memorable poems. The oldest among us, Guv'nor Paul, sometimes honors me with his confidences. He's almost convinced Gus has *what it takes*, and will someday pull off the feat we all dream of.

"One day," he told me, "one day Gus's hideout will be its own museum."

Gus's hideout must be a disused wardrobe, or a trunk abandoned somewhere in a museum attic—the Robinson Museum, or maybe the

Ballantrae, since he hung around there a lot. I swear I bit my lips in disappointment. Guv'nor Paul didn't seem to think my favorite hideaway might also become a museum.

Tuesdays the museums are closed. On Tuesdays alone we emerge in plain day and mingle with the bored tourists. We chat them up for cigarettes and candy. The tourists don't like it when the guards chase us right before their eyes, so the mayor's issued orders, and the guards are nowhere to be seen. But toward day's end, no sooner has the last tourist returned to his hotel, than our enemies, unleashed, hit the streets running. Most of the collars go down Tuesday night. The wariest of us make ourselves scarce long before nightfall. Where do we hide? Everyone's got their secret spot. I know, from having stumbled across Guv'nor Paul's this summer, that he's not too proud to take cover in the bathrooms of the bishop's palace, which was turned into a museum last century, after a subdeacon composed some very pretty Christian meditations there. As for me, every other Tuesday, after making sure I'm not being followed, I make for the former opera hall. I slip in through a manhole that also serves to air out the opera's underground vaults. After navigating a maze of hallways and picking a few locked doors, I reach the prop room. There via a trapdoor built into the shoulder blades of the Commander's statue, I curl myself up in his plaster loins. Every other Tuesday, that is—otherwise I sleep in a cannon up on the ramparts.

A very strange thing happened to me a few days ago. The night before, I'd swiped a bottle of wine, maybe two, from a case a delivery man left by a hotel door. By the end of the night, I'd fallen asleep in Scriblerus House—today the Scriblerus Museum—on the bed where the author of *Sylvie's Baubles* had once lain in state.

The day was well underway when a little old man in a wing collar shook me from my slumber. "Young man! Wake up!"

"Huh? What?"

"Wake up, I say! You've been quite careless!"

I leapt to my feet, despite my state. No doubt I had the museum curator before me. Expecting to see a squad of guards come hustle me out, I eyed the door to the duke's chambers uneasily.

"Don't worry," said the old man. "I haven't summoned them."

He saw the look of surprise on my face. "You see, it isn't every day that a curator has the chance to speak with a . . ."

"A rat?"

The curator nodded. "But you don't seem quite up to satisfying my curiosity yet. Come with me. I'll give you some of my coffee. You'll see, it's excellent; my wife makes a thermos for me every morning."

"So, you're—"

"A rat."

"Delighted! Please, relax! You're safe here in my office. No one will disturb us; the Scriblerus is one of the city's most rarely visited museums. Have no fear of my watchman: he's utterly devoted to me. Would you like some more coffee?"

I took a second cup of the delicious brew.

"And now, tell me . . . What's it like? Have you lived like this for long? Do you have friends? What are they like? Surely you write! Have you anything on you to show me?"

He kept me until the middle of the afternoon, and insisted that I take half his meal home with me: a chicken drumstick and an orange, which he placed in a plastic bag.

"At my age, one hardly eats anything anymore. You'll come back and see me often, won't you? You can't imagine how long I've awaited such a meeting. You...rats, you're life itself, you're hope! The rest of us,"—he waved wearily to include his sumptuous office, that of the Duke of Scriblerus—"the rest of us manage but dust and death. Go on, young man, be careful, and above all, come back. I still have many things to ask you, and some to teach you as well."

I didn't dare confess to Mr. Kingsheart—for that was my new friend's name—that I'd never yet written a thing. We saw each other often; he plied me with beef casserole and rice pudding. Mrs. Kingsheart cooked every dish to perfection. Even reheated any old way in a mess kit over a camp stove, her casserole was a marvel. I hesitated to introduce my benefactor to Gus. I'd have to split the chow. Maybe Gus would even take my place in the curator's heart? That'd be plain dumb of me. No, clearly things were better as they were: genius for Gus and beef casserole for me.

From fear that Mr. Kingsheart might tire too quickly of my company, I took care to dole out the secrets of our band sparingly. Everything interested him: our conversations, our little schemes, our *Weltanschauung*. Sometimes, too, speaking in veiled terms as if he feared to say too much, he broached quite an alarming topic. According to him—if I understood correctly—the township kept us at bay, yet also, in a way, at their beck and call. The mayor had but to give his guards free rein, and they would seize us all in one fell swoop. The trap was set, but the mayor deliberately held off on springing it. *They had plans for us.* They were grooming us as part of some devious design. God, how plain and simple everything had seemed only yesterday! We were Heroes of the Human Spirit persecuted by obtuse Authority. Now I wondered if we weren't merely some kind of livestock, secretly handpicked by some infinitely patient owner...

><

Georges-Olivier Châteaureynaud

I resolved to take Gus to the Scriblerus. He had two short poems on him, jotted in his big, loopy handwriting on endpages torn from valuable volumes of the Ballantrae Museum's library. Mr. Kingsheart read them and reread them with a greediness not unlike that with which I'd initially fallen on the meals his wife made. Tears rolled down his wrinkled cheeks. He pressed Gus to his heart. "My boy! My boy!" he gibbered. Dumbfounded, Gustin let himself be swept clumsily into an embrace. I found both of them fairly ridiculous. From that moment on, I knew I no longer mattered. Gus was the only important one. Of course, Mr. Curator knew how to treat his guests! He began bringing double servings of food, but Mrs. Kingsheart's rice pudding now stuck in my throat. No matter. I put it off for a bit, but eventually wound up following the dictates of my conscience. I didn't think there was anything left for me at the Scriblerus Museum.

It's Wednesday. Last night, Gus was killed. He slipped from the roof of the Robinson Museum, where he'd been hiding from the guards. I went up there with Guv'nor Paul and a few others this morning. I don't know really what we were thinking...a kind of pilgrimage, perhaps.

From above, we witnessed a scene I alone understood. Before a chalk outline traced on the ground the mayor stood stuffed into a camelhair coat. He seemed lost in a bleak reverie. Guards kept the tourists back. Mr. Kingsheart showed up. He walked right up to the mayor and, with all his strength, slapped him. Then he threw a sheaf of papers into his face.

Beside me, Guv'nor Paul's eyes widened. "What's all that about, then?"

"Tell you later."

He stared at me, then, taking closer notice than he had in a long

144

time. "Indeed you will. Come to think of it: time you started writing, isn't it?"

"Yes—it's time."

Below, Mr. Kingsheart had turned on his heel. Leaving the mayor on his knees, busy gathering up the papers the wind threatened to scatter, he strode furiously toward his car.

Bures, February 1983

The Guardicci Masterpiece

I was walking down a quiet street around nightfall. It was fine weather. Even on the ground floor, locals had opened their windows to the warm night. Some had lit their lamps, but others preferred to let night flood the rooms where they sat as the tide floods a grotto. From these submerged chambers drifted snatches of conversation by turns ordinary, amusing, and mysterious. But what struck me at first was the sound of the voices: hushed or muffled, muted, inexplicably distant and musical.

I stopped before a taxidermist's storefront. The pieces on display were bathed in a warm glow confined to the middle of the window by a large parchment shade: a fox and a young boar, a few small weasels (marten, ferret, civet), but also various birds (kestrel, swift, woodpecker, tawny owl). I thought I glimpsed, in the shapes I made out farther back from the light, other creatures, tightly wrapped in bandages, that had been mummified instead of stuffed. My face pressed to the glass, I scanned the depths of the store. There was a jackal, a hyena, then cats, a tall wading bird (stork or heron), and apes—one of which, for all I could see, could well have been a human being.

A brass wind chime gave out a tinkle. The door opened, and the proprietor appeared, an old man in loose brown overalls and a square black hat that lent him a judgelike air.

"Please, come inside! You can't see anything from out here. There's nothing to be afraid of. My creatures are all far less dangerous than any you could meet outside. They're beautiful and well-behaved and pretty as pictures."

I obeyed, mesmerized. He stepped aside to let me pass. "Look! Modern-day mummies! *New* mummies! You won't find these anywhere else. I'm the exclusive distributor."

"But," I ventured, "what about . . . I mean, that—"

I pointed at the human mummy, for indeed a young woman was on display between an ocelot and a baboon. Her mask lay on a table nearby.

"What about it? Oh, yes, quite. Rest assured, it's all perfectly legal, all the papers are in order. Really—no joke!"

She gazed at me, the lamp from the window flickering in her glass eyes.

"Is she for sale?" I asked.

"Everything you see is for sale, sir. Of course, she's my finest specimen, and her price, well . . . Take a closer look, and tell me if you've ever seen anything like it."

I turned back to the mummy.

"If I may, sir, her eyes! Look into her eyes."

The mummy's glass stare had such depth and humanity I found myself more flustered than if I'd been faced with a living person.

"Aha!" exclaimed the owner. He put his hand on my forearm then, a hand white as a stripped root. "You felt it too, then! Her stare is an enigma . . . or rather, a work of art! Have you ever heard of the glass-maker Leonello Guardicci?"

I said I hadn't.

"He created these wonders," the taxidermist continued, pointing at the mummy's right eye. It was so convincing I expected to see it flinch when the shopkeeper grazed it with his fingernail. Despite myself, I turned away.

"Don't do that. It makes me uncomfortable."

"You're too sensitive. It's only glass. A colored marble carefully inset—by a great artist, I'll give you that!"

"It's not just the color," I protested. "It's . . ."

I fell silent. The shopkeeper nodded, as though I'd finished my thought.

"It's a very beautiful thing indeed. A very beautiful thing! A charming subject, consummate craftsmanship. Such skill is costly. The mummy, too, of course—and then those eyes. I dare say, Leonello Guardicci's masterpiece!"

I gave the old man all the money I had on me as a deposit. Ever the professional, he made out a receipt and wrote my name on a tag he tucked into a bandage, right over the mummy's heart: she had been reserved.

I'll admit I was upset the next morning when I remembered my twilight stroll and what had happened. A mummy probably isn't the most essential thing you can buy these days. My apartment was cramped: three tiny rooms already crammed with books and musical instruments. After some thought, I decided to give up what now seemed an extravagance.

I could simply have never contacted the taxidermist again, but instead a trivial concern guided my steps back to his shop: I was willing to pay a penalty, but I didn't like the thought of losing my entire deposit.

I was expecting a niggling exchange. To my deep relief, the shopkeeper made no objection. So I'd changed my mind? It happened. And I wanted to recover part of my deposit? He retained such a tiny amount that I almost felt offended for his sake. It must've shown, for he smiled assuagingly.

"A piece like that isn't an easy sell, but I'm not worried," he said. "She'll be someone's, someday. Just not yours."

In such delicate transactions, a customer's most intimate sensibilities come into play and reveal themselves. Just what was this crude profiteer trying to say? That I was too crass a soul? What did he know? I thought myself worthy of owning such a singular object, at once macabre and sophisticated, almost immaterial. I wasn't merely making a bid on the semblance of a few fleshly remains, but on the glints and echoes of a life cut short. This mouth had laughed and sung, these lips whispered sweet nothings in a darkened bedroom, these hands drawn hopscotch courts, cradled dolls, set balls in flight... I was buying all that and more. I'd changed my mind again, this time once and for all. As the owner of that magical gaze for which the whole mummy was a reliquary, I'd be able to draw on its treasury of impressions and emotions whenever I wished from now on.

I wrote a check for the remainder. The shopkeeper made me out a receipt in due form, accompanied by a certificate of authenticity.

"Hold on to this, for insurance purposes, in the event—fire, theft, nothing's safe. These days, everything disappears or goes up in smoke. Make sure you're insured," he sighed. "I assume you haven't yet decided where you'll display it?

"Not too cold, and not too hot. Watch out for dust and dampness. Leave her mask on as much as possible; it protects her," he said before calling a cab.

When I got home half an hour later, I congratulated myself on the lightness of my precious burden. The elevator was quite old and didn't go very fast. I had time to look myself over in the mirror on the back wall. What was the proper demeanor to assume in an elevator with the mummy of a young woman in one's arms? I reached the eighth floor without finding an answer to this no doubt frivolous question.

>€

My feelings for the mummy whose "proud owner" I'd become followed a predictable course. First, passion: I sometimes stopped in the middle of my work to gaze on her fondly. As a translator, I was lucky enough to work from home. I'd set her across from my desk. My apartment was mostly filled with books and a collection of musical instruments I've since then scattered. I am not a musician. The cases fascinated me more than the instruments themselves. For me, the cases of musical instruments were great brown or blackish shells that harbor strange creatures in their fluffy, satiny, or felt-lined insides. Walking-stick-thin or beetle-round, wooden or metal, matte or glossy, inlaid mandolin, stiff flute, or austere violin, most musical instruments looked like insects, and like them had carapaces bristling with antennae, mandibles, rostra.

I collected instruments in their cases because for me their charm resided mainly in the perfect complementarity of container and content, and the contrast of materials and colors. Contemplating the nickeled keys of a clarinet, set in ebony sections nestled in their padded blue sateen dwellings, or the gleaming body of a concert guitar in plush garnet, inspired feelings of luxury if not lust in me.

How long do we remain aware of the presence of someone or something beside us? Perhaps it's scandalous, in a way, to equate the two ... but what of it? At the time I was greatly inclined to prefer objects, which reassured me, to people, who often frightened me. I was what one called a confirmed bachelor, hardened in his lonely ways. Hardened: well on the way to drying out and becoming a fossil, an object. That was my life when the mummy, and then Delia, came and turned it upside down. But I'm getting ahead of myself. I should tell this story calmly, carefully. It matters little that I should seem at that moment a confirmed young bachelor, prematurely pickled at age thirty-five in his habits and collections.

Sooner or later we wind up tiring of objects as we do people—we

Georges-Olivier Châteaureynaud

lose interest—because other objects, or people, have in turn entered our lives, pushing earlier ones aside. Perhaps what matters most to us in all the world can be safely banished to the very depths of our being. But should disaster threaten our inner attic, it is the one thing we try to save, without regard for all the rest.

My initial wonder dulled as weeks, then months, went by. After so constantly occupying my thoughts, the mummy began to blend into its surroundings in my cramped apartment. My gaze strayed over my possessions and only rarely picked it out; it was just another furnishing.

Then, suddenly...A man who hears a strange voice singing or humming in the night faces a choice: disbelief, rapture, or terror. Should the phenomenon persist, disbelief goes away by itself. Then the choice between rapture and terror becomes one of temperament. One can also waver a long time between the two, to feel them both at once. When this happened to me, I was charmed by what I heard, and at the same time terrified that I was going mad. No one could be singing in my bedroom at that hour, it had to be in my head...The first time I clung to the idea that it was a dream, just a dream, a rather poetic one at that. The late hour and the fact that I was in bed supported this theory so well that I managed to fall back asleep, dodging the essential question: Who was singing?

The second time, both theories, dream and madness alike, were shattered. Someone was definitely singing in my room and not in my head. I turned on the light and got up. Trembling, I looked for whoever had woken me. It was a melancholy tune. The voice was soft and sad, and also muffled. The words remained incomprehensible to me.

I'd given up on a bed to leave my books as much room as possible. All I had instead was a sleeping bag on a sofa between my desk and a French window I opened just a crack, once a year, to air the room out. I'd made my way round my desk when I found myself facing the spot the voice was coming from. It was welling up from the mummy. Her features were hidden by her mask, a simple piece of wood sculpted and painted in a summary but not tasteless fashion. It evoked the face it covered with greater precision than might a mass-produced mask slapped on a factory mummy. And that song issued from beneath this mask, through lips supposedly sealed forever.

I reached out my hand. I'd done so often, my heart pounding at first, and then with less emotion as time passed. Now my hand trembled and my heart pounded anew.

The singing didn't stop when the mask fell away. Had she noticed a difference? Could she even do so? Nothing led me to believe she could. Her expression hadn't changed, her gaze was fixed as ever, mysterious as I'd always known it to be. It was just that her thin lips were moving, rounding or flattening to form words that didn't make any sense to me. What breath, from what oblivion, lent her life? But did I myself even know why I was here in this world? I hadn't the slightest, but did my best to accept my condition. In her way, this creature shared that condition of being alive. None of the rest was any of my business.

Little by little, her voice faded away, like that of someone dying. What was I to do? Call the police, or an ambulance? Alert the press? To do so felt like informing on an infinitely innocent and vulnerable being. I made do with replacing the wooden mask as gently as possible, and then I went back to bed.

On other nights, which followed at ever closer intervals, I was awakened by the mummy singing the same melancholy song. I soon knew it by heart without understanding the words. It sounded Breton to me. One day, while delivering a manuscript to an editor, I ran into Paol Keruzoré. He was known to be neither patient nor polite, but we'd met before. With his surly permission, I sang him the lament I'd learned phonetically.

"You should be ashamed, slaughtering a charming song like that!" he finally said.

"It's because I don't understand a word of it. What does it mean?"

"It means—let's see . . . 'Too early in the season falls the apple, no hand will polish it upon a sleeve to make it shine . . . No mouth will bite into the apple fallen still green, hard as a rock, without sweetness or sap . . . Pity the fallen apple, fear the wind that blows through the orchards, the wicked wind that spared me not . . .' Where did you dig that up, anyway?"

I told him the first lie that came to mind. My nursemaid had sung it to me as a boy.

"A pity you didn't learn to speak Breton at her teat," Paol spat.

Then, with an uncharacteristically civil wave, he walked off, humming a Breton air.

I always took the mummy's mask off when she was singing. At first, for as long as it lasted, I sat on a chair I'd pulled up beside her. Later, I fell into the habit of going back to work. One night, a little while after my encounter with Keruzoré, she stopped and turned her head toward me. Up till then, I'd thought she was only singing for herself. To tell the truth, I wasn't sure she knew I was there. I was proved wrong that night. I saw a pale, thin smile cross her lips. The contrast was striking between the deep, fixed brilliance of her eyes and the hesitant expression on the rest of her face.

I thought she was about to speak, but it wasn't time yet. I was witness to an awakening that could only happen slowly. I suspected that the slightest thing would be enough to hinder, delay, or even ruin it forever.

That was all for now. No doubt that hint of a smile remained on her face after I'd replaced the mask. Three nights later, the mummy spoke her first words.

I'd gotten a Breton dictionary in anticipation, but there was no need. When she spoke, she spoke French. A few disjointed phrases, none of which had anything to do with the situation at hand: something about a younger brother, a house by the sea, a cat. The reminiscing must have exhausted her, for she soon fell silent once more. A bit later that same night, she spoke up again, mostly repeating herself. After that, the situation developed with lightning speed.

When I say "lightning," bear in mind that whatever their nature, manifestations of the vital spark animating the mummy remained limited and intermittent. She lived the way a lamp flickers. She was rather more like a battery, in fact, a depleted battery sporadically calling on its last reserves. From now on, let's use her first name: Gaud. Her parents probably got it from *An Iceland Fisherman*. Gaud had no organs left, and therefore no anatomy. She had no way of replenishing what she'd spent. Of course, her expenditures were negligible. A few words, a few slow and awkward gestures . . . At her request, I undid the bandages wrapped tightly around her body. She reminded me of a newborn fawn, not yet able to balance on her frail legs, tottering with every step. But the fawn would soon grow stronger and bolder, prancing gaily about the clearing where it was born, whereas the unlucky Gaud would never prance about.

Still, she made undeniable progress. It was impossible to speak of a "normal" life for her. She neither ate nor drank, and her attention span lasted no more than ten minutes, after which she grew still, her face frozen. Eyes wide open, she sank into sleep, or a kind of sleep, for an unspecified length of time.

Once I'd removed her bandages, the question of clothes came up. I gave her a blanket, and bought her an outfit the next day. Picture a mummy in jeans and a sweater: that was how Gaud looked from then on. I'd also bought her sneakers and a baseball cap; her shaved head bothered me. Docilely, she assumed the appearance of a modern-day teenager.

She'd come in a Styrofoam sarcophagus, but she didn't like it there. I offered to lay her on a folding cot—like I said, there isn't much room in my place, and she was so slight. She categorically refused my offer, and instead chose to dwell in my double-bass case. Whenever seized by one of her unassailable languors, she'd curl up in this cavity, this womb, with a sigh of pleasure. With a weary wave, she'd ask me to shut the lid, and I obeyed. I was afraid she'd suffocate at first. I feared in vain. She was as likely to suffocate as she was to catch a cold.

She suffered a great deal. Not physically. She was racked by anguish all the more deep-seated since she never managed to give it a name. Everything in her was unsettled, shifting. She sought for words at length to say the least thing. I don't know if you could call what she had amnesia, but the events of her own life seemed distant and uncertain. Sometimes she seemed completely detached from them. The next moment, she was overcome with immeasurable nostalgia as she recalled a possibly invented memory. A moment later, and she'd forgotten everything.

I was used to her, of course. Wasn't she pitiable, and in distress? Wasn't I available? Besides, through the simple act of "owning" this object which was also a being, I'd taken on certain responsibilities. But I'd taken them too lightly. A few scraps to clothe her, a few words to comfort her when she woke chilled through by a cold not of this world...What loved one wouldn't ask more of us? If I'd continued to perform these tasks with my undivided attention, she'd probably have reached the end of her path in peace. Little by little, consuming what energy was left to her, she'd have slowly faded away.

Life, it seemed, had it in for her. Here I was, a man who'd lived alone forever, making do with affairs that ended the morning after, and I had to go and meet Delia! Delia was passionate. She was passion itself. Fierce, fearless, fervent in everything she did. Someone else might've deserved her more, and been better equipped to brave such a human tornado. But through some divine unfairness I'll never be thankful enough for, she chose me. Before her, my life was stale and musty.

I hadn't felt the need to tell Delia there was a teenaged female mummy in my life, more or less alive to boot. She found out by accident, even if that accident was inevitable. We'd been lovers for a few months already. We almost always wound up at her place. It was more convenient, especially because of the size of her bed. So she'd only been to my place two or three times, and had never spent the night there, when a metro strike forced her to stay over. I'd already shown her my instrument collection before, neglecting of course to open up the double bass case. I'd stashed the double-bass itself in a closet. Since I'd started dating Delia, I rarely slept at home. I felt a vague remorse at the thought of all those nights when Gaud woke up and found no one to open the lid and keep her company. I settled this remorse by telling myself that she hadn't ever brought it up. That either meant she hadn't noticed, or that she forgot any hypothetical grief my absence caused her. At any rate, while Delia and I lay entwined on my narrow couch, the Breton lament sounded in the silence.

"Good God, what's that?"

"Don't be scared." I said, "It's just Gaud."

I opened the case. Delia and Gaud studied each other with clear mutual loathing. Could they have been friends or allies? Perhaps in each encounter there's a moment—a split second—when our feelings might go either way. Perhaps the only difference between love and hate is chance. Weren't Delia and Gaud complementary? Together, with one's perfect body and the other's sublime eyes, they could have made the ideal woman. But this miracle failed to happen.

They never spoke to each other directly. Gaud ignored Delia, and Delia pretended to see her as nothing but an anatomical curiosity. Though Gaud sang and spoke, Delia considered her no more sentient than she would a mynah bird. At least in theory, for she never missed an opportunity to humiliate her. Right in front of Gaud, she advised me to let her go because "it wasn't sanitary." I pointed out in vain that Gaud was in fact very sanitary, and when she wasn't needed only a little dusting or occasional vacuuming. A few weeks later, Delia tried another approach. It was not only "unclean," but "dangerous," too. From then on, whenever she found herself alone and free to move about, Gaud played pranks, big and little. She might try to vandalize the apartment in some way within her paltry means, like knocking over a vase or making a minor mess. Reshelving the books exceeded her strength. But she might also leave the gas on, or slit her wrists. The incident with the gas didn't lead anywhere, thanks to the firemen's intervention. Nor did slitting her wrists: nothing flowed out. I kept the box cutter she'd used under lock and key, and put a bolt on the kitchen door, thus keeping her from reaching the gas, any sharp objects, and above all any potentially dangerous sources of heat.

Life went on—an odd life, I'll admit. What Delia and I had shared at the outset of our relationship was ruined. Where she once gave herself to me without restraint, she now refused two out of three times. The woman who'd once seemed so well-balanced and optimistic to me now often seemed willfully sullen or aggressive. For my part—torn between what I owed my mistress and the feeling of responsibility for Gaud that I couldn't quite shake—I was getting gloomy. As for Gaud, well, if a mummy could waste away, it was clear she was also feeling the effects of the situation. We were all unhappy.

All this led us to a vacation. I didn't usually take one. I hate beaches and sunburn. Delia didn't see it that way. She wanted to go to the shore with me. I surrendered on one condition, and remained firm about it: Gaud was going with us. Leaving her alone for a month was out of the question; you couldn't ask the super to look after a mummy the way you would a canary. In truth, I'd long planned to take Gaud back to the Brittany of her childhood. The name of the little fishing village where she'd been born floated to her lips like a cork plucked from a net and tossed ashore by waves. I kept the idea of the pilgrimage to myself. I made sure Gaud knew nothing about it. And as for Delia, who'd reluctantly given in to being burdened with her rival—it was pointless to tell her.

We left one morning in July, in Delia's car. She was at the wheel, with me beside her, and Gaud in the backseat, in her case. Delia didn't say a word the whole way. She'd given in. The vacation she'd dreamed of for so long was ruined in advance. She was determined to make me pay dearly. There was nothing but rain and wind en route.

I'd rented a house in the back country, a few kilometers from the village where Gaud was born. The wet summer made me dig deep into the woodshed. I kept a fire crackling in the hearth in the main room. Unable to swim or sunbathe, Delia was always going out for walks through the waterlogged moors. Never one for slogging through mud, I stayed and worked by the fire. Delia would come back with her nose dripping, smelling of moist earth and the heath. If I offered to warm her up as only I could, she'd turn me down and glare at the case leaning against the wall, across from the bed.

One morning neither more nor less disastrous than the others, I put my plan into action. I'd seen Delia head off in the opposite direction from the village. I carried Gaud's case to the car. Since our arrival the mummy had only stirred from her torpor twice, and quite briefly. I was guessing she had no idea where we were.

A little ways from the village, I turned down a dirt road leading to the sea. The nonstop drizzle had discouraged most visitors. The rare figure stuffed into a jacket, bright yellow or fluorescent pink against the seaweed, punctuated the shore and the exposed rocks.

I parked at the edge of the dunes and got the case from the car. I'd never woken Gaud before. I opened the lid and whispered, "Gaud! Gaud! Wake up! Look where we are."

Her eyes were always open, even when she was asleep. Her nose and lips quivered, telling me she was awake. When she saw the sky and felt the drizzle on her cheeks, she knew, even before she'd climbed out of her shell and looked around.

"You brought me back?"

"Yes. I thought—" In heaven's name, what exactly had I thought?

"Help me."

I obeyed. She crawled from the case and stood up on her wobbly legs.

"Hold me up."

In my study, she'd never taken more than a few steps before, leaning on my arm.

Despite the dull gray sky, it was still too bright out for her. She held one hand up to shield the masterpiece of Leonello Guardicci.

"It was over there!"

With her free hand, she pointed at the slate roofs and the slanting, motionless masts of boats on the beach. Over there, under one of those roofs, she'd had a life, or a childhood, at least. Voices, smells, emotions connected her to one of those houses by a thread perhaps indestructible, or perhaps ready to be severed at last, this time for good.

"Do you want to go down there?"

"No. I know there are people I loved down there, but ... I no longer know who they are. It's better that way. Walking, feeling the rain and wind on my face—this is enough. Help me."

She weighed nothing. Her feet barely left prints in the wet sand. We covered about fifty yards. At one point I loosened my grip on her arm for a second, and I thought the wind was about to blow her away.

"That's enough," she murmured. "That's good. Take me back. Please."

We turned around. She curled back into the case. I put it in the car, and we went back to the house.

During lunch, Delia insisted I accompany her that afternoon. She wanted to show me a cross she'd found by the wayside. Delia was interested in crosses, medieval wash houses, ancient sheep barns ... As though there were something to see in the world. She implied that if I agreed to go out and catch a cold with her, she'd be grateful.

She'd hung her raincoat by the door. I'd gulped down my coffee and, as we were about to head out, went up to the bedroom to find mine. I took the chance to check in on Gaud. She gave me one of those pitiful smiles that moved me so much.

"Nothing can hurt me, you know, but that walk we took did me good," she whispered, as I was worried about how tired she seemed.

"Rest up," I said.

"Yes ... Leave the lid open a little, please. Sometimes I feel like I'm suffocating."

I studied her suspiciously.

"Please! I won't do anything stupid. No more pranks."

Did I believe her? I gave in to her request. When we got back from our walk, Delia and I found her almost completely consumed in the hearth. All that remained was a trace, in relief, of her body curled up on a bed of embers. I wanted to recover the eyes that divine glassmaker had given her, but I didn't have the heart. Delia took the poker from my hands. Digging through the embers, she found only two shapeless drops of glass she gave up on saving. She picked up a shovel instead and patted the reddish burial mound flat.

Later, back in Paris, I remembered what the taxidermist had said when he gave me the certificate of authenticity. "Fire, theft, nothing's safe. These days, everything disappears or goes up in smoke. Make sure you're insured!" I'd followed his advice. Now I called in the insurance. I was reimbursed for Gaud in cash, and with that cash I bought our wedding rings: Delia's and my own.

Lozère, Sept.-Oct. 1995

Écorcheville

When Orne heard that several automated firing squads had been set up around town, he was unimpressed. Of all the innovations constantly being introduced to the surroundings, how many turned out to last? Of course certain amenities, like phone or photo booths, had established themselves by proving their usefulness. But how would the use of an automatic firing squad—one that you used yourself—ever catch on? Once the novelty had worn off, such an invention was doomed never to be more than a gimmick. Besides, from just what point would such contraptions break even and ensure returns? How many shootings would it take per month to pay the upkeep alone? Even though it was all in theory automatic and self-cleaning, someone had to pay workers to remove the bodies and gunsmiths to regulate and reload the weaponry. Orne had trouble seeing how an entrepreneur might make back his investment, cover his costs, and show any profit.

Orne's predictions, pronounced on the terrace of the Café du Centre, in no way surprised his listeners. He was a known disbeliever and belittler. Not a bad sort, though, all things considered. The absence of any unforgivable defect in his personality, aside from a tendency to criticize, brought him, on the part of his acquaintances, a measured attachment more lukewarm than loving, but real. In his circle his skepticism was credited to his frustration. He was a man lucky neither in leisure nor love. Leisure—well, that was a manner of speaking. Orne never relaxed: he worked. And despite the lengths to which he went, his business languished. His glove shop had never managed to attract the refined clientele of his dreams. The dandies and damsels of Écorcheville were faithful to Damien Létoilé, perhaps because his competitor came from the class of which they themselves were part. Damien hailed from the very heart of one of Écorcheville's oldest families, whose prosperity, born of the slave trade, had been further consolidated by the importation of poppies at a time when opium was sold by the seed at every apothecary's. In this gloved, hatted, and cravatted milieu, Damien was related to everyone. The men greeted him with a "Hallo, old sport," and the women kissed both his cheeks upon entering his boutique. From a much more modest background, Orne did his best to sell gloves and ties to those whose parents had lived bare-handed, with unbuttoned collars, like his own. This accounted for fully half his bitterness.

The other half had to do with women. He had long believed that what made them keep their distance was his way of being in the world. He was not all of a piece, simple and adaptable, as they expected a man to be. Reticence marked him, reservations plain as the nose on his face. To all appearances, women wanted men who were men the way women were women, with an almost animal innocence and authenticity akin to a gazelle's artlessness, a crocodile's candor. Whereas he had never managed to forget himself enough to feel wholly within his rights, a fact that lent almost all his acts, especially his amorous overtures, hints of haste and hesitation that most often led to disaster.

The skewed relationship Orne was aware of entertaining with conventional reality wasn't the only cause of his failure. He was also ugly. Large eyes over a large nose that jutted out above a lipless mouth like an open razor wound in winter, the opposite of a lover's mouth, and all of it framed by two oversized, indelicately colored ears. To this was added an extremely elastic expressiveness that led him to underline the slightest proposition with a grimace, as though to reveal bad teeth that no one wanted to see. One wondered how he'd managed to age in such ignorance, but the fact was that after fifty years, Orne was just beginning to suspect he was ugly.

Around the time the firing-squad machines made their appearance, Orne grew quite enamored of Philippina December. This splendid dollop of womanliness had remained single into her early forties. Nor had she been *born* to anything. When Orne fantasized about making a decisive connection with her, he considered the modest origins they shared a favorable sign. But although he managed his trade quite poorly, she conducted her career with verve. This pretty beanpole was generally held to be a lady of means. The fortunes of Écorcheville had few secrets from the woman who saw them file through her office in her position as manager of the region's most prestigious banking institution.

There they were, then, having an aperitif at the Café du Centre, Orne and Philippina and a few members of a small circle of singles, divorcées, and premature widowers. They dubbed themselves the Club of Available Hearts. They applied themselves to the task, in fact, of availing, unavailing, and availing themselves once more of one another in a private *ronde* as the years grayed the men's temples and altered the ovals of the women's faces. The only strangers to these intricate exchanges were Orne and Philippina: Orne because he no longer managed to couple up even temporarily, and Philippina, who'd only have had to say the word, because she refused to say it. Also present that evening were the speculator Macassar; Ludwig Propinquor, rich like all the Propinquors; the dolceola virtuoso Blandeuil, who'd founded a conservatory devoted to his chosen instrument in Écorcheville; and for the ladies, Brunehilde Laurençais and Gina Mordor in addition to Philippina. Brunehilde was a beauty—reconditioned but warrantied, according to the somewhat tactless Macassar, who sponged off her between bouts at the Exchange. Gina Mordor, a peach—golden, velvety, perfumed—had occupied Orne's thoughts before Philippina. He'd gotten nothing from her, and was almost certain she'd mocked him behind his back the whole time he'd wooed her.

"You'll see: they'll all have forgotten it in a month," he flung into the conversation after spitting out the stone from the olive in his cocktail. "If it's death you're after, you do it at home, without making a spectacle of yourself."

"Who said anything about a spectacle?" said Propinquor, up in arms. "The rides are open round the clock. You can go and get yourself shot in the middle of the night, in the wee small hours of the morning... Not so dumb, really, now that I think about it."

"I agree with Ludwig," Philippina cut in. "The designers of these machines must have been counting on a sudden loss of self-control, anguished midnight urges, early morning suicidal impulses—"

"Really, Philippina, have you ever entertained such thoughts?" ventured Orne in what he hoped was an affectionate tone.

"Not personally, no," she retorted, "but it could happen to other people, and such impulses can't always be satisfied when they arise. Even if you don't have a shotgun, a rope, or a sufficient quantity of sleeping pills on hand, you almost always have some cash or a credit card. And these machines take both forms of payment. They fill a real need. With the basics settled, all that's left is adapting to demand: price, availability, selection."

"Perhaps that's where the shoe pinches—in the, um, yes, what you said! Being shot twelve times is a bit harsh, don't you think?" murmured Gina Mordor, trailing her fingertips over the sensitive skin of her crossed arms.

"Twelve? Is it really twelve?" asked Blandeuil.

"It's *à la carte*," Orne replied. "Like oysters on the half shell: a dozen or half a dozen. There's even a little round of just three. Of course, the price varies accordingly."

"I hope they haven't forgotten the *coup de grâce*," rasped Macassar.

"Laugh if you want, but according to the piece by Lupus in the *Rumor*, there is indeed a *coup de grâce*."

Propinquor checked his watch with a worried eye. Homini Lupus, Écorcheville's finest scribe, had promised to join them for dinner. "What's he up to? The owner of the Murky Maw will give our table away if we're too late."

"He knows where it is," said Macassar.

He was hungry, and didn't care much for Homini Lupus, whom he suspected of trying to sway Brunehilde into investing in the newspaper.

The Murky Maw had opened not long ago. It was just as good as, and less expensive than, Chez Pecunious, where its young chef had gotten his start. Orne managed to seat himself next to Philippina. Despite his age, he still never knew whether it was better to sit beside or across from someone you wished well, and from whom you hoped for the same in return. Doubtful that he made for a very inviting sight, he rallied to the solution of sitting at her side. He had reason to congratulate himself on his decision, for dinner went by like a dream in the nearness and immediacy of Philippina's bare shoulders and *décolleté*. Orne was one of those men, to be both greatly pitied and condemned, who couldn't help believing that a woman who smiled while speaking to them was also romantically interested. Philippina didn't ordinarily smile all the time, but that night she was in high spirits, and so she smiled—at Orne, as at the champagne and the lights, the langoustines and the chablis, at the waiter, at Ludwig, at the sweetbread, at Gina, at the profiteroles ... Homini Lupus never joined them; Macassar was secretly pleased. He was suffering losses and would have to seduce Brunehilde for the umpteenth time. Was she taken in? It remained a mystery. Gina pined away. She had always dreamed of an affair with a man like Propinquor. Upon his death, her husband had left her with a pretty stipend, but Ludwig was something else entirely: real money, concentrated, enriched the way one spoke of enriched uranium. She would have liked, much as fans stroke a boxer's biceps or a biker's calves, to press herself against that chest and feel his portfolio beating through his vest. Alas! Respectable women bored Ludwig. It was commonly known that he liked easy women. He paid Gina no mind, despite the licentious airs she tried to put on.

Orne deluded himself with hope. He imagined his dealings were going well because Philippina had smiled at him. He contemplated the best way to bring up, in an aside, the offer of a drink for just the two of them, to finish off the evening. Suddenly, a plump, fortyish stranger, olive-skinned and hook-nosed, with black curly hair and gleam in her eye, appeared at the table. A large gray parrot clung to a wooden perch set in a leather epaulette stitched to her gypsy dress. Frowning, Ludwig Propinquor looked about for the maître d', but the parrot put his suspicions to rest with an amusing stunt. Not content simply to hail the guests one by one, telling men from women without fail, it called upon the former as witness to the latter's charms. The most marvelous part of the act was the aptness of the bird's compliments: it praised Gina's carnation, Philippina's décolletage, and Brunehilde's tresses. In a matter of moments, it had won over the table.

"Ladies and gentlemen," said the mistress of their new feathered friend, "my parrot can speak like you and I, but this is not the only gift God has given him."

She paused. Orne took advantage of the silence to sally forth with a remark he hoped would make Philippina laugh. Oh, Philippina's laugh, that brash workaday guffaw!

"Let me guess—it reads tarot cards?"

His neighbor's reaction filled Orne with delight. She opened her mouth, that pink grotto where frolicked the plump manatee of her tongue, and out came the laugh he'd been waiting for.

"Yes!" The gypsy pointed Orne's way an index finger whose sharp and tapered nail could, he thought, have enucleated rabbit or man with equal ease.

"Yes!" she repeated. "You've guessed it, sir, except that this bird has no need of cards to tell the future. Have you ever asked yourself how long you've left to live? Legends from my native land have it that our hearts know and sometimes warn us in whispers that our minds refuse to heed. Ask the question and my parrot will read the answer in your eyes."

"Is it expensive?" asked Blandeuil.

"Next to nothing. Consider that if the date proves distant, this knowledge will either allow you to go on living more peacefully and happily than ever before—or, on the contrary, to take all the necessary measures. And yet such precious information will cost you almost nothing, for you can ask the bird three questions for the modest sum of one hundred francs each time."

"You mean I'll have to fork over a hundred francs a question?" Macassar asked.

"Exactly," the gypsy replied. "But whether the first answer frightens, upsets, or fully reassures you, nothing obliges you to go on, and you'll only have paid a hundred francs."

Ludwig Propinquor had come by the reputation of a freethinker, which he was fond of upholding. He pulled a roll of bills from his pocket and counted three out on the table. "By God, a Propinquor fears neither death nor spending. Here are your three hundred francs, all at once."

He turned to the parrot. "Well, my little pullet, how much time have I left to live?"

"Pardon me, sir," said the gypsy, "but that's not how to go about it. You must say, for example, 'Handsome bird, have I more than twenty-five years left to live?' And he will answer yes or no. If you want to know more, ask him a second question, framed in the same manner: 'Handsome bird, have I more than or just this many years left to live?'"

"I get it," Propinquor said. "So be it! Let's see: I'm thirty-nine; I belong to a family generally blessed with longevity. 'Handsome bird, have I more than fifty years left to live?'" he asked, imitating the voice and burlesque mugging of Louis de Funès.

Impassive, the parrot waited for the merriment to die down before pronouncing its verdict.

"Yes!" it said at last, with conviction, before turning its head to preen itself.

Ludwig beamed at the applause. With a lordly flourish, he proffered the gypsy three bills. "I'm satisfied with my half century; keep the change!"

"The gentleman knows how to live in style! It's only fair that he should have a long time to do so! Who's next?" asked the woman, tucking the bills away. "Who will delve into Fate's plans?"

Around the table there were light coughs and sidelong glances. Doubtless some trick allowed the gypsy to control the parrot's answers... Ventriloquism, perhaps? Yet the illusion was so convincing it intimidated. There was a moment of uncertainty, almost discomfort. Then in spite of himself—so to speak—Orne jumped in.

"Me!"

He dug out his wallet and laid a hundred-franc bill on the table. "I... well... Handsome bird—"

He would have liked to shine, all the more so because he felt Philippina's gaze upon him, but he knew himself to be pitiful at impressions.

If he couldn't be funny, he could at least be nervy or brave—or seem brave, since it was all a trick anyway. Of course the parrot had no connection with the stars above. It was nothing but a gray bird with a big beak and big round eyes. It answered whatever it was ordered to by the device hidden in the perch and shoulder pad, operated by its mistress.

"Handsome bird, tell me: have I more than a year left to live?"

"No."

"You're not going to believe that nonsense? It's a trick, of course. That gypsy just wanted to have a laugh at your expense."

"I'm sure you're right, but it really rattled me. I'm too impressionable, too sensitive ... Less than a week, according to that stupid creature. What if it's right?"

Orne swayed as he spoke. It could hardly have been called a binge, but all the same, it'd taken him several Irish Coffees to recover. The darkness of the street hid Philippina's irritated expression. Leaving the restaurant, she hadn't slipped away quickly enough, and now she could no longer manage to rid herself of him.

"If it's true," she snapped, "if you die this week, it'll be pure coincidence."

"You really know how to cheer a guy up!" Orne said.

"But why did you keep pushing on? From a psychological standpoint, less than a year feels better than less than a week."

Orne nodded apologetically. To the three questions he'd asked— "Have I more than a year, a month, a week left to live?"—the parrot had answered no three times over. The gypsy had pocketed his three hundred francs, then scarpered off with her parrot on her shoulder.

"Philippina, the more I think about it, the more upsetting it gets, because it's bad business. Predicting the impending death of a client in front of other potential clients is bad business! If you ask me, it wasn't a trick. The parrot spoke the truth."

"That's ridiculous—oh my, it's late!"

"Don't leave me! You don't understand: I've maybe less than a week left ... Philippina, I wanted so much to spend my last days with you!"

"Excuse me?"

"I've been crazy about you for months now. I didn't dare tell you. Now, in the face of imminent death, all my shyness has disappeared. Philippina, be mine, even if only for a few hours, so at least I'll have known happiness!"

Philippina rolled her eyes skyward. Just her luck. Her gaze, finding no help in the heavens, fell once more to the world below. She picked out headlights on the avenue, an available taxi. Saved!

"Dear, dear friend! I'm very touched, really, and also very flattered! You're a man who's so—but excuse me, please, here comes a taxi. At this late hour, it would be a crime to let it slip away!"

She lifted her arm and practically threw herself onto the taxi's hood. A moment later, the cab carried her off into the night.

As he was crossing Market Square, Orne stopped short before one of the machines. According to the article by Lupus, there were three in all: one behind City Hall; one in front of the elementary school, its use forbidden to minors; and the one now before him. He drew closer, curious. The automatons of lithographed iron, in their bas-relief firing squad, gleamed in the moonlight. Their uniforms evoked the Empire, without Orne being able to say which, exactly: First or Second. In any case, the soldiers looked quite distinguished in their dress blues and gold-buttoned trousers, white gaiters and leather bandoliers, the appropriate expressions on the twelve faces individualized by mustaches and sideburns of varying shades, a military cap tilted to the right or the left, jammed tightly down or tossed back behind the head. Both arms, the only moving parts, were for the moment drawn back to the chest, in their hands carbines that a mechanism permitted them to aim at a post a few steps away. You were shot more or less point-blank, so there was no need to fear any inaccuracy of aim. The customer was sure to have his fill of bullets. To one side was a mechanical officer, identified by his pistol and epaulettes, mounted on a little cart that slid along a rail, bringing him to the dying man in order to administer, for the sake of good form, the *coup de grâce*. Peering more closely at the post, Orne found a clever adjustable pedestal allowing each user to adapt it to his or her own size. Thus the *coup de grâce*, delivered of necessity at a standard height, would not run the risk of missing. A duly lighted notice clarified a few operating procedures. The requisite restraints consisted of thin iron hoops that automatically closed around the body of the self-condemned. As for the body's disposal, a diagram outlined the workings. A door opened behind the post, which turned, then pitched forward as the hoops retracted into their housings. The freed corpse fell into a temporary casket that slid into a slot in a morgue chambered like the barrel of a gun. They'd thought of everything, reflected Orne admiringly.

A discreet cough made him jump. He turned around. In the lunar clarity, he made out a woman of about thirty with a small boy.

"Excuse me, sir, but are you going to use—"

Orne said no. He had no intention of using the machine. He was interested, very interested, of course, but he could not foresee resorting to it for the time being.

"Then, please—we're in a hurry."

He stepped aside, absentmindedly at first, as if before a telephone booth, but at the sight of the woman placing her hands on the child's shoulders and nudging him gently toward the post, he couldn't stop himself from speaking up.

"What are you going to do?"

"It has to end," the woman answered in a woeful voice. "My little boy and I are too unhappy. My husband's dead. I'm unemployed. My landlord just threw us out. We're so alone, all alone, oh God! That's why they made these things, right? So we could be done with all the misery and the loneliness?"

"Maybe, but—but you don't have the right!"

The woman shrugged. "Of course I do. I've got the right to use this machine because it's here. I didn't invent it, did I? They put it here so I could use it, and if I've got the money I will, that's all there is to it!"

"But the boy—!"

"What do you suggest, sir? Will you marry me, feed and raise him? No, of course not!"

She pulled a gaunt coin purse from her coat and set to counting out change.

"I'm not even sure I have enough for the half-dozen," she said. "Would you be so kind as to help me out?"

"Absolutely not!"

"Whatever happened to charity? Oh, wait...I think I've got enough. Be good, sweetie, just a moment and we'll be in heaven," she told her son.

She made all the adjustments with an eye to her child's execution, covered him with kisses one last time, inserted the coins into the slot and then pressed herself to him before the firing squad.

A tinny recorded voice burst from a speaker hidden in the officer's head: "On my order... Ready! Aim!"

With a single synchronized screech, six of the metal soldiers drew their rifle stocks to their shoulders and took aim at woman, child, and Orne.

"Out of the way, you fool!" she yelled.

He only had enough time to obey.

"Fire!" cried the officer.

The salvo shattered the night.

Only the child was entitled to the *coup de grâce*, since there was only one per round, and the woman had in a way snuck in for free. Fortunately, she expired quickly, while the machine swallowed her son's body. After the tragedy, Orne remained rooted to the spot, shivering before the unhappy woman's corpse. What could he have done? Everything had happened so fast! The woman's words still rang in his head: "Are you going to marry me, feed him, and raise him?" No, obviously not. But what was a man worthy of the name supposed to have done? Surely not panic, stammer, and let widows and orphans die before his eyes. Feelings of guilt and impotence all but drowned him. It crossed his mind that to redeem himself he might wait for the next would-be executee and devote himself to saving him, by force if necessary. Then he remembered that he had less than a week to live. His hour might even come that night. He no longer had time for anything. Wasn't he exempt from all responsibility? The living could struggle with life, he was but a dotted outline now, barely even there. After all, who cared about him? Leaving the restaurant, his friends had all vanished, abandoning him to face the prospect of his imminent death alone. And the women! Brunehilde with her silky tresses, Gina with her peach-down skin, Philippina with her splendid bosom...Gone, flown, nowhere to be found! What was the world coming to if women no longer bestowed even the least consolatory favors on the dying?

The sound of steps interrupted his thoughts. He recognized the gypsy from the Murky Maw. She was biting her lip and her eyes glistened worriedly. "Sir—would you have seen a large gray parrot?"

She hadn't recognized him. She didn't remember having predicted, less than an hour earlier, that he had but a few days, perhaps even only a few hours, left to live.

"Did it escape?"

She shrugged. Would she be looking for him otherwise?

"I'll help you look! But please, tell me—it's a trick, isn't it?"

Orne's voice was pleading. The woman studied him more closely.

"Ah . . . You're one of the gentlemen from the restaurant."

"Yes! Tell me it's a trick!"

The worried gleam in the gypsy's eye gave way to one of irony. As she opened her mouth to reply, the parrot, with a great beating of wings, passed by above.

"That's him!" the gypsy cried. "Coco! Come back!"

"Coco, come back!" Orne echoed.

Indifferent to their cries, the bird stayed its course, alighting for a moment on the head of the statute of Mathieu Chain, then setting off again toward the square.

"Quickly," the gypsy panted, "follow, we can't lose sight of him!"

God alone knew why, but Orne found reason for hope in the fact that she wished him to join her in pursuing the bird. He fell in beside her. Luckily, the parrot's plumage was a very light gray, and could without too much trouble be made out in the gloom through which, with no particular hurry, it glided in an almost stately getaway.

Palaiseau, July 2001

Sweet Street

Some people never wonder what they were put on earth to do. When the time comes, a voice pipes up inside and says, be a linguist, or a bridgebuilder. The voice speaks; they listen. The earlier it speaks, the earlier they set out in search of dialects to master or rivers to ford.

Moe had found out on the late side what his purpose in life was. By all appearances, it was to read and daydream in his taxi while waiting for a fare. He wasn't proud of it. He'd rather have taken the century head-on, but, aware his own limits were quickly reached, he'd let it go.

As with many other blessings in his life, he owed his late calling as a cabbie to his godmother. She was a building super. A guardian super. A fairy godsuper. Even something of a mer-super, maybe, the way her fragrant basement apartment, bathed in a blue glow and reaching back into the building depths, reminded him so much of a marine grotto carved out by tides at the foot of a city block. For her godson, sick of scraping by at twenty-five on a string of jobs from intern to part-time temp, she painted a rosy picture of the taxi driver's trade. The tenant in 4B—one of her favorites—had plied it four straight decades without noticeable weariness or disappointment. For him, the hour of retirement had come. He was willing to sell the license that for so long had been his daily bread.

Between minimum wage and social security, Moe hadn't a penny to his name. His fairy godsuper brushed his objections aside. If it'd help get him set up on his own, he could borrow the money at a token rate. That woman was living proof evil and despair hadn't yet conquered every last corner of the world. She lent Moe enough for the license, and the car, too. The make didn't matter—it was some foreign car. It had about as many miles on it as a trip to the moon. The seller claimed there was still enough under the hood to make it back. And he was right. Seven years later, it was still running. For Moe, it wasn't only a way of getting around or making a living, but the carapace or exoskeleton he'd always lacked. He needed a protective barrier between himself and the world or, since he was a citydweller, between him and the streets. This finally materialized in the form of an automotive chassis. Himself within and the universe without, was how he imagined it. In his safe space, he saw the steady stream of fares less as intrusion than (economically necessary) distraction from a sometimes onerous solitude. His fares were his guests. He sized them up as quickly as he could—as soon as they'd sat down in the backseat—and treated each according to his observations. He left those he felt hostile to all attempt at conversation to their own interior monologues. He and the others—most of them—exchanged a few passing thoughts on weather or traffic: was it staying good or getting worse? Were they moving or not? Some people could only parrot back the news, some had been brainwashed by the boob tube, some were demented sports fans. He adapted. "You got that right!" he'd say. When his head was filled to bursting with baloney, he met the minimum of polite conversation with an occasional nod. Sometimes he picked up a man of learning. There was no mistaking the type. Most fares, surprised, managed a polite question on seeing the scuffed spines, with their faded gilt, crammed into a glove compartment gone bookshelf. It usually had to do not with the books themselves, nor their titles and authors, but the strangeness of their presence in the cab. They clearly weren't new.

Brownish, yellowish, or tannish, nick-pocked and stain-spotted, the old bits of leather dated back to the times of wigs, swords, and kings. They aroused a limited curiosity in most: when was it from, how much was it worth? Only a few asked to see, sniff, or feel them, to open them up and read a little. Moe readily complied with their requests. His beloved books were in no danger. They were already falling apart. He liked them like that. Miraculously restored copies were in fact beyond his means. His passion didn't balk at browned or worm-eaten pages. Quite the contrary: time had placed its seal on the book. Moe haunted flea markets, buying what he could: what others scorned, orphan volumes, incomplete copies, books with warped or broken bindings, fossils, wrecks, scraps, and fragments. He never turned his nose up at anything. Like a beachcomber, he picked up whatever came his way, collecting memoirs, educational and religious treatises, prayers and pamphlets, comedies and tragedies, philosophical dialogues, novels frivolous and edifying alike. Everything nourished him; everything challenged him. From this silt—from the rare nuggets and the blackest follies of eras no more or less foolish than our own—his imagination extracted a compound of almost hallucinogenic qualities.

Slowly, he had started to get older. He'd married Maria, his kind of bohemian, an Ecuadoran art-school graduate, who regilded cherubs for the diocese. They were bringing up two olive-skinned kids in a small apartment whose prevailing greenhouse temperatures were kind to the tropical plants Maria couldn't live without. Moe expected nothing more from life than for this torrid, unassuming happiness to continue when fate, in the form of a seemingly ordinary fare, stepped into his cab.

It was toward the end of a rainy autumn afternoon. Since morning, every other fare had coughed or blown his nose right into the back of Moe's neck. He was sure he'd caught something; his nose was already tingling. The man in his fifties who'd just climbed in seemed to have dodged whatever was going around, Moe thought as he looked him over in the rearview mirror.

"Evening, mister."

"Good evening. Sweet Street, please. Number forty-two."

Moe must've heard wrong. He tried to think what other streets might sound like Sweet, which he'd never heard of. Not coming up with anything, he decided to ask the fare to repeat the address.

"Sorry, but . . . where'd you say again?"

"Forty-two Sweet Street."

"Sweet Street? You sure? I don't know any Sweet Street in this city, or around."

"Few do," the stranger said. "Head for Granary Hall, and I'll tell you where to go from there."

Moe pulled out, awfully intrigued. After five years of driving around, he thought he knew his territory. A little more and he'd have had doubts about his passenger's seriousness. How could so "few" know of a street that a cabbie hadn't heard of it at all? But the man's gaze had fallen on the stash of books.

"Say, those books . . . Pardon me for being nosy, but I'm in the business: I'm a book dealer. Are you a collector?"

"Collector? Yeah, I mean . . . I collect them!"

"Hmm . . . eighteenth century? May I?" The book dealer extended a hand over the front seat. Moe grabbed two books and passed them to him.

"Thanks. Let's see now . . . ah! Father Margolin, an old friend! And what have we here? Mesambierre! Have you read these? What I mean to say is: Have you actually read them?"

"Sure, you gotta, it's a book. I mean, what else . . ."

Moe trailed off. In the rearview mirror, the book dealer frowned slightly. For him, books were for buying and selling before reading.

"Quite. But take fine wines, for example . . . Some bottles are so old, drinking them is no longer a possibility. They've become utterly undrinkable. Still, we don't pour them down the sink. So we keep them for display, like works of art."

"I read my books," said Moe.

His fare opened his mouth, as if about to say that Father Margolin's sermons and Mesambierre's pastoral odes were completely indigestible today. He must have been afraid of insulting Moe, who gave every impression of having thoroughly enjoyed them. He changed his mind, shut his mouth, and set the dreadful octavo on the front seat.

"You sell books like these?" Moe asked.

"Yes, I deal in rare books. I traffic in books as old, but also as new-looking, as I can find. That's the trick of it, you see. You have to dig up three-hundred-year-old books that look fresh as newly laid eggs...Make a left here, and go straight. Where do you find your books?"

"Flea markets and yard sales."

"Yard sales can be good. It's surprising, what people put out on the sidewalk sometimes. Sorry, left, then the first right. I get most of my stock from auctions or private collectors. You have to take the good with the bad, buy whole libraries to treat yourself to a few nice pieces. I've got boxes full of Mesambierre, if you're interested."

Moe's eyes lit up. "Really?"

"Mesambierre and more...eighteenth and seventeenth of course, not very sought-after, but in good condition, at modest prices..."

"Stop here, please. Number 42 is just a bit farther down."

Moe felt cheated. Captivated by the conversation, he'd unthinkingly followed the book dealer's directions, his lefts and rights, and now they'd arrived at their destination, catching him off guard.

"This is Sweet Street? Are you sure?"

"Positively," his fare replied with a little laugh. "How much do I owe you?"

He paid, got out, and disappeared. The street was narrow; Moe had parked to let the man out, so he didn't have to drive off again right away. Now that he was alone, his curiosity about the little-known street got the better of him. He cut the engine, rummaged through the glove box, and pulled out from between two books a city map almost as worn out as they were. He knew it like a priest knows his breviary. With a quick glance, he gave himself a religious refresher. Sweet Street didn't exist, since it wasn't in the holy writ. But if it didn't exist, where had he brought his fare, and where was he right now? He swore. He stepped out of the car and, in his annoyance, slammed the door.

He looked around. Night was falling on Sweet Street. He took three steps without noticing a thing, then froze. There was something...in the air, or the light. Or in himself? No, not in him. He was just the same as before, when he'd picked up the book dealer. The same as he'd been at lunch, sitting down to lamb stew at the diner. The same as that night in Maria's arms, his face buried in her armpit. The same as last night at the apartment of his benefactress and godmother, whose birthday they'd been celebrating. The same as a year, a decade, or two earlier. So if the cause of this sensation—at once foreign and familiar, brand-new and very old—wasn't in him, it had to be somewhere around him.

Rain can be a friend—even a gray city rain. It can settle on your hands and forehead like a caress. Evening can hover in the air like a perfume, and the modest lights of daily life give off a glow like lanterns at a festival. Despite being unknown, Sweet Street was still lively and bustling. Without a care for the shower, a relaxed crowd thronged the sidewalks, clustering about the shop windows. The owners of a large fruit and vegetable stall praised their product in stentorian tones. Moe had to admit he hadn't seen apples that beautiful since...He tried to find something to compare them to, but all he could come up with were things he'd read. No apple in his memory could equal them except the golden ones from the Garden of the Hesperides, in a little book of stories from Greco-Roman mythology. Taken all together, the jumble of fruits and vegetables on display recalled to him the cornucopia on a banknote long since out of circulation. Right away he bought a small bag of apples and another of tomatoes for Maria and the girls. A few yards down, a baker right out of an operetta, plump and tempting as a cream puff in her white apron, sold him an archetypal loaf that seemed to have come more from an artist's brush than a breadmaker's hands. He brought his purchases back to the car before heading off again in search of the street sign the sight of which would alone settle the disbelief that continued quietly to haunt him.

He struck out toward where his fare had vanished: the far end of the street. He soon passed forty-two and had reached sixty-four when he stopped again in surprise. In the lengthening shadows, the street that appeared on no official city maps, which he himself had never heard of before tonight, was in fact quite a long one. He kept walking. The shops went by one after the next. Pigs' and calves' heads in the butchers' windows—their eyes closed, their nostrils stuffed with parsley—seemed to be laughing contentedly in a dream. Before a scene of garter belts and gauzy stockings, thongs and the lace-eyeleted brassieres in a lingerie boutique, he stopped, filled with wonder like a child before a nativity scene. Just as he was tearing himself away from his examination, a human projectile shot out from a porch and ran straight into him. He went hurtling backward. His skull smashed into a lamppost, and he collapsed, taking a scooter parked by the sidewalk down with him as he went.

He woke to find himself in a chair, in the neon glow of a pharmacy. An assistant was tapping his right hand while another bandaged the wound on his left. An older woman, also in white, was dabbing at his head with arnica. Their kindly faces were pressed together before the window, in the sign's green light. Right in front of Moe, her skateboard under her arm, a girl in a hot pink tracksuit with green stripes was watching Moe with relief.

"At least you're not dead! That's good, less trouble for me that way."

"Yep, the troubles would all be yours. I wouldn't have any more."

Once he'd thanked the pharmacist and apologized for the inconvenience, the girl dragged him firmly off to her parents' café just across the street. Her father, the owner, had a round, lumpy head, crooked teeth, and was generous to a fault. Her mother was of composite elegance—50s beehive, 60s pancake makeup, and a 70s short skirt— and an outstanding human being. The cordial they offered Moe to help him back on his feet soon turned very cordial indeed. From pear liqueur (under-the-counter) to plum spirits (from the back), he soon found himself singing an old folk song in an ambience of fellow-feeling that now and then drew a tear from his eye. Later there was couscous at an Arab place nearby, impromptu dancing in the back room of the café, cha-cha and slow dancing with an older sister, a nightcap at her place, and then it was late, so late . . .

At the crack of dawn, Moe staggered off to his car. A truck had broken down a few yards ahead, blocking the street, leaving him the choice between a long way in reverse or a difficult U-turn, given the narrow street. Moe went for the reverse. Though his head didn't hurt that badly despite the plum, the pear, and the Boulaouane he'd had with couscous, he couldn't remember the name of the girl in pink, nor that of her sister, with whom he'd . . . And what about all those nice people he'd spent the evening and part of the night with? He saw their faces again, heard their voices and laughter, but their names eluded him as a piece of cork in a glass of wine eludes the spoon. He shrugged. He'd be back. For now he had to get home. Maria was probably worried. In five years of marriage, he'd never spent the night away. She'd probably called the hospitals, the police. Moe didn't feel guilty. He was bringing back marvelous fruit, bread just like they used to bake it. When he reached the foot of Sweet Street, he reflected that he was going to have to tell a lie, and forgot to lift his gaze to the name of the next street he took.

He told Maria some unbelievable story about a childhood friend he'd had to keep from suicide. She believed him, or pretended to. The girls bit into the apples and tomatoes and found them delicious. The bread, toasted with jam, was astounding. Life resumed it course.

In the days and even weeks that followed, Moe searched for Sweet Street like a man possessed. For a while, his quest began to look like an obsession. He circled the city like a beast in a cage. He sought information from the roads administration, the land registry, the police, the tax authority ... all in vain. Against his fellow citizens' conclusive unanimity, he had but his personal conviction. Sweet Street was real, because for a few hours he'd been happy there. Had he lived centuries ago he would've plunged his hand into hot coals and sworn to it. Thank God no one asked him to do anything like that. Besides, he was careful not to assert that the street existed. All he'd say was, "I heard about this Sweet Street ... Is there any chance you ...?" He pretended to side with whomever he was talking to: if a street had a name like that, we'd all know, right? Right? Right. But no one knew. The name meant nothing to anyone.

He'd kept his story to himself. Telling Maria about it would have upset her. After all, he'd cheated on her with neither hesitation nor remorse. The other cabbies were too caught up with soccer. They wouldn't have understood. That left his godmother. He thought too late to ask her if she'd ever heard of Sweet Street. She had to die someday. The dead each take a piece of us with them when they go.

Summer came. At the Breton shore where he and Maria took the kids every summer to give them memories of wind and drizzle, the smell of cow dung and fallen fruit rotting in the orchards, he had the feeling of not quite being entirely there anymore. When they came back from vacation, the memory of Sweet Street already troubled him less. Bit by bit, though he never entirely forgot it, the episode melted back into the hazy mural of dreams that we walk beside all our lives without really noticing, except in furtive glances. Months, years went by. Moe was graying at the temples; the wrinkles deepened around his eyes. A streak of white parted Maria's dark hair. His daughters' minds and bodies changed. They didn't want to hear anymore about sea breezes and abandoned orchards, swearing instead by the sun of the southern coast and the huge mirrorballs of dance clubs.

Moe had bought a new car. He'd gone with the same foreign brand. This time he'd gone for a model with enough under its hood to take him to Mars and back. He still toted around, in that magnificent vehicle, his pitiful books. These days he dipped mainly into the 19th century, which had no shortage of bores, either. Sweet Street was a distant memory. He began to dream of a house for later on, in the wind and drizzle, with at least one apple tree he'd leave partly unpicked, leaving some fruit to rot at its foot. Preferably at the far end of the backyard, because of wasps.

And then one night a man got into his taxi and asked him to take him to Sweet Street. Moe's heart started pounding. Over time, he'd stopped believing in it. He looked at the man in the rearview mirror. It was the same one. Well—the same, but older. His hands and forehead were spotted. The flesh of his cheeks shook when he spoke. His head trembled almost imperceptibly. Out of reflex, Moe felt his own forehead, his own cheeks.

"Sure, mister. Number forty-two?"

The man leaned forward to peer at Moe, then let himself fall backward in his seat. "Number forty-two, of course."

"You'll have to give me directions, 'cause—"

"Don't worry, just drive! Head for the old Granary Hall..."

They chatted about the nineteenth century and romanticism. Now and then the old man stopped to give directions. Moe tried hard to memorize the route, but entertained no illusions. He knew the ins and outs of all the streets he drove. He could've drawn a complete map of the city from memory. He knew that Sweet Street began and ended nowhere, that to get there you had to *leave the map*...And one way or another, that was what happened. After fifteen minutes or so, they were there. The last sign he'd seen before arriving was Guardicci Avenue, but it might just as well have been any other, Delaunay Lane or Mathieu Chain Boulevard. It was random, Moe thought. His throat tightened. Time had gone by. What would he find?

The gentleman paid and got out. Moe hesitated. Wouldn't it be wiser to leave right away and return to a simple life, the lukewarm yoke of happiness and the sleep of days just like the sleep of nights? No, he'd waited too long for this moment. He stepped out of the car and locked the doors with the remote. He turned around to look for the fruits and vegetables vendor, the shop window with the beaming calves' heads, the pharmacy where he'd been cared for, the café where he'd danced...It was all there, but closed or decrepit, as though stricken by disaster. The stall had nothing to offer but overripe fruit and shriveled greens. In the entrance to the bakery, between the lowered grille and the glass door, soggy wrinkled flyers, old social-security letters, and court notices lay in a heap. He crossed the street and entered the café. The crowd was sparse: a few regulars clung crablike to the bar, watched over by two old harpies. A woman was drying glasses like in some sad blue-collar ballad. Moe recognized the little girl in pink, but she no longer shone. She looked wan and six months pregnant. He ordered the first thing that came to mind. A red wine spritzer. She served him without a word or a second glance.

"Don't you recognize me? You ran me over in the street with your skateboard. It was ... a while back. They patched me up at the pharmacy across the street, and then you brought me here. Your dad offered me a pick-me-up, one thing led to another, and ... remember?" Moe heard the pleading in his own voice. He tried to control himself. "You were what, ten? You were wearing this hot pink tracksuit with apple green stripes. You were so sweet, and really sorry about knocking me over. Remember?"

She stared at him a few minutes with a doleful look, then, slowly, shook her head.

"C'mon! You had a sister, I even danced with her. What was her name again?"

"My sister's name was Dora. She's dead now."

Dora. How could he have forgotten that name? They'd loved each other for a night, and now she was gone. He didn't dare ask how, or how long ago. All he said was, "That's awful!"

The girl nodded and went back to drying glasses.

"What about your parents?"

He was happy to hear they were doing well, aging gracefully out in Brittany, where they'd bought a small house in the middle of an orchard overlooking the sea.

"Great, great, good for them ..."

He left some coins on the counter. She put the glasses away. She said good-bye without looking up.

Night had fallen. Blackest night, with a few stars here and there as if to say, this is the sky up here since there are stars in it, though perhaps it wasn't the sky at all. Everything was quiet. Moe remembered the first time, the hubbub of voices and laughter, jokes ringing out from all sides, the impromptu dance music, Dora's kisses. Dora was dead. He wondered if he was dead, too. Were you ever sure? You lived step by step. What makes us think we're alive and nothing's happened is continuity. But as soon as that was shattered, you knew nothing, you could very well be dead and keep right on going same as ever for a while, like a ball dropped down a flight of stairs. It might bounce from step to step, but finally it was bound to stop. He chased these outlandish ideas from his head. He was alive, period. He resolved to walk all the way to end of the street this time, like a mustachioed explorer from a past era tracing a river to its source, all the way to the initial rivulet trickling out from between two rocks, to know once and for all, to dispel all doubt. As he moved forward, the night began to look like soup separating as it cooled—thin in spots, thick and clotted in others. The sidewalk rang hollow beneath his feet. He glimpsed a cat between two trash cans, a stroller chained up in a vestibule, an old abandoned refrigerator against a wall like a disused sarcophagus ... The street was almost real. Behind its facades, families were having dinner, men and women were yawning in front of TV sets, bickering, embracing, or sleeping in all too believable ways. He thought of Dora, who'd pulled him with her to the other side, behind the scenes. He had difficulty recalling her face. He'd never seen her in daylight, only beneath the muted lamps in the back room of her parents' café, and then in the darkness of her bedroom. Above all he remembered her warmth, her perfume. He stopped suddenly, letting out a cry of fear. Before him yawned a chasm into which he'd almost disappeared without a trace. He stopped himself just in time, catching hold of the last lamppost at the edge of the abyss. There was nothing at the end of Sweet Street. No lane or avenue, alley or boulevard, bridge or crossing. Only pitch-black nothingness. He froze, gazing on it for a moment, breathless, heart pounding, before finding the courage to let go of the lamppost and move back. After a few shaky steps, he managed to break into a run, then fled toward his cab. He started it up, sweating blood and tears

Georges-Olivier Châteaureynaud

to make a U-turn in a street too narrow for his huge sedan. He finally
gave up and threw it into reverse, afraid some vehicle might come up
and block the entrance to the street at any minute. None did. This
time, he deliberately looked away from the sign showing the name of
the street he'd backed onto. He didn't want to know. He was done with
Sweet Street. He'd send the next fare who asked to go there packing.
Ten minutes later he was back home. The soup was on the stove. The
girls were mooning over the bleached highlights of some TV pretty
boy. Maria had her tongue stuck out in concentration, painting a small
bouquet of anemones on a napkin ring of blond wood.

Palaiseau, February 2002

The Bronze Schoolboy

The apple of the world is not yet ripe..." or "There's no such thing as chance—*perhaps*..." Dorsay loved tossing out these sorts of phrases before select audiences, in his fine poet's voice. Yes, he had a fine voice. A bit finer, and it might have been an actor's. But it had too big a string section and not enough brass for it to carry on stage. Yet, like an actor, its owner knew how to dramatize a silence. When he said, "There's no such thing as chance—*perhaps*..." he was careful to leave the *perhaps* hanging over a pool of silence, like a line from a fishing rod.

Dorsay numbered among those men for whom a life of obscurity was no life at all. Not so much full of himself as uncertain of his own existence, he needed the stares and attentions of others to confirm it as often as possible. Of course, he took care to draw these stares, these attentions, and fasten them to himself. In this game—so vital to him—his fine voice and the effects he plied from it were far from his only assets. He'd declared himself a poet at quite a young age. And indeed—tall, erect, slender, with a face at once manly and childlike, and the somewhat vague expression of a man whose life wasn't as simple as it seemed—he was the very semblance of a poet.

What—or perhaps whom—did he resemble? The idea of a poet, let's say.

It would be a mistake to look on him and see nothing but a *poseur*.

His aphorisms and insinuating questions weren't mere verbal grenades thrown into conversation. He had given thought deep and true to the world's hypothetical unripeness. He'd quite honestly wondered if the word "chance" ever concealed anything besides our intrinsic inability to untangle the knot of causes and effects. Since no step we take can ever be completely inconsistent with those that came before, it is written from our first stumbles as rug rats that we will one day cross the threshold of this church, that nightclub, that museum, or any other place where we set foot, unremarkable as the sight of it may seem. On such things Dorsay reflected readily, and his reveries nourished his work.

It was work few concerned themselves with. He knew as much, and usually spared himself the attendant suffering. As he saw it, humanity was headed right down the tunnel of the future without a lantern. Soon, no doubt, it would fall into an abyss, and that would be just too bad. While waiting for the apocalypse to prove him right, he put out a collection every two years, on a subscription basis. Sowing words on costly paper. Even free, verse was no longer possible. But the word remained: raw, naked. He used them like unmixed colors. He stopped with the word, just as they'd stopped, for a while, with the atom in sundering the universe: because you had to stop somewhere, cling to something to catch your breath for a minute in all this metaphysical slicing and dicing. Of course, since the days of Epicurus and Leibniz, the atom had had its share...Was it time to dissect the word now? Dorsay couldn't bring himself to do so. Perhaps someday he'd take that step. Then it would be his turn to venture forward without a lantern.

The world: well, there always came a time in every life when you gave up trying to save it. And man? A runner who set out at a sprint and, after a while, slowed to a jog and was satisfied. Dorsay jogged along at the center of a small crowd of close comrades. Old friends, former mistresses, vague hangers-on. He usually printed three hundred copies of his collections, twenty on Japan imperial paper. A good village baker did better with his apricot tarts on any given holiday. Dorsay had come to see himself as *just one more* little maker of poems. *Just one more* poet, husband, lover, and father. He had come to this humility fairly early, all things considered—at the stroke of forty. A secret, shameful humility, for he'd been careful not to admit it. Would others ever admire us if we didn't throw them a line? In reality, if he kept on pretending to the uniqueness of an artistic temperament, it was to avoid disappointing his faithful flock. They needed him, he thought, as he needed them. Many people draw a powerful sense of comfort from the feeling of being close to another consciousness. He vampirized them without their knowing it, sucking the warm blood of their presence from them through painless, invisible bites. Predator and shepherd to his insiders, he didn't like any thinning of the ranks, even if these days he rarely added to them. The death of one grieved him as much as it aggrieved him.

It was exactly what he held against Hostia: she'd died without his permission. While alive, Hostia had seemed less a woman of flesh and blood than a memory incarnate. A body like a path you'd once taken. A face you now saw only in dreams. A friend—just a friend. At first, news of her disappearance caused Dorsay only middling sorrow. Not grief, even, but annoyance. "Hostia's dead, dammit! Just my luck!" At first it had seemed a minor loss. They hadn't been lovers for a long time. Her kisses, her embraces: he wasn't going to miss them. They saw each other rarely, and never alone. Two or three times a year, Hostia would show up at one of his parties, one of those weekends that seemed fortuitously to happen when he was around, but which he'd actually planned under the table. With each new publication, one of the two hundred and eighty copies on regular paper (a handsome ragstock nonetheless) was set aside for her. She'd write him to discuss it after reading it. Had those letters perhaps kept up, in a way, their former amorous commerce? At any rate, he would no longer get letters signed Hostia. He'd understood as much before the publication of the next collection. Of the two hundred and eighty ragstock copies, one would have no owner; the fireworks would be short an echo and a gleam. The unavoidable fact made its way into him. Hostia was, if not the first, one of the first to fall; with time, others would follow, and the poet's cohort would go on thinning out. It was something successful writers never considered. They advanced at the head of an army of a hundred or three hundred thousand comrades. How could they tell, when they turned to take in this enthusiastic crowd with a glance, if it was smaller than before? Dorsay knew each one of his "happy few" by name. Hostia's death had been a sign: they were getting older, just like him. He saw himself, in twenty years, staggering through a Sahara of Letters between his last ailing readers. He imagined himself abandoned to the implacable sun of posterity, which withered his works. The winds of History would scatter the words he had so lovingly chosen. Taken individually, they weren't heavy enough to withstand such torture. He'd made a fatal mistake in not stringing them together one to the next. Now there was the secret to lasting works: the mesh, the network, the weave . . . Without them, words were wisps of straw. And as expected, the prettiest were the most deceiving. "O poet! Trust not in words," he moaned. "If you don't bend them to your will, they'll impose their own . . ." Shortly after Hostia's funeral, he dove back into reading his own poems. He reemerged defeated. The words he'd thought to tame had toyed with him. He'd sorted them like stamps in an album, or plants in a herbarium. And what comfort would they have brought to Hostia, in her new abode, if by some miracle she could hear them? Poetry addressed itself not to the living, but the dead; it was something like their mail. Overwhelmed by this sudden intuition, he junked the precious volumes whose creation and publication had given his life meaning until now. When the garbage-men pulled up the next day at dawn, he almost went down to snatch his papers back. He was stopped only by the thought of his read-ers' stupefaction when they learned he hadn't bothered to keep even a single copy of each of his books. He recalled Bert Jansch, the guitarist who hadn't owned a single instrument during the most productive period of his career. In the studio as in concert, he used whatever was lent him. No doubt they took care only to give him the best... Still, the image of an offhanded Orpheus had amazed Dorsay. And what amazed him even more was that he too had dared free himself of his reverence for the sacred object. He listened to the rumble of the gar-bage truck grow faint down the cold, dark streets, taking away the fruit of twenty years of labor and rumination. Dirtied, dog-eared, soon to be crushed, his books jostled among potato peelings and sticky yogurt cups toward the ruin of a public dump. And he couldn't care less. Incredulous at first, then with a kind of arrogant elation, he saw that he really didn't give a damn. He was free.

He had to put this freedom to the test right away. He pulled a jacket on. He needed a hat—but no, it was raining; he wanted the rain, the cold, black rain, to bathe his forehead. He hadn't let himself get soaked for... twenty, maybe thirty years, even! The life he led was too comfy, too neat. How could he bear witness to the strangeness of being in the world—a heart alarmed under the stars—if he no longer felt anything? The world burned and froze, bit and scratched; it was haunted by women with mad or famished gazes, roaming up and down the streets in search of someone. Wasn't that how he'd come upon Hostia, long ago? One night, in the street. It was raining, he remembered. A cold, black rain. He slammed his door shut and ran down the stairs four at a time. Somewhere, a woman with a famished look in her eye was looking for him: Hostia's replacement, her relief, sent by fate.

He walked for a long time. He hadn't buttoned his raincoat. The rain wasn't that cold. Or that black. Actually, it fell black on the empty streets and red, green, blue, and yellow on the busy boulevards. Dorsay walked unhurriedly, searching for a face. How to know? How to tell some instinctive complicity tied you to a stranger? You'd feel it, right? Was it really something you could feel? He made an effort to remember the first moments of his meeting with Hostia. But he had to admit that if she hadn't agreed to follow him, he probably wouldn't have any memory of the encounter. Even so, he could recall little of what had preceded their embrace . . . and precious little of the embrace itself! It was like a story someone had told, leaving out all the details. They'd touched—there was that—and then they'd coupled: nothing unforgettable, nothing everlasting about it. But then how was it that Hostia belonged to his life forevermore, like a cast member in a show with but a single performance?

That night, at any rate, he met no one. Many people crossed his path. They had no faces. He probably didn't have one to them, either. Around midnight, he came to a halt in a deserted square. Before an imposing edifice stood what seemed to be the bronze statue of a child. Not an idealized child—an allegory of childhood—but, he thought to make out in the dark, a simple schoolboy in a cap and duffle coat, satchel in hand. He was idly surprised. You rarely saw statues of children, except perhaps on graves. He looked around in vain for a plaque with some information about the unusual sculpture. He vowed to find someone who'd shed some light on it . . . when it was light out, perhaps. He felt weary, with no idea of where he was, nor how far from home. What with his great idea of going out without a hat, his hair drooped in dripping strands down his forehead. He'd walked right through puddles, his leather shoes waterlogged; he was cold, tired, willing to bet he'd pay for his childish behavior with a raging cold. He looked around for a taxi. No taxis. The sign for a hotel drew his eye.

The Museum Hotel was on the other side of the street, across from the statue. Its name stood out in bluish neon letters over a glass door, through which could be glimpsed the usual faux marble lobby decked with potted plants, and one of those sofas too soft and squashy to be comfortable. The iron plaque set beside the door boasted three stars. Dorsay thought that if he could take a hot bath in the next five minutes, he had a chance of avoiding a cold. Then, for the same price, he'd stay the night. Of course he clung, like anyone else, to his little habits. He wouldn't have his mouthwash at hand, or his bedtime reading (Milosz one night, and the next Baudelaire). But hadn't he just tossed his entire body of work overboard? Surely it wasn't to batten himself down in routine again so soon! After all, perhaps life began anew with every step only for those with the courage to strike out from marked trails. If he went home tonight, either by cab or by walking an hour in the rain, he could be sure of one thing: nothing would happen. But if he pushed open this glass door and slept at the Museum Hotel like a traveler without any bags, maybe... Maybe he didn't know what, but that was exactly what he wanted: knowing nothing in advance. The principle of uncertainty that seemed to have steered his youth hadn't been working for a long time. Likely it alone had brought him discoveries, lovers, friends, everything that had really counted. Dorsay wanted it back in his life, to enrich it once more.

He crossed the street and pushed the door open. A middle-aged blonde welcomed him coolly at the front desk. Travelers without bags weren't well-loved in the hotel business. But he paid up front, and it all got better. She handed him a key to Room 305, on the third floor. He hurried up to draw as hot a bath as possible, and after the first scalding minutes lazed there a long while. When at last he got out, he rubbed himself down vigorously and donned the terry robe he'd found in the bathroom. He would've like to top off his preventative treatment with some grog, but all the minibar had was whisky. He downed two minis in two gulps as a preemptive strike, then poured another into a glass that he planned to nurse before going to bed. Glass in hand, he went to the window and drew back the curtains. On the other side of the street, atop his pedestal, the bronze schoolboy turned toward him a face streaming with bluish tears. Shocked, Dorsay shrank back, letting the curtains fall shut. Was it exhaustion, or the alcohol he'd guzzled? He thought he'd glimpsed expectation, even supplication, in the statue's gaze. He shrugged, yet almost drew back the curtains to check again. He shook his head. It was pointless: bronze schoolboys weren't expecting anything from tired old poets. He took another swallow of whisky. All that whisky, straight up! But if he'd added soda, he'd have upset his stomach. He'd be a better "heart alarmed under the stars" if he didn't have to put up with a host of other organs.

The next morning, his first thought was to congratulate himself for having dodged a head cold. He'd woken up refreshed, sinuses clear, his head astonishingly light. Next, he noticed that sacrificing his own works inspired not the slightest regret. The freedom he'd felt the night before was intact. It even seemed that he hadn't gone far enough in getting rid of just those copies. He would have liked to destroy everything. Part of him rebelled at the idea. Everything? Erase it all? But all that was his life! protested the familiar voice that had whispered to him, one by one, the words enshrined on the Japan imperial and creamy ragstock of his collections. Another voice croaked that the copies in circulation weren't worth worrying about. Too thick and stiff, neither Japan imperial nor ragstock lent themselves to wrapping fish; for the same reason, they'd make catastrophic toilet paper, but they'd right tables, stuff shoes, and light pipes well. As for the copies that found no practical use, like all things in the world, they'd dissolve in the river of time, a river of acid.

Dorsay had breakfast in his room. Before going to bed, he'd taken care to lay his clothes out by the radiator. This morning they were wrinkled but dry. He dressed and readied to leave the hotel. As he was, in truth, incorrigible, he couldn't help but secretly draft an entry on the establishment for a future history of French literature: "The Museum Hotel—that ordinary spot—became the site of a veritable *satori* when poet Jean-Pierre Dorsay took refuge there one November night in 19—"

A girl with a healthy glow had replaced the wary woman of the night before at the front desk. He settled his breakfast and the three minis of whisky. As she was handing him his change, he noticed that her nails were well-manicured. Not overlong, but well-manicured. How he loved women's nails! The ones with dodgy nails appalled him. He'd never be able to bear an affair with a woman whose nails were black or even grayish. He shivered at the thought. But this girl's were flawless, from where he stood. He lifted his gaze to study her. She had pleasing features. Her pink cheeks—almost pink—contrasted with her pale throat and forehead. She was no less delightful for not quite being fashionable. She conjured up old prints, English paintings— that kind of thing. He smiled at her. She smiled back. An innocent smile. For a few years now, he'd been able to detect innocence in others, to sniff it out like the scent of a rare herb. His expression darkened. Faced wih this young woman, he felt impure, unworthy, his soul all warty and callused. He spied sudden worry in her eyes. She'd been surprised by the change in his expression, and was wondering if she'd done something wrong. O innocence! He abruptly blushed. Foolishly, he set down one of the bills she'd returned on the faux marble countertop. Then, muttering a vague good-bye, he turned and left.

He crossed the road double-quick, without looking right or left. He hadn't heard a single car since waking. When he was on the island, in the shadow of the statue, he stopped. The bronze schoolboy stood out against a pure blue sky with pure white clouds. The pale sun seemed suspended from the heavens' vault by a plastic line. High, high up, Dorsay saw the unmoving silver cross of a plane. He thought to see in the Currier-and-Ives sky an intent, a kind of crushing irony, as though someone were mocking him from the heights of heaven above. He ceased his scrutiny of the skies, and turned his gaze back on the bronze schoolboy. At once, his heart began to pound in his chest. It was him. Him, ten years old, in that hat with earflaps Aunt Marthe had given him to go with the Christmas duffel coat from grandmama. He recognized his satchel, his scarf, and his canvas hiking boots. Many hiking boots had been sold that year. They seemed to have come straight from some military surplus, which the kids had liked.

"Sir—"

He lowered his gaze. The girl from the hotel was standing before him, holding out the bill he'd given her a moment ago. He'd made a mistake ... or she didn't want it, for innocent reasons.

"Sir, you forgot this."

"I didn't forget it. It's for you."

"For me? But—"

"It's a tip. Don't you ever get tips at that hotel?"

"I don't know. I'm just helping out my aunt for the first time—"

"Ah. Well, then, this is your first tip. You'll surely get more, nice as you are!" He bit his lip. She wouldn't get tips that big often. Unless she was *really* nice ...

"Well ... thanks!" She folded the bill and stuck it in her pocket.

"You're welcome. Say—"

"Yes?"

Those fawn's eyes, that young voice, that confident tone. He hesitated. She'd think he was insane. But he didn't have to go about it so directly ... He pointed at the statue. "Do you know who that kid is?"

She glanced at the bronze schoolboy. "No idea. I don't know this neighborhood. I came from Niort to help out my aunt, so—"

"Don't you think ... don't you think he looks like me?"

She looked up again, and this time stared at the statue longer. At last she said, "It's hard to tell, since I didn't know you then. Why? Is it you?"

"No. I was just kidding."

She didn't laugh. Which was worse, coming across crazy or stupid?

"You're very sweet," he said. "What's your name?"

"Julia."

"Julia? Well, Julia, I hope you'll buy yourself something you like with that money." Was he ever in form today! To think he'd once considered himself a seducer.

"Sure ... Can I go back to the hotel now? Someone might be waiting to pay—"

"Of course! Off you go!"

Before going through the glass door, she looked back again to thank him, flashing the wadded-up bill. A little girl! He shut his eyes. He reflected that he'd been left to his own devices once more. He could pretend he'd never seen the statue, and walk away quickly. If only there'd been a taxi in sight! All he'd have to do was get inside and bark his address at the driver. But a taxi wasn't the only solution. He could walk, like yesterday. Just around the bend, and everything would probably seem familiar again, fall into place ... But what was he on about? What was out of place? What needed to be *normal* again? Everything *was* normal. He'd let himself be unnerved by a coincidence, that bronze whippersnapper up there, with his false airs of ... Quite simply, he'd gotten in his head that it looked like him. Eyes still shut, he thrust out his hand. His fingers brushed the pedestal's rough stone. The statue was still there. It existed, of course. It existed with all the atoms of all its molecules. He couldn't pretend to ignore it. There was but one way to have it rejoin the ordinary things from whose ranks it had stepped to torment him: he had to give a name to the child it depicted. He walked around it, looking for the plaque he couldn't find last night, or a signature. After all, statues were signed! Once he knew the artist's name, he'd have the mystery all cleared up before long. Suddenly, the idea came to him that there might be a link between the statue and the museum before which it stood. He turned from one to contemplate the other. He'd barely spared the building a glance till now. It was a handsome edifice, of medium size and yet perfectly proportioned. Its neoclassical façade was adorned with columns and a pediment of indistinct figures that nevertheless gave off a happy impression. Without lingering to inspect them—in a place like this, they had to be the usual mythological suspects—Dorsay swiftly crossed the street. In a few bounds, he climbed the steps that led him to a great portal whose leaves were mostly open. He entered the lobby, looking around for a ticket counter, and soon saw a sort of booth or cage of glass and lacquered wood that surely served the purpose. He walked up to it. The cage was empty. There was every indication it usually housed the person whose job it was to sell visitors tickets and souvenirs: to either side of a boiled cardboard blotter lay a book of tickets and bundles of leaflets and brochures he couldn't make out the writing on, as well as envelopes that probably held postcards. He pressed his face to the glass for a better view of the inside of the cabin. He could see no personal effects that might lead him to believe whoever manned (or womanned) it was somewhere in the building and only momentarily away from the booth for one reason or another: a quick trip to the bathroom, idle chatter by the coffee machine, or a service issue to be taken up with management. Dorsay would've liked to have one of these possibilities to cling to, which the situation, in its bareness, did not allow him: there was no one to sell him admission or give him information about the statue. No one at all? The ordinary sound of a mop and bucket rekindled his hopes. A cleaning woman had just appeared at the far end of the lobby.

"Ma'am! Ma'am! Is there anyone up front?"

Was she from some far corner of the world, or even another altogether? She spoke no language that Dorsay knew. And yet she didn't lack common sense. As he was gesturing wildly at the empty cage, she urged him, with a single, briskly eloquent movement of her chin, to pay no heed and enter the first room of the exhibition.

Kids' outfits of all ages, swaddling clothes, diapers, and onesies, all kinds of woolens, bibs, pajamas, and bodysuits, variously frayed, worn, and unraveling—these were what the first display cases Dorsay bent over featured. The frames of theses cases were of the finest oak, and outfitted with thick glass and heavy locks, as though they held jewels or manuscripts of incredible value. Moving along, Dorsay found even more display cases. In these, with a piety worthy of a collection of Noah's fishing hooks or Xenon's arrowheads, were bits and pieces of toys in a neat row. The axles of tiny cars, torsos of pilots exiled from their cockpits, gas-station signs, railroad-crossing gates, canoes with garish redskins, surviving pawns from the shipwreck of a board game, corsairs with gaping holes midhull, nurses eternally well-behaved in their unmussable skirts, the heads of high-wire electricians, battleships on casters, spavined sawhorses . . . Dorsay understood perfectly that he was fainting. In fact, a mist seemed to be descending from the coffered ceiling, but the sight of this didn't fool him. He congratulated himself on losing consciousness in utter lucidity: he'd recognized the toys, and had decided to faint. For the sake of form, he tried to hang onto the top of the display case. He managed only to slow his fall a bit, or perhaps stage it better, like children who practice their dying fall artistically before the wardrobe mirror.

He was lying on a sofa, and his head was in a woman's lap. She was stroking his forehead, brushing his hair back with two gentle fingers.

Georges-Olivier Châteaureynaud

She was sitting too far back for him to see her face.

"What happened?"

He knew quite well, but he wanted to hear the stranger's voice. Besides, she wasn't a total stranger to him: he recognized her perfume, was sure of having smelled it once before in a woman's arms ... But which one? Hostia, perhaps? It had been so long, my God, so long!

"You fainted. The watchmen brought you here."

The voice was deep and beautiful. He didn't like twittery voices. O Verlaine! "And her voice, distant, calm, and deep ..." He felt relieved; the voice that had responded wasn't Hostia's. Hostia had a rather deep voice, too, but less husky, more velvety.

"Who are you?"

"I'm the director of the museum."

"And where am I?"

"You're in my office."

"But this museum—"

"Shh, don't get excited. Relax. Isn't it nice here, just like this?"

The gentle fingers slipped from his forehead to his right temple and began lightly massaging it. Dorsay was torn between the anxious curiosity this place inspired in him, and a languor close to the utter relaxation of a well-fed infant or a sated lover. The woman's voice, her perfume, the warmth of her thighs beneath his neck, her calming caresses, produced a hypnotic effect on him. He felt like he was about to go under again, but voluptuously this time, as one might under soft eiderdown. And yet the incongruity of his situation provoked a flash of pride.

"Ms. Director, what do you think ..."

The woman smiled. He knew without seeing her that she was smiling, and when she spoke again, the almost tender irony of her voice proved him right.

"Let yourself go," she said. "Forget everything. Here, with your head in my lap, you're right where you belong at last, and I fully in my role—"

"No!"

He wasn't sure what rebellion of his entire being lifted him from where he lay. But just as he was about to turn toward the director and order her to explain this so-called museum, this building's true purpose and the role she'd boasted of playing with regard to him, his strength deserted him. He fell to a crouch at the foot of the sofa, out of breath, about to be sick.

"Really, you're impossible!" She rose in turn. He heard the sound of her heels on the parquet floor. "I'm going to call an ambulance. They'll take you to the hospital, if that's what you want."

The voice was curt now. It no longer held the complicit inflections he thought he'd heard earlier, even when she was mocking him.

"No—no, not the hospital," he stammered in a strangled whisper.

She stopped, picked up a telephone, and dialed a number. "Hello? Emergency? This is the museum. One of our visitors has just had a little fainting spell."

"Don't!"

The voice continued, implacable. "How long? All right, I'll notify the watchmen; they'll keep an eye out for the ambulance."

She hung up.

"You're ... mean!"

Could she even hear him? With great strides, she crossed the room again, and passed near him without stopping, in a whiff of perfume. Her indistinct figure disappeared through a tall padded door.

It was as though, in leaving, she'd taken Dorsay's weakness with her. He got enough strength back to stand up. He was tempted to follow the director, but what was point, since the damage was done? Part of the room had remained out of his sight until now. He swept the room with his gaze. It contained a library with overloaded shelves, armoires, and assorted filing cabinets, and an executive desk on which great inventory ledgers bound in black canvas stood beside piles of documents and photos. There were also masses of documents that awaited cataloguing, in boxes or stacks, plopped here and there on chairs, even the floor.

Two windows overlooked the street. He walked over to one and spotted the bronze schoolboy, this time from behind. Beyond the traffic island and the statue, he made out the glass door of the Museum Hotel. He had a fleeting thought of the girl. With its waters of unmoving asphalt, the street seemed a river on whose other shore she awaited him like an unlikely little fiancée. He shrugged. Always with the fancies! He walked to the desk. He picked himself out easily from a group of young people in the first photo his gaze fell upon. Royan '65. In Bermuda shorts and a short-sleeved shirt, he held a short brunette with blandly pretty features in a tight embrace. He'd forgotten her name, but remembered that in the end she'd preferred Macassar. Good old Macassar! He was one of Dorsay's three hundred subscribers. Banker. All-time ladies' man. He rarely missed a launch party. He'd show up, jovial, the *Financial Times* sticking out of his blazer pocket. He never stayed long. "Bad timing. Got a date. A real squealer. I insisted on coming, but I have to run. Save me a Japan imperial, won't you?" A faithful friend, Macassar, but never introduce him to your woman. Dorsay had never introduced him to Fulvia. He put the photo back down. In the next he was sitting at a table, probably at La Palette, with Lozec'h and Doblinon. The young guard. The dream team. That photo was from the '70s. Before Lozec'h made it big. They were rapier-thin, all three. Thin and well–dressed, and by God, funny-looking! But what a fire in their eyes! He was touched. Here was the whole of youth in a snapshot: hope, fervor, and now . . . What? A novelist with a print run of a hundred thousand copies, a poet of three hundred, and a philosopher of a hundred twenty-five. A hundred twenty-five in a good year, because Doblinon's recent Heraclitus was, well, sorry, a bear to get through. He felt a prickling in his eyes. He sniffed, and went on to another photo. He started. Him and Hostia, naked, entwined on a bed in black and white. It wasn't pornographic—just private. So private that Dorsay couldn't imagine who'd taken it. He hadn't asked himself that question with the two before because they hadn't at all been of a private nature. Anyone could've snuck away from the group or the table for a moment and snapped a shot. But this third photo was completely different. He was sure *no one* had ever taken a picture of them like this, him and Hostia, even without their knowing. Since Hostia was still living in the dorms then, and he was single, they'd always met up at his place, where there were no two-way mirrors or voyeur's peepholes. Besides, their affair had remained a secret, without either of them actually meaning for it to turn out that way. Well, then? What eyes had spied on their embrace? What hands had framed and captured it? How many similar photos were there in this bundle, these piles, these filing cabinets? Admittedly, the indiscreet image was still almost chaste by the standards of the age. But if, in fact, as Dorsay had reason to suspect, the material in the museum's collections consisted of his entire life, there had to be other, less "artistic" ones . . . They had no right! The simple fact of that snapshot belonging to a third party without Dorsay's consent amounted to a criminal offense. Privacy? It was first among the rights of man, from which the rest followed! And yet, amidst his anger, he was flooded with doubt. Hadn't he, over the course of his poetry collections, taken an oath of shamelessness? That pathetic and accursed specimen, the authentic archetype of the Artist—wasn't it that poor devil of a flasher by the high school who offered up to sudden gusts and the laughter of little girls a strip of trembling flesh? Unless he'd only pretended, only aped the poets with his phony words set in the sham ivory of the page . . . A pretend-poet: a fine fate!

Georges-Olivier Châteaureynaud

An ambulance siren brutally yanked him from his reflections. Photo in hand, he ran to the window. That was it, it had come for him; all this was of a piece: the blue and white van with its garish flashing lights and electric shrieking, and the photo showing him and Hostia cheek to cheek and belly to belly. His calling was reduced to an eccentricity and his loves to casual encounters. The ambulance parked in front of the museum. Two men sprang out and hurried around the back of the vehicle, which they opened to pull out a stretcher. Dorsay realized that if he remained standing here like a stick-in-the-mud, in two minutes they'd come and take him away on that stretcher despite his protests. He thought he heard, closing on him in succession, the doors of the ambulance, then the hospital, then the common room where they'd coop him up with actual patients suffering from disgusting, terrifying actual diseases . . . He tore out of the director's office.

Much later, when Dorsay ventured out of his broom closet, he saw that night had fallen and the museum was closed. At night, the building was placed under the surveillance of a single soused watchman. Curled up at the back of a booth wallpapered with truck photos, he was sleeping with his head on arms crossed atop a table, his slumber shot through with terrible visions. Sometimes he woke with a cry. Then he remained upright for a moment, wide-eyed and covered in sweat, before plunging in again like a man fishing for horrors. It went without saying he was no bother to Dorsay, who borrowed his flashlight and visited the rooms of the museum one by one. These explorations confirmed all his suspicions. He came back down embittered from the attic, where all the pains and humiliations that lay ahead in his final days were evoked. It was one thing to know what abyss we were all drifting toward, and another to see ourselves sinking there through letters, documents, photos, and objects testifying to our decline. The poet's cane, his hearing aid, his supporter underwear. Worse yet, the exhibit didn't settle that obscene question no creator could evade: would posterity remember his name? This museum—absurd, *in posse*, or premature—limited itself to recounting the life of Jean-Pierre Dorsay. Nothing in the heaps of relics it held led him to suppose that they would be worshipped one day. Still, he hadn't hesitated to look for the slightest trace of the survival of his body of work after his death, which he now knew down to the day and hour, reasonably distant in and of themselves . . . Emptying the file cabinets, upending boxes, he'd tracked the posthumous reprinting, the theses, the redeeming essays, the least article that would acknowledge him. In vain. The period covered by the Dorsay collection stopped short at the date of his death. When at last he was convinced no evidence existed, hope returned. No hand had yet been played. His adventure had but pushed back by a few years the lid of smoke or fog that kept all mortals from seeing the future. Someday, in a few hundred or even few thousand lofty souls, his name might awaken the same fraternal impulse he always felt on hearing those of his favorite poets. Nothing guaranteed it, but nothing ruled it out. The idea perked him up considerably. As a result, other curiosities came back to him. Since he hadn't reached the end of the road, would he write again, love again, before the distressing deadlines of the attic? He began emptying drawers and cabinets again, without finding anything at first. Finally, as he was losing hope, his gaze fell on a black and white photo quite similar to the one that showed him in Hostia's arms. But it wasn't Hostia nestled up against him, nor any of the other women in his past. Nor was it a stranger. In fact, he had met her this morning for the first time in his life. It was the young woman come from the provinces to help her aunt at the hotel, the girl with rosy cheeks who'd stepped out of an English print. Dorsay's heart filled with joy. If life still had such a godsend in store, then he wanted to face it once more, with its gray vagaries and black certainties.

He slipped the photo under his shirt and made his way back to the closet where the watchman was moaning in his sleep.

"Wake up! Good God, wake up!"

"Huh? What? Who are you?" The man's eyes widened at this apparition, for once not even monstrous.

"A visitor. I didn't notice what time it was; you have to let me out, I want to go home!"

The poor lout did as he said without being asked twice.

"Good night!" Dorsay yelled back from the bottom of the steps.

"Good night, yeah right!" the watchman grumbled.

He locked the monumental door and drew back into the depths of the museum to pick up the thread of his nightmares again, as a reader might get back to a book.

The night was clear and cold. Dorsay crossed the street, skirting the pedestal of the bronze schoolboy. The Museum Hotel was still open. He walked in. The hotelkeeper welcomed him with a surprise not entirely free of suspicion. A traveler without bags who slept in the same place twice: what was he hiding?

"I'll pay in advance, like last night," he told her.

"As you wish," she replied, relieved.

He didn't have enough cash on him. He paid with a debit card. "I'm going to go out and have a bite before bed."

"There are hardly any restaurants in the neighborhood. I can bring a meal tray up to your room."

He wondered what it would consist of. Parma ham, salmon steak, apple pie? In truth, he felt ready to devour almost anything.

"And wine, too, please—white."

"Chablis?"

"Chablis."

"Very good, sir. I'll bring it up in half an hour?"

"Perfect. Um...your niece isn't here, is she? Maybe she stepped out?"

The hotelkeeper looked him up and down with an icy eye, all her prejudices instantly restored. What did this fellow want with the girl? "My niece?"

"Yes, the young lady I saw this morning. She's quite friendly!"

"She's only here in the daytime."

"Ah! So I'll have the pleasure of seeing her again tomorrow morning, then...Make sure the Chablis is nice and chilled, won't you?"

"I will. I keep it in the fridge."

As he slipped his key into the door to his room—305, the same as last night—Dorsay let out a victorious little laugh. The old lady could wrinkle her nose all she wanted; the girl with the rosy cheeks would inevitably be his. It was written—or rather, photographed!

He walked in, hung his raincoat and his blazer in the closet, kicked off his shoes. On his breast, between shirt and undershirt, the photo rustled. He undid two buttons and removed it carefully from its hiding place. He gazed upon it. The young woman was beautiful— so beautiful! And he was...well, less handsome, of course, and not as young, but as though transfigured by the brilliance of his companion, regenerated by her grace. He pulled the bedspread back and hid the photo under the pillow. The meal was in...half an hour? He had time for a bath. He turned on the tap. While the water ran, he walked to the window. He drew back the curtains. In the moonlight, with a gaze turned directly on him, the bronze schoolboy was smiling.

Lozère, December 1994-January 1995

The Pavilion and the Linden

Upon his return from a war in the course of which he had, as was his custom, defeated many an enemy and reduced many a citadel to gravel and ash, King Guita wished to take the air beneath a certain aged pavilion. In the most solitary courtyard of the palace it stood, of simple stone, its floor adorned by a mosaic of no great originality. No legend clung to its grounds. A linden hung over the pavilion, whose furnishings in their entirety consisted of a single wooden bench. In his now-distant childhood days, King Guita had spent many a long and easy evening there, playing in the wan scent of lime at his governess' feet.

When, on his return, he found the pavilion leveled and the linden felled, he flew into a royal fury. He summoned the palace architect and demanded he explain himself. In a quavering voice, the man pleaded for his life. Wasn't it his duty, foreseeing as he did His Majesty's victory and the treasure he would certainly bring back, to enlarge the palace storehouses? And since that courtyard, forgotten by one and all, with its crumbling pavilion and its ailing linden, adjoined one of the storerooms already overflowing with the spoils of earlier wars . . .

King Guita saw that the architect believed himself to have acted rightly, and so for a time spared his life. But a feeling of irreparable loss overcame him whenever his thoughts returned to the coolness of tile beneath his knees and the scent a light wind from the tapering leaves wafted toward him. Then it seemed that he had lost much more than a city, more even than a province: something like his kingdom's secret heart. One day, when this feeling assailed him with greater force than usual, his gaze settled on the architect. He frowned, and had him put to death.

He ordered the man's successor to erect the pavilion once more in a faithfully recreated courtyard, and to have a tree, like the first in every way, transplanted there. When all was done at last, he went one night and sat alone on the wooden bench. And lingered there, sniffing the air in vain. The tree's very odor seemed foreign and unnatural to him. When the light had grown so dim that the mosaic might no longer be made out, he let himself slip from the bench onto the floor, onto the very spot where he had spent so many peaceful hours as a child. He ran his fingers over the mosaic's surface without finding the same terrain of tiny ridges, the same infinitesimal fissures, the same traces of wear his fingertips remembered. The pitiless ruler wept. He who had never before trembled was terrified. The pavilion and the linden, so lately but a memory, were a reality once more. Suddenly the king doubted his powers of recall, his own name, his very kingship. And if he were not King Guita, who was he, by God, and what was he doing in this strange palace on this hostile night?

To ensure he might never again suffer so nightmarish a feeling, he forbade henceforth any change, be it even in the tiniest detail, to the city. It could of course grow, and maintaining it would always be a sacred duty, but what already was would forever so remain, enjoying inalienable rights and total precedence over what was yet to come, over all the unformed and inchoate future.

The king's character and project seemed to capture the imaginations of his subjects and their children, as for many years, almost unto the present day, his will was done. Today, few dare venture into the city's distant heart where, on days of high wind, the last buildings from the

Founder's era finish breaking apart, waves subsiding in a sea of rubble. Abandoned, too, are the plans to preserve the knotted and dangerous maze of medieval alleys. We have our people's long allegiance to the folly of a single man to thank for this our dwelling place: the sole existing urban order aimed at totality, a concentric and cumulative keep, time and the city turning ideally round a memory like a wheel around an axle.

Lozère, December 1990

Another Story

For anyone who feels deeply about property, there's nothing like owning an island. Nothing comes closer to pure possession; nothing else goes quite so far in confirming the illusion of sovereign, absolute selfhood. When a man has almost everything, buying an island is the next step.

That's what Erwin Laurençais did. To sniff out where the rich get their riches, you have to be one of them, or else few things seem so vague and nebulous as money. You see it all around, bathing those who have it in its light and warmth, filling and transfiguring them . . . And yet the average man, who manages food, clothes, shelter, warmth, and transport without undue worry or exertion, will sometimes want a slightly clearer idea of the gulf between himself and the truly wealthy. A pointless, even spiteful, curiosity. Just as well, then, that money isn't my subject. The Laurençais fortune plays but an incidental part in this tale. Erwin Laurençais was so rich he'd bought himself no tiny islet, but a good-sized island.

I went there at his invitation—by air, to my acute dismay. You'll find no creature more earthbound than I. I'm so naturally averse to flying I usually give up on any trip that can't be made by road, rail, or sea—but the area around the island happened to be so dangerous the only way in was by plane or helicopter. For Laurençais, and for his legend, I made an exception. The money that pours into his hands drives him to undertake a certain number of *secretly necessary* things almost no one else on earth could see to completion. A hunch about these things is essential to understanding the great eccentric billionaires...For a billionaire (I believe the word falls short), Laurençais was unique in this respect: he wasn't satisfied with owning the most expensive things or mingling with the most famous people. He loved surrounding himself with what was least known as well, objects and people alike. I found his invitation flattering. I am a writer—a French writer, to boot—two qualities worth less than nothing these days. I was astounded that a Laurençais (despite the sound of his surname, a Venezuelan) wished to make my acquaintance.

Laurençais' island is beautiful, in its way—thanks to him. It was once a picturesque rock, an actual desert isle: pretty mountains, but no shelter, no beach, no fresh water, and as a result, stunted vegetation. Laurençais' money changed everything. Planes brought in soil for gardens and meadows now irrigated by processed seawater. For private use, Laurençais built a desalination plant that would've been enough for the average emirate.

On the island's most stunning side, where Laurençais had chosen to build his palace, a steep and sudden drop lay between the coast and the line of reefs barring the seaward approach. The tycoon could have flattened the coast with dynamite and brought in all the sand he wanted, but nothing in the world would have kept the ocean from licking the shore clean. Never mind, then—Laurençais had a second shoreline, set back from the first, designed, dug, and shaped to his liking. Beside an artificial lagoon, a landscaped beach secured the master of the house and his guests all the charms the site supposedly refused them. The sand was so fine each grain seemed handpicked. Nearby, the birds that sang above their heads were, like the trees where they dwelled, chosen from a catalogue. So were the people...but I'll get back to that.

I mentioned a palace; don't go picturing alabaster columns, marble staircases, and golden roofs. In Laurençais' jaded gaze, luxury—the spirit of luxury—had left materials behind to seek refuge in form. He wasn't completely indifferent to materials, of course: for the most part his palace was made of solid mahogany and pristinely white, freshly cast concrete. Yet with this bias in mind, the architect Benito Guardicci (yes, a relative of the famous artisan glassmaker) was able to work wonders. The residence he created for Laurençais was beautiful without being reminiscent of any other. Its beauty was for those who lived there. As the days went by, you became aware of the balance, the harmony emanating from the rectangular structures amid the rocks and the greenery. At first, they seemed scattered haphazardly about the lagoon, itself irregularly shaped. You had to stay there a while to realize that Guardicci had conceived it all with a rich man in mind, for Laurençais and his select guests, in accordance with the truth of the setting: a world without neighbors, prying eyes, or unwanted onlookers.

I didn't quite know why I'd been invited. For my talent, they'd said, my works. I wanted to believe it. Nevertheless, everyone else in my batch enjoyed actual international fame, except me. I won't name names. A golden voice, a sex symbol, a director, a guitar hero; two champions, one in boxing and the other in tennis; a Nobel laureate in medicine; a painter only slightly less well-known than Leonardo or Vermeer; a physicist, all torso, whom the media that year claimed was Einstein reincarnated—there were ten of us all told. Needless to say, none of these people traveled without an entourage: lovers, mistresses, confidants, nannies, secretaries, trainers, doctors, and fortune-tellers...With diplomacy and a firm smile, Laurençais' butler had managed to spread the crowd of underlings out in the estate's many annexes. I was the only one who'd come alone. Which meant that I was scared stiff at first among egos all bloated to varying degrees. Most knew nothing about me and mistook me for a bartender. I cleared this up three or four times before everything got sorted out. Since Laurençais vouched for me, granting me a status like their own, be it in ever so narrow and obscure a field as French literature, the celebrities all followed suit. They lowered their guard and showed themselves for what they really were: creatures superspecialized in their chosen fields and by the same token off-true, even crippled, at once pitiful and admirable, so many products of a limited shelf life. Take the guitarist. He was from a working-class background. A hard worker, he honed riffs on his lucky Telecaster eight hours a day while smoking joints his roadie-dealer rolled. He allowed himself a line in the evening the way people had a drink after the daily grind. We became friendly, and he didn't forget to offer me a sniff from his little box. I held up my glass of scotch. He shook his head in sorrow.

"That stuff's poison!"

I also liked the porn star, an oversensitive young woman, plaintive beneath her statuesque exterior. But she had a sense of humor about herself, her line of work, and her smutty fame.

"God," she'd moan, "I grew up wearing little white socks and blue dresses and crying at *Bambi,* had my first kiss at nineteen, and now I'm the biggest slut on the planet. What's wrong with me? Eew! A rash! Get my doctor quick, he's around here somewhere. Tell him I'm dying!"

I didn't hit it off with everyone. The golden voice really annoyed me, and no primate deserved to be compared to the boxing champ. I found the Moldo-Wallachian director, whom I believed and still believe to be a great artist, standoffish and incapable of camaraderie. At any rate, an unusual apparition soon made me forget my disappointment. We'd been there for two days when a young woman literally sprang from the lagoon. I happened to be watching Laurençais when she joined us. I thought I spied great relief in the eyes of our host. He introduced the newcomer to us as Ligeia. She greeted us with brusque timidity, surprising for such a beauty. For though I'd called the actress statuesque, Ligeia gave the word an altogether different, more impressive meaning. The actress—call her Cindy, or Christie—embodied an admittedly stunning but eminently consumable, even comestible kind of femininity. On first sight, everything about her woke in men a predatory instinct strongly tinged with almost cannibalistic overtones. But when you met her in the flesh, this initial impulse soon faded away because of the irony she employed at her own expense, and others' when needed. In real life, Cindy/Christie was only sexy for the first three minutes, before becoming endearing and sisterly.

Ligeia was another matter. A fierce presence, an aura of sexuality heady as an odor that persisted after she walked away. For I never saw her stay in any one place for long: she was always passing through. In the same way, I never heard her start a conversation of her own initiative. She answered, with a single precise sentence requiring no clarification or additions, then fell silent, as though she'd discharged a tiresome duty. I had to admit it wasn't very pleasant. Her charm lay elsewhere. What we mean today by the word "charm" in no way describes what she exuded. You'd have to restore to the word the powerful associations it possessed in antiquity: a purely physical appeal so violent it was frightening. By day she lived in the water and wore only a G-string. By night, she donned a tunic, very simple and very short. The muscles of her arms, legs, and belly were free of the softness and tenderness of Cindy/Christie's. She looked like one of Arno Brecker's valkyries. Even while admiring her you thought to detect something not alienating but alien, something animal and disconcerting that confounded compliment. Who was she? Where had she been born? Who'd raised her? I tried to imagine her at the age of ten. It was one of my favorite games: picturing how the adults fate put on my path had looked as children. With Ligeia, no image came to mind; I found it impossible to conjure her up in any normal professional environment. She gave me the impression of being able to exist only the way I saw her—that is, more than half-naked in or near the water. Laurençais had left us in the dark as to their exact relationship. There was no evidence that she was his mistress. Two or three unassuming and very young things filled that role, behind the scenes. Was Ligeia his daughter, then? She didn't look like him at all. His niece? His ward? I wound up asking her. She was slow to answer.

"Erwin? He...He fished me out of the sea!" she said at last, unsmiling. With that, she left me standing there and dove into the blue lagoon where she spent most of her time.

I never go anywhere without a good pair of binoculars. Thanks to them, I feel like I'm flipping through a picture book rather than observing reality. The general outline of things looks different. Planes of vision remain distinct instead of blending into one another. A clearly decipherable world emerges, with the false and beautiful lucidity of childlike perception. I liked to follow Ligeia with my binoculars from my room. To say she swam like a dream was an understatement. But I wasn't simply struck by the excellence of her front crawl. In the water, her face conveyed a tranquility totally lacking on land. Another woman revealed herself, resurfaced, far from the world of men...

One morning, as I was spying on her movements from my room, an incident occurred. Having swum the lagoon from one end to the other, along the craggy and impassable original shore, I saw her plunge a few dozen yards from the edge. She often went skin diving. I expected to see her come back up at any moment, but time went by and I began getting impatient. I soon panicked, dropping the binoculars and picking them up again, straining my eyes to spot the figure that would convince me my fears were ungrounded. Without success. Had I just seen someone drown? Perhaps there was still time to do something? A feeling of responsibility oppressed me. I spotted Laurençais talking to a gardener in the path beneath my balcony. I called out to them, and tried to communicate the fear that gripped me. Faced with their incomprehension, I jumped down onto the path to reach them more quickly and explain myself.

"What? Someone drowned?"

"Maybe. Over there. Ligeia—"

"Ligeia? Impossible! Where did you say?"

"Over there!"

Laurençais turned to look where I was pointing. A vague worry left his face. "Have no fear, my friend. If you saw her disappear over there, she's completely safe!"

"But—"

The Venezuelan clapped me kindly on the shoulder. "Don't worry! She went for a rest in the grotto. It's an artificial lagoon, as I'm sure you're aware . . ."

He dismissed the gardener with a look.

"When they were digging the lagoon," he said, "I had them make an underwater grotto . . . We all have a fantasy like that, about one thing or another. Now that mine has been satisfied, I hardly ever go there. Besides, Ligeia's sort of made it her own private spot. She spends a lot of time there."

A submarine grotto, with lighting, decorations, and a sound system, no doubt. I'd forgotten I was dealing with a billionaire.

Laurençais took a cell phone from his pocket. "Let's check, just to be sure."

He dialed and waited, shooting me a sideways glance. "You can visit if you'd like. There's a stairway, too, of course! Now, what can she be doing—ah! *Holà, eres tu? Como estas? Muy bien! Figa te que el señor . . .*"

The conversation was brief.

Georges-Olivier Châteaureynaud

"She had a good laugh when I told her you'd seen her drown," he said, putting the phone away.

"She's quite an individual...individual!" I said. "What does she do in life?"

"What does she do in life? Since you're a writer, I assume you've already pondered the strangeness of that expression, right?"

"Indeed I have."

"Indeed, it reveals the full extent of its strangeness when applied to a creature like her. What does Ligeia do in life? What do lions do in life? Or wild geese?" He laughed with relish. "Ligeia swims in the lagoon, she haunts the underwater grotto, and when she comes back to the surface she snorts and falls asleep in the sun. *Voilà!*"

"But how did she come into your life?"

"It was I who came into hers, to her misfortune, I fear." He fell silent. He'd intrigued me, of course.

"What do you mean by that?"

"No more for today. I must confess something. I didn't ask you here for the same reasons as the others." He gestured offhandedly toward the buildings where the demigods were lazing about. "I collect stars. For me, these people are objects I line up on a shelf in my head. Handsome items, of course! Mostly. But you're something else. I have a story I can't keep to myself. I can't imagine dying without having told it to someone. And you're one of the people I plan to tell. However, it isn't time yet."

"If you've read my work," I said, "you must know I'm not much interested in true stories."

"Precisely. Precisely!"

"I'm leaving soon. You'll have to make up your mind."

"The main thing is knowing what you'll make of this story."

"Probably another story, if it sets the little wheels in my mind spinning."

"There you have it! Another story! And I'll also tell two or three of your professional brethren, who will do the same, I'm sure. Thus Ligeia's true story will give birth to three or four fictional ones. People will read this one, or that, in New York, or Mexico, or Paris, without knowing they're reading a variation on a true story. Anyway, no story is entirely true, or entirely false. I want Ligeia's story to make its way around the world. I want it to escape the dangerously close circle of those who know it. When the time comes, you'll help me!"

To keep my curiosity at bay in the days that followed, I settled for Cindy/Christie. She had to have a story, too. I undertook to make her tell it. But the life of Cindy/Christie, as told by hers truly, was but a humongous, incoherent, and wildly proliferating lie. She'd gone through every conceivable kind of upbringing, every kind of mis-fortune, and every excuse, but also every rebellion, every ambition, and every kind of courage. She was Juliette, the victim of universal lust; she was Justine, priding herself on challenging the status quo by displaying her own infectious lubricity. Then she turned sweet and amusing when you stopped analyzing her soul to concentrate on her boo-boos and ailments.

Laurençais knew life and in lordly fashion assessed the loss of earn-ings a week of inactivity implied for the sacred monsters he hosted. A practical lord: the lavish gifts he gave his guests at their farewell party could easily be converted into cash. We could choose to keep them, or exchange them for dollars, yen, or Swiss francs, in which case they'd be used for the next lucky visitors. How many guests with their checks in their pockets had pretended to gush over a Sèvres vase or contemporary sculpture they'd leave behind without regret?

Georges-Olivier Châteaureynaud

When it was my turn, I played the game as sanctimoniously as anyone else. I found myself faced with a check, or selections from *The Odyssey*. Flustered at first, I clapped like a child when, beneath a sorry-looking binding, all sooty and crumbling, I recognized an authentic incunabulum, all the more precious because ancient authors, along with their great contemporaries, were the least well served during the first century of printing. I set out to look for Laurençais and thank him. He was nowhere to be seen, which surprised me, since the party was in full swing and he should've been the life of it.

It was barely noticeable from the glass-walled rooms overlooking the lagoon, but the weather was dreadful at sea. A raging, rain-laden wind swept the terraces and even the sheltered paths set back in the bowers. Rounding a corner in a hallway, I ran into one of Laurençais' young assistants, and asked after the master of the house. She bade me follow her down a narrow spiral staircase of white concrete. I recalled Laurençais' invitation to visit the grotto, which I hadn't given further thought to taking him up on... Come to think of it, hadn't he told me he was hardly ever down there? Why tonight then, while a bevy of celebrities cracked open the champagne without him?

The young woman bowed and stepped gracefully aside to let me pass. I stepped into the green light that bathed the grotto. I found it childlike in spirit and Hollywood in its actuality. Surely the austere Benito Guardicci had never had a hand in this. Still, it was pleasant: the womb we should never have left, the ideal lap to lay our head in and fall asleep on returning from a terrifying adventure in the world.

Laurençais called out to me. I spotted him, haloed at the far end of a golden beach that gently sloped down to the emerald water. He seemed to take a long time reaching me, though the distance between us couldn't have been more than sixty yards or so.

"Hello! Have you made up your mind?"

"I wanted to thank you for *The Odyssey*. A princely gift! I have a few misgivings—not about accepting it, but owning it. These things are really only safe in museums or major libraries."

"Bah! If your apartment catches fire, that book is probably the first thing you'll try and save. In any case, I'm happy you like it."

I jerked my head, indicating the grotto. "I should've come earlier. It's a stunning place."

"I'm not sure it's in good taste, but I wanted it. You can adjust the lighting to suit your mood, like in a theatre."

"Ligeia's not here?"

"No. I'm worried, I'll admit. As always, at spring tide—she goes out, see? She can't help it, she has to go back..."

"Where? This entire island is yours, and we're—how many miles did you say, the other day? Eleven hundred nautical miles from settled land?"

Laurençais shook his head. "I see I'm either going to have to tell you everything, or keep my mouth shut."

"Is this about—"

"Yes. The story. Let's go back to the past. A short hop: twenty years. Picture me twenty years younger, stronger, more adventurous... but already rich enough to be offered certain experiences exclusive to a handful of individuals for whom money no longer has any reality. This time it's not about sex, but rather sport. I can still picture the man who contacted me. He was a sailor, a Chilean. He died later, of delirium. He was possessed—but that doesn't matter. This man said: 'I hear you're a fisherman, *Señor* Laurençais...' As a matter of fact, I went deep-sea fishing at the time. 'I'm offering you a fishing trip the likes of which you've never seen. This is an opportunity not to be missed, *señor*! It might be the last time...' I shrugged. I'd hunted every creature of the sea, even whales! But the good man smiled in commiseration, his eyes agleam: he had a billionaire on the hook. '*Señor*, there is a creature you've never caught before—the one I'm bringing you! Of course it'll cost you a great deal, but only if you're satisfied…' I'll spare you the negotiations and the details. Finally the Chilean convinced me."

"What was he talking about?"

"I thought you'd understood. Sirens!" sighed Laurençais, turning his gaze on the unruffled green surface of the waters.

"So Ligeia—"

"I caught her twenty years ago, a few miles from here, on the reef." Laurençais' voice grew soft. "I'd never seen death so close-up before. Siren-fishing is no doubt the most dangerous sport in the world. I know a few others—very few, over the years—did it before me, and maybe even a few after. You're in a tiny boat, deliberately hurling yourself at the shoals. That's where you'll find them by night, at spring tide. It seems a nightmare now, twenty years later. The roar of the waves, the howling wind, the foam on the jagged rocks, those pale bodies glimpsed in the dancing flashlight beams, and in the space between two breakers, when the storm was catching its breath, their song—"

"Their song?"

"Of course! Have you forgotten your Homer? My present will refresh your memory. But the *aoidos* was mistaken, like every poet who's tried to write about mermaids. Their song isn't meant to draw men, but males of their species, undines. They're the wanderers; the sirens never stray from their shoals. How many still exist on our planet today? Our wars have decimated them, our waste poisoned them, and we hadn't even the slightest suspicion. In a house that's been bombed to bits, roaches in the basement, mice in the attic, or even crickets by the hearth aren't counted among the casualties. It seems the nomadic undines were at once less numerous and more exposed than their mates. Their fraught mating habits couldn't have helped the species survive, either. They reproduced at spring tide, between sheets of foam, on half-exposed reefs, in an often fatal love-drunk rapture.

When I came from the open sea with the Chilean and his crew, we surged up with our nets in hand right in the midst of this conjugal trance. It all went very fast. A terrified creature rolled into our legs. We threw a net over her blindly. A breaker swept someone away. The Chilean gave the signal to depart. There was no question of turning back. Our only chance at survival consisted of clearing the reef and landing on this island. It would've been as deserted and hostile as on the first day of creation if I hadn't set up a base there in advance. We reached land and made it to camp, by what miracle I'll never know. More dead than alive, we examined the siren by floodlight. She was a young girl, wounded; she'd broken her leg trying to flee. While Chilean and his men patted one another on the back for having made it through alive—and rich, for they'd earned their bonus—our catch seemed so pitiful to me that I was crushed with shame. This was the result of my money and passion: this pain, this terror! Aware at first glance of the gravity of my error, I decided to turn my guilt into responsibility. I'd torn this creature from her world; I had no choice but to help her while waiting for a chance to send her back. So—you see!"

Laurençais spread his arms, as though to take in not only the grotto but, beyond its walls, the entire complex he'd built on the island.

"All for her?"

"How could I take her away from the reef? Confront her with our world, with curiosity of every stripe—government, scientists, the media—how? Never! So I built this refuge for her. But I'm getting ahead of myself. My initial intention had been to heal her, then bring her back to the reef by helicopter in calm weather. The time it took her to heal decreed otherwise. She was too young, too impressionable, too close to us . . . in a few months she'd grown too human. When I realized it was impossible to throw her back in the sea like a fish, I bought this island and converted it to suit her needs. She can neither live fully there nor here . . . and it's my fault."

"You said she'd gone human. Are you sure? She feels so distant, aloof ..."

Laurençais gazed at me ironically. "What would you have her be, a flirt? For her, humanity consists of me and two or three other people who looked after her the first few years. Her emotional vocabulary stopped developing long ago."

"So ...?"

"So she watches out for undines at spring tide. She sings in the whirlpools to call them, like her sisters. And I'm terrified a wave will knock her senseless."

"Is she out on the reef right now?"

He nodded. "She never tells me, but I know. She comes back exhausted, often wounded, and sleeps entire days at a time."

"And you can't—"

"Can't what? Hold her back? What would be left of her then? She's barely tame. When she was younger, afraid of the dangers out there, I wanted to shut her in when the tides came. She threw herself headfirst against the door. I gave in, of course, and away she swam, her forehead still bleeding. That night I thought she'd never come back. But she did, silent, distant. So I promised I'd never do that again."

We went back to the party. Cindy/Christie was showing the Nobel laureate her latest rash, and the guitarist was talking with the tennis player about highs and which drugs went best together. In the wee hours, I ran into Laurençais again. He was beaming. Ligeia had returned home once more.

It was high time I started to drink in earnest if I wanted to get into that helicopter tomorrow with any semblance of composure—that is to say, dead drunk. To think that as a boy I'd dreamed of being a pilot! When I was ten, I lifted my gaze upward and thrilled to the blue above, seeing myself up there, free in the light...What is it that terrifies me now? The skies? The light? Freedom? Bah! I became myself by giving that all up. I managed to fall dead asleep at last on Cindy/Christie's shoulder just as the helicopter flew over the reef.

Several years have passed since my visit to Laurençais Island. I hear people talking about him from time to time, in the paper or on TV: he lost a bundle of money in phosphates, he made a bunch in rare earths...I like to believe he still manages his empire from his rock at the far ends of the earth, and still trembles at spring tide, waiting for Ligeia to return.

I entrust these pages to my safe. Fifty years after I'm dead, Ligeia will be beyond reach...I leave it to anyone who reads this to decide if what they're holding is a true story, or another story, the one I promised Laurençais.

Paris-Bazas, Jul.-Nov. 1996

About the Author

Georges-Olivier Châteaureynaud is the author of nine novels, two young adult novels, and over one hundred short stories. Despite a lifelong fear of flying, he has been to Peru—his only time on a plane—and lived to pen a travel memoir about the experience. He is the recipient of the prestigious *Prix Renaudot*, *Prix Goncourt de la nouvelle* (for short stories), *Prix Giono*, *Prix Valéry Larbaud*, and the *Grand Prix de l'Imaginaire*. His work has been translated into fourteen languages.

Born in Paris in 1947, Châteaureynaud was a solitary child who became a voracious and unprejudiced reader, ingesting *Treasure Island* as avidly as *Lady Chatterley's Lover*. He studied English at the Sorbonne, discovering Stevenson, Shelley, Stoker, and Wells, and later took a degree in library science from the École Nationale Supérieure des Bibliothèques. In 1968, he embarked on a series of odd jobs—including antiques dealer and auto assembly line laborer—that comprised, in his words, an "apprenticeship in human nature," cementing his sympathy for the marginal, outcast figures who would become his luckless, well-meaning, Everyman heroes and narrators. Grasset published his first collection in 1973, *Le fou dans la chaloupe*.

With novelist Hubert Haddad, and fellow Goncourt winners Frédéric Tristan and sinologist Jean Lévi, Châteaureynaud is a founding member of the contemporary movement *La Nouvelle Fiction*: "New" because it rose up against the prevailingly minimalist and confessional tendencies (*autofiction*) of recent French writing, seeking to rouse it from what critic Jean-Luc Moreau called "the slumber of psychological realism," and to restore myth, fable, and fairy tale to a place of primacy in fiction.

In 1983 and 1990, Châteaureynaud was a representative of the Foreign Services Ministry to Quebec and then to Greece. He has been consistently involved with the Centre National du Livre and the SGDL (Société des Gens de Lettres de France). He plays an active part in fostering new talent, serving on the juries of such diverse prizes as the Fondation BNP-Paribas Young Writers Award, the international Prix Prométhée de la nouvelle, the Prix Renaudot, and the Prix Renaissance. Châteaureynaud sees his enthusiastic participation in these institutions as a way of repaying the literary community that has allowed him the luxury of dedication to his craft. An Officier des Arts et Lettres of France, he is currently the editorial director of foreign literature at Editions Dumerchez. In 2006, he was made a Chevalier de la Légion d'Honneur.

About the Translator

Edward Gauvin has published George-Olivier Châteaureynaud's work in *The Southern Review, Harvard Review, AGNI Online, Conjunctions, Words Without Borders, LCRW, Joyland, F&SF, Postscripts, Epiphany, The Café Irreal, Eleven Eleven, Postscripts, Sentence,* and *The Brooklyn Rail,* among others. A graduate of the Iowa Workshop, he has received a Fulbright grant as well as fellowships from the Centre National du Livre, the American Literary Translators Association (ALTA) and the Clarion Foundation and residencies from the Maison des Écritures Midi-Pyrénées, Ledig House, and the Banff International Literary Translation Centre. Other translations of his have been featured or are forthcoming in *PEN America, Tin House, Interfictions 2, Subtropics, Silk Road, Two Lines,* and *Absinthe.* A consulting editor for graphic literature at *Words Without Borders,* he translates comics for Archaia, First Second, and Tokyopop. He has lived in Austin, Pittsburgh, Los Angeles, New York, Taipei, and Amiens, France.

Translator's acknowledgments

Merci mille fois à Paul and Sylviane Underwood, and the many readers and editors who've supported these tales along the way. Time to work on this manuscript was generously provided by the Banff International Literary Translation Centre, to whose director, Susan Ouriou, I owe special thanks. For his kindness, his generosity, and his stories, a debt of gratitude to G.-O. C.

Original Copyright Notices